What They Said

About Luisa

What They Said About Luisa

a novel

ERIKA RUMMEL

DUNDURN PRESS

Publisher: Meghan Macdonald | Acquiring editors: Russell Smith and Kwame Scott Fraser
Cover designer: Laura Boyle
Cover image: Miguel Cabrera, Pintura de Castas, 5: Collection of Lydia Sada de González (public domain); Vista de Sevilla, Anonymous (public domain)

Library and Archives Canada Cataloguing in Publication

Title: What they said about Luisa : a novel / Erika Rummel.
Names: Rummel, Erika, 1942- author.
Identifiers: Canadiana (print) 2023048526X | Canadiana (ebook) 20230485278 | ISBN 9781459752771 (softcover) | ISBN 9781459752788 (PDF) | ISBN 9781459752795 (EPUB)
Classification: LCC PS8635.U56 W53 2024 | DDC C813/.6—dc23

We acknowledge the support of the Canada Council for the Arts and the Ontario Arts Council for our publishing program. We also acknowledge the financial support of the Government of Ontario, through the Ontario Book Publishing Tax Credit and Ontario Creates, and the Government of Canada.

Care has been taken to trace the ownership of copyright material used in this book. The author and the publisher welcome any information enabling them to rectify any references or credits in subsequent editions.

The publisher is not responsible for websites or their content unless they are owned by the publisher.

Printed and bound in Canada.

Dundurn Press
1382 Queen Street East
Toronto, Ontario, Canada M4L 1C9
dundurn.com, @dundurnpress

For Gregor Medinger, who inspired this
book with what he said about Luisa.

PROLOGUE

A silver mine in Zacatecas, 1575:

Jorge

THEY SAY WHEN YOU ARE close to death, the whole of your life passes before your eyes. It's an act of God giving you a last chance to repent of your sins. It didn't happen to me on the day the mine collapsed and buried me under rubble of stone and ore. I thought of nothing. My brain seized up like a rusty wheel the moment I felt the earth shaking and heard the cracking of the beams. The lantern that I had hooked up fell to the ground, and the candle inside hissed and died. For a moment I glimpsed the light of day at the entrance of the mine, the last rays of the slanting sun. Then it too was gone, as if a giant hand had shut a door. Nor did I think of my sins when I felt a rock lacerating my shoulder, when the weight of the collapsing walls brought me to my knees and my fingernails scraped the rough ground. My mind gave out like the candlewick.

I don't know how much time had passed in that blind darkness before I woke to a stabbing pain in my shoulder and left arm, a deep ache in my bones. My throat was dry, but I had nothing to quench my thirst or still my hunger pangs. I raised my head, thumped against wood and sank back again. I couldn't shift my body or straighten my legs, but I was able to move my right hand to explore my surroundings. There was a wooden barrier mere inches away, a toppled beam hemming me in, running along the whole length of my body. It pinned me down, but also protected me from the falling rocks and formed a hollow space around me that allowed me to breathe.

I had been working close to the mouth of the mine when the shaft collapsed, and the fact that I was now surrounded by darkness told me that the way out was blocked. Not even a ray of light could penetrate to the spot where I lay. I was shut up in the mine as in a tomb. The silence surrounding me was complete, except for the ghostly rumbling of shifting rocks somewhere in the depths of the mine and gravel raining down on the beam above me.

After what seemed like many hours, I heard more rumbling nearby and saw a glimmer of light. A new rockslide had opened up a crack no wider than my hand. However close I was to the surface, it did not help me because I was trapped by the beam and could not move even an inch toward the source of light. At least I will not die a wretched death of suffocation, I thought. That tiny gap in the wall of rock assured me a fresh supply of air.

Then my thoughts turned to Luisa, my poor Luisa. She was far away but as I spoke her name, I was comforted. Her image sustained me in the darkness, and I realized that I had been wrong all these years when I thought love was a meaningless word, no more than romantic nonsense. I didn't believe that there was true love between men and women. There was only self-interest or lust or, at best, companionship. But the memory of Luisa's sweet voice settled on me like a balm, and I realized that love did exist and had bound me to her all along.

1

Seville, 1575:

Ana Rodriguez, widow

INCREDIBLE.

Luisa is back from Mexico and has set up shop here in Seville. If that's true and she has that kind of money, she made it by selling her body. That girl has always been good at wiggling her arse. That's how she caught Diego, and I haven't forgiven her for it.

The morning started out like all the others, not worth getting dressed for, not worth squeezing into a bodice as stiff as a suit of armour and sweating under a damask skirt — even if it is a lovely feeling to pass your fingers over the delicate embroidery. Sitting in the courtyard, I was thinking I should have stayed in my chemise, in the darkness of the bedroom, with the shutters closed tight against the sun. It was early in the morning, but the pleasant coolness of the night had already worn off.

Not a breeze, not a wisp of air in the courtyard, where I had taken refuge from the servants rattling around in the house. They think if they make enough noise, they'll convince me that they are working hard. They are a lazy bunch, all of them, but what can you do? It's in their blood.

It is going to be a long day, creeping by like all the others, I thought. I felt tired at the very thought of the empty hours ahead of me. I closed my eyes against them and wanted to doze them away, sitting there in my wicker chair, leaning back into the cushions, my feet resting on the footstool — but then the clanking of the door knocker jerked me awake. I opened my eyes again, blinking against the hazy sunlight, and there was Lela beside me, curtsying. She always looks dishevelled, that girl. I could see a spot of grease on her apron.

"Doña Eugenia here to see you, señora," she said in her squeaky voice.

It was rather early for Eugenia to pay me a visit. The bells of Santa Maria calling the faithful to mass had barely stopped ringing. Eugenia always attends the morning service. She is a devout woman, sitting in her pew "without the benefit of a cushion" — her daily penance, as she calls it. On most days she drops in after church to complain about her poor health, her aching knees, her sore back, her swollen ankles: nothing that I don't already know and suffer myself. Anyone less charitable than me would have thought up an excuse not to listen to the litany of her aches and pains, but I know my Christian duty, especially to a neighbour.

If Eugenia was skipping morning mass, it could mean only one thing: She had a juicy bit of gossip and couldn't wait to tell me — a delicious secret or a scandalous rumour or an offer of marriage for her daughter, Cecilia. I hoped it wasn't an offer.

Cecilia would make a good match for my son. Unfortunately, Ramon isn't ready to settle down. I don't know what he is waiting for. You couldn't ask for a larger dowry, I tell him, but he shrugs me off. "I'm too young to be shackled to one woman," he says. "I want to enjoy myself a little longer." He is his father's son and has inherited Diego's unfortunate taste for servant girls. I wish he had inherited his business sense as well. So let's hope he comes to his senses while Cecilia is still available.

Meanwhile, Lela, that stupid girl, was standing by my chair, waiting.

"What are you waiting for?" I said. "Show Doña Eugenia into the drawing room. And how often have I told you to take off your apron when you are not working in the kitchen and to put on a clean pinafore before you answer the door?"

"But I *was* working in the kitchen, Doña Ana, helping cook —"

"Don't talk back to me, girl," I said. "Shut your mouth and show Doña Eugenia in. Say I'll be with her in a moment."

I watched Lela hurry away, untying her apron as she went, but I was sure my dear neighbour had spotted that splash of sauce on her apron when the girl opened the door to her. I could already see her putting on a patronizing smile. "It's a pity, Ana, that you allow your maids to go into the kitchen," she'd say with that ring of false sympathy. "Their clothes will take on the smell of boiled beef, you know. You'll never get rid of the fug. It stinks in your nostrils."

Eugenia prides herself on keeping the house servants separate from the kitchen servants. But that's easy for her. She has a dozen. I make do with five, including Jacinto, who is now too old to do more than muck around in the garden. And Lela is hopeless. Such a scrawny thing. Diego got her cheap, years ago when she was a little girl. He thought that with proper care and feeding, she'd grow into a decent servant. No such luck. She's still a runt.

I stepped out of the brightness of the patio into the opaque shadow of my bedroom. The maid hadn't made up the bed yet. The tumbled sheets gave off the smell of night sweat — I must tell her to brush them with lavender. I opened one of the shutters to let in a ray of light, just enough to check my image in the mirror, and couldn't help sighing when I saw the passing years reflected in my face and figure, the cheeks no longer full, the skin under my eyes pouchy, the slenderness of youth gone. I noticed that the lace at the neck of my blouse was loose and re-tied it, straightening the starched edges. It would not do for Eugenia to see me in disarray, even though she herself has no sense of fashion, poor woman. She is rich, certainly, but she has no taste.

I stopped for a moment at the door before entering the drawing room and cast an eye over the scene. Everything was in order there. For once, the servants had done their work. The satin cushions on the sofa were plumped up, the dark console tables gleamed, the crystal of the chandelier sparkled.

Doña Eugenia was standing by the window. The shutters were half-open to allow a slight movement of air, or else we would surely have suffocated in this brooding heat. She turned. Pearls of sweat glistened on her brow; her cheeks were as red as if she was wearing rouge. It's the layers of fat that make her perspire. That's what you get when you eat like a pig. Put sweets in front of Eugenia, and she wolfs them down without restraint. The plate is half-empty before the serving girl is even out the door.

"My dear Ana," she said, grasping my hand and kissing me moistly on both cheeks. "You won't believe what I just heard."

She paused and looked at me expectantly, as if I could read her mind.

"Well, what have you heard?"

"Luisa is back from Mexico."

What? I didn't believe my ears. The day was no longer boring. The news galvanized me.

"You don't say. That little minx who waggled her hips and batted her eyes at every man around? She is back?"

Eugenia was breathless with excitement. She lowered herself onto the settee, careful to centre her rear end or, I swear, the sofa would have tipped sideways under her weight. She fanned herself vigorously with one of those expensive but ugly fans made of ivory sticks.

"Yes, she is back and has set up shop in San Bernardo," she said, huffing and puffing. "She must have struck it rich in Mexico. She bought a house and opened a candle shop, or so they say."

"Hah. I'll believe it when I see it," I said. "Not that I ever want to lay eyes on that ungrateful girl again."

"I don't blame you," Eugenia said. "After what she put you through. Or rather, what Don Diego — may his soul rest in peace — put you through, but that's men for you. You give them everything, you bear them a son, and they cheat on you with a young girl, a mulatta by preference, because they say they are better at — well, I won't say any more. All men are ingrates."

"Right you are, my dear, but what can a wife do? We have to put up with their foibles."

I had known about Diego's affair, of course. Everyone did. A blind woman couldn't have missed what was going on between Diego and Luisa, but I thought I'd let him have his fun with one of the house slaves. They don't count. And they can

9

be had for free. Better that than spend his money in one of those houses of infamy and pick up some awful disease from the whores. Besides, God knows I'd done my duty by him, and was tired of being pawed in bed when I'd rather sleep. Only sometimes I think, *If I had been more loving to Diego* ... but no, it wasn't my fault. Luisa knew how to rouse a man's desire. She was only twelve or thirteen when Diego bought her and already strutting her wares, her budding breasts and her mobile hips. A beautiful face, but the very devil within, and sneaky too; never said a word more than she had to, just looked at you with those large eyes full of hidden plots.

"I was prepared to overlook it for the sake of keeping the peace," I said to Eugenia. "But what a shock when the lawyer read Diego's will to us!"

I still run hot and cold when I think that Diego left that girl a hundred ducats and set her free. A hundred ducats! Enough to buy a pair of mulattos — at that time, at any rate; now they go for eighty apiece, what with the inflation.

"It was a shocking thing, and we all felt for you," Eugenia said. "I don't know why he set Luisa free at once. He might have left her to you in trust, the way my father did with Egidio, his favourite slave. He willed him to me with the proviso that he must work another five years before getting his freedom. And it cost me a pretty penny to replace Egidio because the inflation is ruining us all."

I could only nod. I couldn't say another word, couldn't push out a single sound, because I felt choked at the thought of my helpless jealousy and the indignity I had had to suffer, and that girl raking in a hundred ducats. Although it's almost ten years ago that Diego died, the memory still leaves a bitter taste in my mouth. How he carried on! To see him give Luisa a radiant smile and look through me as if I didn't exist. My heart throbbed with pain. Some nights I cried myself to sleep. I was tired of his passions, yes, but I was not tired of love, and I missed his endearments.

Then Diego died, and the provisions of his will added insult to injury. Ramon was certainly disappointed. He had expected to inherit a larger estate from his father. Diego never said a word, either to me or to our son, about selling a number of fields three weeks before his death. We were struck dumb when the lawyer, Miguel Aguirre, told us.

Aguirre came back to the house with us after the funeral, on which we had spent a fair amount of money because we didn't want the neighbours to think we were cheap or didn't know what was due to a man of Diego's standing. The door and the balcony and all the mirrors in the house were hung with black cloth edged with gold. We hired keeners to beat their breasts. We did not stint on hospitality during the wake, to the point where several guests got drunk and acted in a most undignified manner. Nor did we stint on flowers, wreaths, and funeral masses. And then the lawyer tells us that Diego has squandered that kind of money on Luisa!

I was sitting on the sofa in the drawing room, in my new black mourning dress of taffeta and Flemish lace, dabbing my eyes with a delicate black handkerchief — of which I had a dozen made for the occasion — but my tears dried up when I heard from Aguirre what Diego had done to us.

Then Ramon said to the lawyer, "Perhaps my father wasn't in his right mind when he gave the instructions to sell those fields. I mean, was he *compos mentis* after he suffered that fall from the horse? What with the pain and the fever and the drugs the doctor gave him, he was not himself."

"We discussed the matter before his accident, if that's what you mean," Aguirre said. "And I assure you he was perfectly lucid when he put his signature to the document of sale, which my groom and I witnessed."

"And where is the money he got for the fields?" Ramon asked.

"That I cannot tell you," he said. Or, more likely, didn't want to tell us. Those fields were worth a few thousand ducats.

Diego had been in the best of health until the day his horse shied and threw him off. He struck his head on a stone balustrade and split it open, an ugly cleft on his right temple, spilling his lifeblood on the pavement, the servants said, when they brought him into the house.

He was unconscious by then. We called the doctor immediately and he put a dressing on the wound, but gave us little hope that Diego would survive. There he was, lying on the bed piled with extra cushions and fresh coverlets, deathly pale, his eyes closed, his lips half-open as if he wanted to say something, but no words came. I sat by his side through the night, sick to my heart with grief and sorrow. In the morning he woke from his coma, feverish and raving. The doctor returned and gave him a tincture of opium to calm him down and lessen the pain, but I knew — and Diego himself understood in his more lucid moments — that the end was near. He lingered for another week, but never left his bed again.

Ramon and I took turns staying with him during all waking hours. I saw Diego looking around the room, passing his eyes over everything: the bed curtains, which I had looped back, the fine wall hangings, the carved wardrobes, the tall windows he asked me to open so he could look to the garden beyond. It was as if he wanted to say farewell to his possessions and the very sun in the sky.

"Do you want me to call a priest?" I asked him.

"No," he said. "Call Miguel Aguirre while I can still think and talk."

"What do you want to talk to him about?" I asked, but he waved me off, saving his breath for the lawyer. I could guess, of course, that it had something to do with his will.

The lawyer came, and Diego asked Ramon and me to leave the room so the two of them could talk in private, which I thought was most peculiar, as did my son. We waited in the hall, walking up and down, stopping at the door from time to time to listen, but we could hear only a murmur. After a while, the lawyer came to the door and asked us to call his groom. He wanted him to come and witness Diego's signature on the papers he had drawn up.

"Wouldn't it be better if Ramon witnessed them?" I said.

"I am following Don Diego's instructions," he said. "He asked for my groom."

"Can the man even read and write?" Ramon asked.

"There is no need for him to read or write," Miguel Aguirre said. "I only want him to put his cross beside Don Diego's and my signatures, as a witness."

"The old man has something up his sleeve," Ramon said to me the moment the door closed on the lawyer and his groom. "I hope we aren't in for an unpleasant surprise."

But I couldn't believe that Diego would do anything to disadvantage me — his wife of thirty years — or his one and only son.

As soon as the lawyer was gone, I went back into the room and sat down by Diego's bedside, thinking he might tell me what was going on or that I might coax it out of him, but he only said: "Now I'm ready for the priest."

Don Francisco, the parish priest, came with a flask of chrism and gave Diego Holy Unction, anointing his forehead and hearing his last confession. After that he lived for another two days, and at the very end he asked for Luisa to come and see him.

I was scandalized and had a good mind to defy him and refuse to fetch the girl, but Ramon said, "Let the old man have his last bit of fun."

So I asked the girl to go in to Diego, trusting that he was too weak for any fun, although I wasn't so sure about that, especially when I heard her singing in there.

She was with him for a good half hour, while I sat in the anteroom with an aching heart, crying for shame because he preferred her to me even when he was staring death in the face. When she finally came out, I dug my fingers into her arm and gave it a yank.

"You hussy," I said. "Singing in a dying man's room!"

"He asked me to," she said, looking at me in the mulish way those half-castes have.

I was going to slap her face, but Ramon took both of my hands in his and said, "Let it be, mother."

Then I went into Diego's room again and sat by his bedside.

"Are you feeling better now?" I asked him, still hoping for a sign of love, for a few words to let me know that I — the mother of his son — was closest to his heart, after all. But he gave me no reply, just turned his face to the wall.

The next morning, we found him cold and stiff.

All that was going through my head when Eugenia said that Luisa was back.

She was looking at me expectantly, and I pulled myself together.

"That little chit!" I said. I could still see Luisa in my mind, coming out of Diego's room, moving like a cat, smooth and slinky. "She had a way of looking at men demurely from under her eyelashes — that's how she trapped them."

"Yes, there was something demure about her," Eugenia said. "She was a very quiet girl, hardly ever said a word at all."

"She was close-mouthed, all right. Didn't give anything away."

"But you know what I remember about her? That her embroidery was superb, and that she made the most delicious quince preserve. I never could get my cook to produce the likes of it."

That's Eugenia for you! Sweets are all she ever thinks about.

"The quince preserve was good. I give you that," I said.

"And, you must admit," she went on, rubbing salt into my wounds, "Luisa was handy for entertaining your guests at a fiesta. Such a beautiful singing voice she had, and the way she danced the zarabanda or the chacona. There was something charming about that girl. And although she didn't talk much, she was always pleasant and smiling, unlike the others, who are sullen and scowl at you when you tell them to do their work."

"She was good at wiggling her rear end, you mean, and the men couldn't take their eyes off her," I said, impatient with Eugenia paying compliments to a hussy who didn't deserve them. "But how did you find out that she is back?"

"I have it from my maid, and that girl is never wrong. She tells me that Luisa lives just around the corner from Our Lady of the Angels. She has bought a tidy adobe house there, she says, with a large *sala*, a storeroom, and a candle shop out front, and she has a helper, too."

The barrio of San Bernardo is where the freed slaves who have made good live. They hold their heads high and act as if they measure up to any Spaniard. And the Church lets them get away with it instead of preaching modesty to them and deference to their betters.

"What's going on in San Bernardo is a scandal," I said to Eugenia. "Those freed slaves are getting too uppity."

"You are right, of course," Eugenia said. "But my husband is sorry he didn't invest in some building lots there earlier. The houses in San Bernardo have gone up in price. It's becoming a respectable quarter."

"Respectable? I don't know about that. Those freed slaves are allowed to gather on feast days and perform their own godless dances and songs. I'm asking you: What is this world coming to? Soon they will claim to be our equals."

"Yes, they are taking too many liberties. They have asked and gotten permission to organize a fraternity like regular craftsmen and they are running their own hospital, I'm told."

Eugenia tends to go on and on, keeping up a steady stream of tattle. At any other time I would have found it gratifying to listen to her because, I must say, whatever her faults and lapses in taste, Eugenia is the very best source of news. Nothing escapes the eyes of that woman — or rather, of her maid — but after hearing about Luisa, I couldn't wait to get rid of her.

I was keen to make my own inquiries. The day, a blur of hours until I heard the news, had suddenly taken on form and substance. I had things to do!

After Eugenia finally took her big rump out of my drawing room, I called Jacinto. He came tottering in and stood there with his shoulders sagging, looking down to the floor as if it was too much work even to raise his head. I told him to go to San Bernardo and find the candle shop around the corner from Our Lady of the Angels.

"You remember Luisa?" I said to him. "The girl who went off to Mexico some ten years ago?"

He looked at me with his rheumy old eyes. "It's not likely anyone would forget her," he said. "Such a nice girl, and jilted by the apothecary's helper."

It looked like Luisa had worked her charm on everyone, even old Jacinto.

"She's back in Seville, keeping a candle shop," I told him. "Look her up and tell me how she is doing and find out how much she paid for the house — at least, that's what Doña Eugenia tells me, that she owns the house she lives in."

"Go to San Bernardo!" Jacinto said. "Mercy me, Doña Ana, that's a long way off. I don't know if my old legs will carry me that far."

The nerve of the man! That's what you get for keeping an old slave for charity's sake, when he can no longer do any useful work and looks like a rusty pitchfork. I am ashamed to have him in the house.

"It will do you good to get some exercise," I said. "Sitting around all day makes you stiff and weakens your legs."

He sighed and nodded meekly. "As you please, Doña Ana."

Then an idea struck me. "Jacinto!" I called after him. "On second thought, ask her to come here tomorrow after siesta, and I'll find out for myself."

If she really had a candle shop, she would no doubt ask me to order my household supply from her. Let her ask, and I will tell her: If you want my business, I expect a healthy discount. That girl owes me!

After Jacinto was gone, I went back into the courtyard and sat in the shade of the myrtle tree.

"Lela!" I called. She came and stood in the door, awkwardly twisting her pinafore. You can't teach that girl manners. "Bring me another cushion for my neck."

She turned to go into the house, but I stopped her. "I can smell the kitchen fug on your clothes, Lela. Air out that pinafore and put your apron back on. No sense in getting two things dirty when one will do."

She curtsied, but I could see the stubbornness in her eyes.

"And don't stare at me like that," I said, and she lowered her head.

She took her time bringing me the cushion. She is not only awkward, she is slow as well, but never mind that incorrigible girl.

I leaned back leisurely and watched the play of the sunlight on the glazed tiles of the fountain. Pots of basil and rosemary and sweet-scented jasmine lined the steps to the portico and perfumed the air. I listened to the finches in the cage by the door and thought about Luisa and her unhappy affair with the apothecary's man — what was his name again? Jordan. The moment Jordan heard that Luisa was a free woman and had inherited money, he came to me and asked permission to court her. Of course I said yes, to get her out of the house faster. I couldn't stand seeing her pale face and hearing her sniffle over Diego's death. The nerve! What right did she have to grieve for Diego? I would have thrown her out at once, but the will had to be proved first, and Ramon said he would challenge the bit about Luisa's manumission before the tribunal. It wasn't right that she should be set free just like that.

"You'd better hold on to her until we know where we stand," my son said, and I saw his point. "Don't allow the apothecary's man to take her away yet," he said, but there was no harm in allowing the fellow to come and pay his attentions to Luisa, especially when he showed his gratitude by bringing me little packages of herbs and a compound for headache, which he had probably filched from his master. Then he stopped coming, and Luisa was again slinking around, looking dejected. I lost all patience, seeing her moping like that, and spoke to her sternly.

"What's going on between you and that man, Jordan?" I said. "Why doesn't he come around anymore?"

"He asked me to be his wife," she said, "but now he has jilted me and is going to marry another. It was wrong of him to act like that. A promise of marriage is as good as a marriage."

"Only when it is consummated," I said. "Was it consummated?"

She had the decency to blush. "I'm not sure what that word means, señora," she said, "but I can guess. I didn't do anything improper with Jordan. You know very well that I never left the house unaccompanied."

But I had my doubts about that and about the validity of the man's promise. I went as far as asking the opinion of Don Francisco, the parish priest. Not that I think much of his opinion because he is of peasant stock — or has a peasant's broad face, at any rate — but he is God's representative. I thought I'd better not delay until Sunday to see him and get his advice right away, so I looked him up at the parish house, in case he had anything useful to offer. Just looking around the bare reception room told me that I had come in vain. Whitewashed walls with no more than one large cross for decoration, a bare plank floor, and hard chairs such as you would expect in a poor man's house. I wondered whether he kept the room like that on purpose to get rid of his visitors faster, for no one could suffer those uncomfortable chairs for very long. But I think it was a matter of principle with him to live like a poor man. What advice can you expect from a fool who doesn't enjoy the good things in life when he could afford them?

So I didn't expect much when I asked him about the promise of marriage exchanged between Luisa and Jordan.

He said these private promises were a bane and shouldn't be allowed.

"The Church frowns on them. Promises of marriage must always be witnessed. The rest is just an invitation to sin," he said. "Young men make all sorts of promises to lure girls into indecent relationships. 'I swear to God I'll marry you,' they say to an innocent young woman, and she believes them and allows them to take liberties."

That was probably what happened in Luisa's case, I thought. After the man had taken his pleasure with her, he left to marry another woman, who had the wits and the character to keep her virginity intact. And nobody can blame him for that.

Don Francisco was right to condemn such goings-on among the servants. The problem is that he doesn't know where to draw the line. He treats everyone the same. In the case of Luisa, he was absolutely right. But I would have expected him to be more lenient with people of standing. When I think how often I had to placate him because Ramon had not been at mass or hadn't gone to confession during Lent. You'd think Don Francisco would look the other way and excuse a young man like Ramon, considering who his father was: a man of rank who gave alms and paid his tithes on time,

who was generous to the Church. Too generous. But I put a
stop to that after his death. What's the use of paying a parish
priest extra if he doesn't help you? Especially a parish priest
like Don Francisco, who doesn't know how to act his part.
Above the altar in the parish church is a painting of God the
Father on his Heavenly throne, with a bejewelled crown on his
head and wearing a purple mantle of royal splendour with an
ermine cape, and Don Francisco, his representative on Earth,
runs around in a plain cope and sandals down at the heels, like
a beggar. God cannot be pleased with a man who shows no
respect for his dignity. From me he won't get even a peso more
than the tithe I owe. I'd rather spend my money on a dozen
wax candles for the Virgin, who surely has God's ear, or buy an
indulgence from the bishop. At least I get something tangible
for my money — a document stating that I have bought fifty
years off purgatory. When I look at the figure written on the
indulgence certificate in large print and at the bishop's red
seal beside it, I know what I paid for. I won't be lingering in
purgatory or be licked by hellfire.

What a fuss Diego made when I asked him for money to
buy indulgences for him and Ramon, to secure their salvation
and keep them out of purgatory. They certainly needed to be
pardoned for their sins more than me, what with Ramon going off God knows where every night, and Diego carrying on
with Luisa.

"You, more than anyone in this household, need an indulgence," I said to Diego, as we were going to bed. I wanted to
remind him of his sins so he wouldn't importune me, because
I could see he was in the mood for getting his hands on my
body. A few glasses of jerez after dinner had that effect on him.
I knew that the moment I snuffed out the candle, he would

start groping and pushing his salivating tongue between my lips, but my words stopped him.

"Nonsense," he said, rolling back into his half of the bed. "Those indulgences aren't worth the paper they are printed on. You think it's that simple? You put down a ducat, and God fetches your record from the ledger, totals up your sins, and takes ten years off purgatory with the stroke of his pen?"

"Diego!" I said. "God will punish you for talking like that."

"God has nothing to do with it," he said. "I tell you what's going on. The bishop is trying to fill his coffers with our hard-earned money. He makes dupes out of silly women like you, and stupid old men, too, preying on their fear of hellfire. As if you could buy your way out of purgatory. There's nothing in the Bible about indulgences. And nothing about needing the bishop as a middleman to obtain God's forgiveness. I will make my peace with God directly, and I advise you to do the same."

"No," I said, "you are wrong, Diego. Those indulgences are worth every maravedi. And to talk the way you do comes close to heresy."

God is just. He gives back what you put in. I do my bit: I go to mass and drop my money onto the collection plate. I give alms to the beggars sitting on the steps of the church. I light candles before the saints — not the cheap tapers that most people buy, but the fat wax candles that burn for hours. I pay for indulgences and, whatever Diego's blasphemous thoughts, I firmly believe that every coin I spend on the Church is entered in God's books and I will receive my just reward from him when I go to Heaven. I only hope that God took mercy also on Diego — may his soul rest in peace.

As for Luisa, Don Francisco was right, of course. The apothecary's man had probably made her grand promises, and she let him have his will. Not that I cared about her going to hell, but while she was under my roof, I kept an eye on things. What would the neighbours say if word got out that Jordan had taken liberties with her in my house? I told him he had to wait until the question of Luisa's manumission and inheritance was settled by the tribunal. Oh, he said, it is before the courts? Well, yes, I said, it's still under consideration. You mean she might not have a dowry after all? he asked. I shrugged. I suppose he didn't want to run the risk of marrying her without a dowry, so he started looking elsewhere for a wife.

"I just hope the fellow didn't get her pregnant," I said to Ramon, because he was the master of the house now and I took all my concerns to him.

But he only laughed. "If Luisa is pregnant," he said, "and if the court case goes in our favour and the clause in the will that grants her freedom is set aside, you'll have two slaves for one. If the clause is upheld, what do you care if she is pregnant? Just show her the door, and make sure she doesn't take along anything that isn't hers."

But the will was proved, and we could do nothing about the clause that granted Luisa her freedom or about the hundred ducats Diego had left her.

"The old man was batty about her," my son said. "He was head over heels, you know."

His words cut me to the bone. "How you talk about your father!"

"It's the truth, mother. You might as well face it."

"But I tell you one thing," I said. "If she asks for her letter of manumission to document her freedom, I won't pay Miguel Aguirre for drawing it up. He can take his fee out of the hundred ducats."

23

And you know what that fool of a lawyer said to me? That he was embarrassed to charge Luisa for drawing up the document of manumission. If we didn't want to pay, he would absorb the cost himself.

"Let him," Ramon said. "Perhaps Luisa will pay him in kind."

When the lawyer brought the letter of manumission for me to sign, I saw that it contained another clause that might allow Luisa to ask for even more money out of the estate.

"Don't say a word about it," Ramon said. "She can't read, and it's unlikely she'll ask questions or understand what it's all about. Just hand her the paper and tell her it's the letter that sets her free."

"But what if —"

"Don't worry, mother," he said. "Just keep mum about the clause and get her out of the house as quickly as possible."

That was my fondest wish as well: to be rid of Luisa, forget her existence, and heal my broken heart. As it was, I did not have to urge Luisa to leave. The very day I gave her the letter of manumission and paid her the hundred ducats, her "dowry," she bundled up her possessions — her Sunday outfit and a few trinkets — and went away.

A year later, I heard from Don Francisco that she had married a sailor and gone with him to Mexico.

And now she is back. What happened to her husband, I wonder? Did he die, or did she leave him? I wouldn't put it beyond her. That girl has no decency, or she wouldn't have carried on with Diego the way she did.

The heat in the courtyard is making me drowsy again. I untie the lace at my neck, loosen my stomacher, and close my eyes, but I can't shut out thoughts of the unfortunate will. That

Diego would do such a shameful thing to me! True, we had our arguments, but who doesn't after twenty-eight years of sharing a life, and it wasn't fair of him to interrogate me and call me to account over every little expense, when all I wanted was to keep up with the neighbours, an obligation that can't be denied. It was expected of me to dress well and wear my jewels proudly and return my neighbours' invitations and make an earnest effort to trump them. It was all for the honour of the family. And yet Diego begrudged me every new dress and every new "bauble," as he contemptuously called my jewels. I was doing my duty as the mistress of the house, but he was interested only in my "marital duties." What did he expect? We were no longer young lovebirds. After suffering through two miscarriages and a stillbirth, I gave him a son, and yet he kept importuning me at least twice a week until I demanded a separate bedroom.

Perhaps that was where I went wrong. Perhaps he would not have favoured Luisa if I had indulged him, but I had made discreet inquiries among my friends beforehand and knew that separate bedrooms were by no means an unusual arrangement. To be on the safe side, I asked Don Francisco's advice as well. Not that it did me much good. He is such a stern man. His speech is like his shabby cassock: plain and unadorned. He has no smooth words for his parishioners. I wish the bishop had sent us a different parish priest, one of those fine gentlemen canons who say mass at the cathedral. They understand what dignity is all about. They understand that some people are better than others.

"All acts of fornication and all vile desires are sinful," Don Francisco had said when I consulted him about my marital obligations, sitting on those uncomfortable chairs of his in that cheerless reception room. Just looking at those bare walls was a penance. And that plain language of his! It made me blush. You would think he'd choose more polite and elegant words when talking of marital duties to a woman.

"Copulation is permitted within the bonds of marriage," he said, "but only for the purpose of procreation. Indeed, the apostle Paul says, 'it is better to marry than to burn,' meaning marriage is a man's refuge if he cannot contain his burning desires."

"And if a woman is no longer of an age to make procreation likely?" I asked.

He sighed as if I had asked him a particularly hard question, one he would rather not answer. The man was absolutely useless as a counsellor. But I pressed on. A parishioner is entitled to an answer from her priest, and I didn't let him get away with sighing.

"What if that's the case?" I said, looking at him steadily.

"Then it is incumbent on the partners to suppress their desires, especially at this time of year."

It was the time of Lent, when we are all commanded to remember Christ's suffering and death, to refrain from eating meat, and to keep from any other enjoyment, such as singing, dancing, and, of course, vile thoughts.

"And after Lent?" I said to Don Francisco.

He looked at me with his unforgiving eyes. "Thereafter I advise you to remember the vows you made when you stood before the altar, promising to love and obey your husband."

Oh, he was a hard man! I cried out in anguish, "When I stood before the altar, I didn't know what I was promising. I was a young girl, with the mind of a child. My parents arranged the marriage —"

"Are you saying that you did not enter the marriage of your own free will — that you were coerced?" he asked sternly. "As you well know, a promise of marriage is valid before God only if made freely."

"No, I'm saying only that I was naive. My parents praised Diego — he is rich, they said. He is a hidalgo, a nobleman, a man of standing you can be proud of. They made it sound like a marriage made in Heaven. They did not force me, unless persuasion is a kind of force."

"I see," he said, and his voice softened a little.

"And then came the miscarriages," I said. I could not help tearing up when I thought of the heartbreak I had suffered, the unbearable pain, the fear of death. Men have no idea how women suffer. If they, rather than their wives, had to bear children, they would be more careful about sowing their seed.

"But then God rewarded you with a son," Don Francisco said.

"And I thanked God with all my heart, believe me, Father. You will remember that Diego had a mass said in gratitude for my delivery, and I donated a new altar cloth with a pattern of gold thread. It cost me a pretty penny. And now I think I have done my duty by Don Diego and his family, and I deserve peace at last."

That's what I said to him, but what does a parish priest know about marriage and the things that go on in the privacy of a couple's bedroom? He can only quote the Bible. And so I decided not to listen to his admonitions. I asked Diego for separate bedrooms and, although he was disgruntled, he agreed in the end. I in turn shut my eyes to his carryings-on and never complained when he stayed out all night or indulged his fondness for jerez or, for that matter, his fondness for Luisa. Yes, perhaps I did wrong, perhaps I should have been more loving to Diego, but even so, that last will of his came as a great shock.

It was almost as if he wanted to punish me, or perhaps punish Ramon, who was not, it must be owned, a dutiful son. Diego had good reason to complain of Ramon's habit of attending bear-baitings and cockfights. He frequently had to pay his betting debts —

I am roused from my thoughts by a sudden noise and commotion in the house. I hear Ramon's boisterous laugh and Lela's squeal, "No, señor — please, señor." She comes running out into the courtyard, her hair flying.

"Oh, señora!" she says, passing her trembling hands over her face to hide the tears in her eyes. She pulls the strings of her apron straight and escapes.

Behind her, Ramon appears in the door, yawning and stretching, his shirt rumpled and stained with sweat, his hair sticking out from his head in unkempt tufts.

"Ramon, my dear," I say, "you shouldn't show yourself like this, unwashed and with your clothes in disarray. It lowers the respect of the servants."

"Oh, bother the servants!" he says. "And that Lela in particular. She never does what you want her to do. You ought to teach her a lesson. A little bit of melted pork fat dropped on her arm would go a long way, I bet."

I am shocked by his suggestion. He can't be serious. Hot fat would leave a mark on Lela's arm. He must be stupid with drink. I can smell a sour whiff of yesterday's wine on his breath.

"Ramon!" I cry. "How can you say such a thing? Would you disfigure Lela and damage your own property?"

"Don't get into a funk over nothing, mother. I was joking, but it's the truth. You can't get a friendly word out of that girl, not to speak of a friendly bosom to rest my aching head on — not that she has a bosom to speak of. She's as flat as a pancake."

I am glad Eugenia has gone home and didn't witness this scene or the sorry sight of Ramon. It would have been the end of my hope for obtaining a suitable daughter-in-law.

"If you got married, you would have a sympathetic bosom to rest on," I say to Ramon.

"Are you still trying to fix me up with that walleyed girl next door?"

That is my hope, indeed. If only Ramon could snag Eugenia's youngest daughter. Cecilia is ugly, it must be owned, with those staring eyes of hers and that wine-red birthmark on her cheek. She won't attract many suitors, but her father is willing to give her a large dowry to make up for her personal defects and his own lack of standing. Eugenia has married down. She comes from a noble family, but her father married her to the highest bidder, a spice merchant. She herself has naturally coarsened over the years and turned into a common merchant's wife. Her husband is generous, I'll say that much for him. He doesn't object to her spending money as if there is no tomorrow. She orders silk gowns from Venice and cloaks from Lombardy, but their design lacks elegance. Last Sunday she wore one of those ridiculous high hats, pushed all the way forward. It looked like someone had stuck a green taffeta cylinder to her forehead. I thank my good fortune and my father for finding me a husband like Diego — may his soul rest in peace; a man of honour and property, a hidalgo who never left the house without proudly carrying his sword and being attended by a slave or two. He had his faults, of course, but he never forgot what he owed to his standing, at least in public.

"Cecilia may not be the most beautiful girl around, but she has a respectable dowry," I say to Ramon, making my voice as hard as I can. I do, of course, know it is not just her looks that keep away suitors. She always has her nose in a book and prides herself on her fine drawing and writing skills. What man cares about writing skills, I ask you?

"Leave me alone, mother, will you?" Ramon says. "You are giving me a worse headache than I have already, just by mentioning her name. She is so ugly she gives me the creeps."

Ramon forgets that he himself is no catch for any girl. He is handsome enough: he has the noble features of his father, the nose of a Caesar, and he needs no padded shoulders to make him look like a man, but he is a spendthrift and has a roving eye. Still, if Cecilia's father agreed to the marriage, I suppose the girl would prefer Ramon to the cheerless life of an old spinster.

He goes to the fountain in the centre of the court and splashes water over his face and rubs his head vigorously. Then he wipes his face on the sleeves of his shirt and sits on the stone steps, in sodden silence.

Thank God for my annuity and the provision in Diego's will that gave me the house for life and made me secure in my old age. Ramon inherited the rest, a solid sum of money and a substantial property even after those fields were sold, but he is a wastrel and God knows what will become of him. He has already gone through half of his inheritance and may yet end up a burden to me, unless he makes a lucrative marriage.

I am racking my brain what to say to him, how to encourage him to propose to Cecilia, when Jacinto returns from his errand.

Ramon looks up at him without moving from his seat on the steps.

"You look all pooped, old man," he says. "What's going on?"

But Jacinto hasn't enough breath left to answer him. He leans against a pillar, clutching his chest, breathing heavily.

"I heard that Luisa is back in Seville and sent Jacinto to find out if it's true that she is the owner of a candle shop now," I say to Ramon. "That's what Doña Eugenia told me, at any rate."

"Luisa? What Luisa — Father's jade, you mean?" When he sees my hurt look, he pulls back. "Come now," he says, "I meant no offence, mother. His favourite slave, shall we say. I thought she went to Mexico."

"She did, but now she is back and has set up shop in San Bernardo. I told Jacinto to look her up and tell me how she is doing."

"Why didn't you send me? That's an errand I would not have minded. Father had good taste in women."

"Ramon!" I choke back tears.

"I meant that as a compliment to you, of course," he says, mirth dancing in his eyes. He has no pity.

Jacinto has recovered his breath, meanwhile. He found the candle shop and went in, he says. Luisa was behind the counter, serving customers, and her helper was busy fetching wares from the storeroom. On the shelves, there was a good stock of tallows and wax candles.

"Even some of beeswax. The scent was all over the store, although I don't know who can afford that kind of stuff in San Bernardo, unless the priest buys them for special masses."

"And did Luisa recognize you?" I ask him.

"She recognized me at once," he says, "but she had no time to talk."

"Or didn't care to, because she never was one for talking," I say.

"I did give her your invitation to visit tomorrow, señora, but she said she couldn't leave the shop. Business is keeping her on her toes."

What impertinence! That's just like her. Luisa never had any respect for her betters.

"That girl was a looker," Ramon says, "but that was ten years ago. What does she look like now?"

Jacinto opens his mouth, but I cut him off. "Never mind her looks," I say. "The shop was busy, you say?"

"Yes," Jacinto says. "I didn't want to be in the way, so I left. But I did get to talk to Luisa's helper because he was heading out with a delivery and going in the same direction as I. He is a good-looking lad, except that his right cheek is marked by a great, ugly scar. 'How did that happen?' I asked him. 'A mule kicked me,' he said. Some mule! More likely he got cut up in a fight — that's what it looked like to me."

"What I want to know is how Luisa made enough money to buy the house," Ramon says with a leer. "I bet you she had help from a generous patron."

"The lad told me that her husband was a silver miner in Mexico," Jacinto said.

"And what happened to him?" I say. "If she was really married, that is."

"I don't know, señora. I didn't ask. I thought she was a widow."

"You know those girls," Ramon says. "They call themselves 'widows' when they reach a certain age and have to give up the profession."

"I think you are right," I say. "I myself never believed the story going around at the time, that she married a sailor. She ran off with a sailor, more likely, and exchanged him for a miner in Mexico."

"I wouldn't know about that," Jacinto says. "But now, Doña Ana, I must beg you to let me sit down and rest, because I'm all done in from the walk."

"Go and rest, then," I say and, against my better judgment, tell him to go into the kitchen and ask the cook to give him a glass of sweet lemonade. I know I am too soft-hearted.

2

Seville, 1575:

Don Francisco, parish priest

THE BOY WHO USED TO help me in the garden — whatever happened to him?

I wish my mind wasn't in such a blur.

The nuns are looking after him, yes, that's what it is, but I worry that Sister Maria will get her hands on the child and hurt him. God has struck her with madness and filled her head with dark and bloody fantasies, thorns and arrows and knives.

No, wait, I no longer have to worry about the boy. Luisa is back and will take care of him. She always acted with a firmness you didn't expect from her soft looks and tender voice. She had to make some difficult choices after Diego's death, but she never flinched. She did what she had to do.

I didn't expect to see Luisa again after she married and set out for Mexico so many years ago. When she came to see me at the hospice yesterday, I thought at first she was a figment of my imagination, a ghost of a memory. My mind has been wandering lately and playing me tricks. There are times when the past is more vivid to me than the present. I become a child again and walk on a dusty road by my father's side, holding his hand. Or I watch my mother shelling peas in the yard in preparation for supper. Or I am once more a postulant and stand before the altar, looking up at the painting of Christ suffering on the cross, an oil painting darkened by age. I kneel down on the flagstones in the church, worn smooth by a thousand shuffling feet, and am ordained by the bishop. I hear the echo of footsteps and voices extinguished long ago, and glimpse the faces of my parishioners: a parade of rich and poor, well-fed and hollow-eyed, old and young, haggard and rosy-cheeked, hidalgos and slaves, like Luisa. I hear their confessions and their complaints floating up to me through the dark, and repeat my advice and my admonitions to them and wonder whether I was right. The present blends into the past as I lie on my cot, staring up at the whitewashed ceiling of my room in the hospice.

They have put me into a room like a monk's cell to let me die in peace. There is a small, barred window high up in the wall that tells me the time of day. I see only a patch of sky, hazy in the morning, bright blue on a sunny day at noon, turning mauve in the later afternoon and at last blending into the velvety night. The room is facing the orchard, I believe, because it is so very still in here. I lie beyond the sound of human voices except when the attendant comes in three times a day to bring me a bowl of gruel and to refill my water jug, or when the orderly rolls me over, like a sack of bones, and changes the sheets, for I am like a newborn again, pissing and shitting myself without shame. The very room stinks of death, and the taste of death is in my mouth. It will not be long now before God calls me from this world. I have begun to examine my conscience and am spending long hours in thought, going over my past actions, repenting my sins.

I wonder what God I will meet: the God of wrath we read about in the books of the Old Testament, or the God of mercy to whom the psalmist sings his grateful song, or Christ the Redeemer who is one with the Father, or the Spirit of God who is joined to them in the Trinity. I have never understood God, but I expect I will once my soul has shed its mortal coil and stands in his presence.

God has given me a long life — whether that is a blessing or a punishment, I do not know. A long life has given me more opportunity to sin as well as to do good. From childhood on I wanted to dedicate myself to God. Not that I was a particularly holy child. I did my share of mischief and practised all the vices usually found in boys — lying, cheating, fighting, shirking work, and idling — but even as a young man, I was never bothered by two vices commonly found among men: avarice and lewd thoughts. I did not cast lusty eyes on women and I had no desire to accumulate money. Fortified against those two temptations, I led a blessed life.

Dear God, what am I saying! Is it a blessing that you have never visited me with those temptations, never struck me down with sickness before, or made me suffer poverty or the horrors of war? Does a man deserve such happiness? I am afraid I will be judged all the harsher for it in the afterlife. A poor, sick cripple has done his penance on Earth, and God will pity him. A fortunate man like me will face an interrogation on Judgment Day: What have you done to deserve a happy life? I can only cry out, *I served you as best I could, oh Lord.* I tried to be a good shepherd to the flock you entrusted to me. Was I compassionate enough with the sufferers, stern enough with the sinners, or did I fall short in my obligations?

I fear I will meet the God of wrath and judgment. He may be merciful to the common herd, but he will be demanding of the elect: his representatives on Earth. How confident I was once, thinking that I was equal to the tasks of a priest. I thought I could make of my flock the lambs of God, but I did not succeed. I did not make them better. I listened to their confessions and wearied of the sameness and the repetitions. I saw that I had not changed their hearts. And now that the day of judgment draws near, I am afraid I will be weighed and found lacking.

Dear God, I prayed yesterday, lying on my cot in the hospice, *Make me ready for the final journey*. And so, when I opened my eyes and saw a woman standing at my bedside, I took her for an angel of God come to carry me away. Then I strained my poor eyes and recognized the woman speaking to me. It was Luisa.

I recognized her even though I hadn't seen her in years and she was no longer the slim, lively girl I had known. Her slenderness had turned to angularity; her face is careworn now and her dark hair shot through with grey as if she had suffered some terrible ordeal, but her smile was as sunny and warm as ever and her voice as melodious. At first, I could not make out what she was saying. Her words seemed to float in the air, but slowly they descended and penetrated my mind, and I realized that she was asking for my help to get the boy back from the Clares.

Then I licked my dry lips, opened my mouth and said, or tried to say, "You will have to fight that battle yourself, my dear girl. You can see that I am a helpless old man now. I barely have the strength to draw breath, never mind argue your case with the Abbess of Saint Clare, who is a very determined woman."

A garbled sound came out of my mouth, but I think she understood me. She sat down at the edge of my bed, reached for my hand, and pressed it a little too hard; my bones are brittle now and my skin painful to the touch.

"I know you have done a great deal for me, Father," she said, "and I am sorry to see you laid so low."

"Growing old and dying is the fate of every mortal," I said, and she bent down, straining to hear my words. I wanted to add, "And I hope to have conducted my life in such a manner that I will be permitted to look upon the face of my Maker and be deemed worthy to share his glory on the Judgment Day." But my voice gave out.

"I'll pray for you, Father," she said, "and do say a prayer for me in turn because it's more likely God will listen to a good priest than to a sinner like me."

After she left and I was alone again, I raised my eyes to the wooden cross hanging on the wall across from my bed and silently beseeched God to help Luisa in her quest for the boy she boarded with the Clares all those years ago. I thought about her for a long time, wondering whether she had told me the truth about the child. She said he was the son of a friend who died in childbirth, that she had promised to look after the baby, but she was no longer able to do it and had to give him up. Could I find a good home for the child? I had my doubts about her story. Was the baby truly her foster child or was he her own, a child born out of wedlock? But then, who was the father?

I felt sorry for Luisa. Whatever Doña Ana thought about the provisions of her husband's will, it was only fair that he set Luisa free and left her money. A hundred ducats is a large sum, but I question whether it can compensate a girl for the loss of her virginity. Diego seduced her when she was barely fifteen. He made her his mistress in defiance of the laws of the Church and my earnest admonitions. I was afraid it would come to that after Doña Ana told me in so many words that she was done with her marital duties. I could not very well insist on her continuing with carnal relations, which the Church allows only for the purpose of procreation. I did, of course, remind her that when they stood before the altar and became husband and wife, she had vowed to love and obey Diego. Diego, I knew, would not abstain. His spirit was weak. He was a man of the flesh, and Luisa was in the house, her considerable charms always before his eyes. Diego made his annual confession, of course, as he was bound to do by the laws of the Church, but I have my doubts that he truly repented of his sin. He offered a thousand excuses.

"Luisa was willing," he said. "She baited me. She is a beautiful girl and likes to parade her beauty before my eyes."

"Then you must resist," I said.

"I can't," he said, "but I try to be careful not to impregnate her because I realize that childbirth is risky, especially for one so young. I wouldn't want to lose her. You have to give me credit for that."

"God will not give you credit for that," I said. "On the contrary, he will debit your account, and those sins of yours will weigh on you when you stand before the Heavenly judge."

Then he tried another tack.

"But Luisa is my slave, after all. She is my property, just like my house or my horse. I take care of my property, of course, but am I not entitled to use it as I please?"

"We are talking about the laws of God, not about the laws of men," I reminded him.

"And are relationships with heathens governed by the same laws as those with Christians?" he asked, kneeling there in the dark confessional, his face obscured and his voice muffled by the heavy wooden grid, so that I could not tell by his looks or his voice whether he was penitent. His arrogant question pointed to an unrepentant mind.

"Luisa *is* a Christian," I said sharply. "All your house slaves have been baptized."

"But they remain heathens at heart," he said.

"Never mind *their* hearts. We are dealing with your heart and your conscience here," I said to him. "You are a married man, and it is a sin to fornicate and commit adultery. Do you repent of your sin?"

"Of course," he said. "I repent it deeply, every time."

What could I do? If a man professes repentance, he can't be denied absolution. I did make him pay a hefty penance, but a fine is no deterrent for a rich man. I knew Diego would sin again and felt helpless in the face of such goings-on, which had become almost routine among the wealthy men in my parish. "The love of money is the root of all evil," as the apostle Paul says. And when I looked around the parish church, the gold-embroidered cloth on the altar, the communion chalice garlanded with rubies and emeralds, the rich votive offerings and the row of tall wax candles lit before the statue of the Madonna, when I heard of the great sums of money my parishioners spent on indulgences to buy their way into Heaven: If I contemplated all that, I saw that the root of evil was entangling the very Church together with its bishops and perhaps even the Pope, and was sprouting new and monstrous shoots every day. The thought of the Church's wealth and my own impotence troubles me a great deal, until I look upon my own bare cell here at the hospice and think of the words of Jesus, "Blessed are the poor in spirit, for theirs is the Kingdom of Heaven," and for a while at least I am comforted and savour peace in my heart. Then my thoughts turn to Luisa again.

It may be true that she was a willing participant in those sinful carnal acts and that she was even a little in love with her master, the silly girl, or flattered because he singled her out among the servants and paid her attention. He was a good-looking man and had a way with words. What could I say to her or to Diego? The work of a parish priest is never-ending. I had to divide my care and attention among so many people, give advice and make decisions on so many cases, and consider so many circumstances. It was a task that exceeded human wisdom.

Take Doña Ana's marriage, for example. The Church requires a bride to enter into the union freely, but very often it is the parents who make the decision. Doña Ana's heart may have been engaged elsewhere, but they urged her to marry Diego. No doubt they pressed their case, as parents do: He is rich, he comes from a good family, he will keep you in style. And Diego himself was a man who knew how to use fine words and might have persuaded her that it was for the best. That is how young girls enter so serious a contract, not because they decide freely, but because they are obedient and ignorant and easily persuaded. How often have I listened to tearful brides, shocked by the events of the first night, asking me how this could be right in the eyes of God, and I could only quote them the Bible, "Be fruitful and multiply," and hope that love would smooth their way.

Poor Doña Ana had a phlegmatic temper and would have been better off marrying an old widower who didn't make too many demands on her, rather than a lusty young fellow like

Diego. She suffered two miscarriages and felt sheer terror at the thought of another pregnancy, and when it was all over and she had given Diego a son, she wanted only to be left in peace.

At least Luisa knew what to expect when she got married. She was no virgin when she stood before the altar in my and God's presence and said "I do" to her bridegroom. She was more like a widow about to remarry. When Diego died, she was certainly as distressed as if she had been his widow. Her tears were genuine. She felt more sorrow perhaps than Diego's lawful wife and his son, who seemed to care only for the dead man's fortune.

Luisa was a beautiful woman and did not lack suitors when word got out that Diego had provided a dowry for her, but Doña Ana should have kept an eye on the girl when Jordan, the apothecary's assistant, came calling. She was responsible for Luisa as long as she was in her house and should have protected her against the sinful intentions of that man. I told her as much when she came to see me one day to ask me about the significance of the promise of marriage he had given Luisa, privately.

Doña Ana came to the parish house and looked around with disdain at the simple room where I received my visitors. She had no respect for my clerical office. I was a nobody in her eyes. She measured the worth of a man by the weight of the silver goblets on his sideboard, the size of the jewels on the fingers and earlobes of his wife, and the number of slaves serving in his household. I am afraid my words did not carry much weight with her after she had summed up the value of my poor furnishings. But she was my parishioner, and when she asked me questions, I answered them, even if I did not have much hope that she would follow my advice.

She wanted to know what to do about Jordan, who had given promises to Luisa and then jilted her.

"You must confront him," I told her, "and keep him to his promise."

"But what I want to know is am I responsible for the girl?" She looked at me defiantly. She had been meeker during her husband's lifetime. It was as if she felt entitled to hold the reins now and no one could tell her how to run her household. "I am not even sure that Luisa is still my slave. Diego has set her free, as you know. I am only waiting for his will to be proved to settle it all."

"Even so," I said. "Luisa is living under your roof, isn't she? It is the duty of the mistress of the house to maintain order in her household, to protect her servants and tolerate no immoral goings-on."

"But the man seemed eligible to me, and so I saw no harm in allowing him to meet Luisa. You cannot say that I neglected my duty. I have come to you the moment the girl told me that he had made her a promise of marriage and then jilted her."

There was no use arguing with Doña Ana. It was hard to keep a man to a promise for which there were no witnesses, and she seemed almost gleeful that he had jilted Luisa. I knew the reason, of course. She was bitter and resentful that her husband had carried on with the girl and that he had left Luisa money. Ana was sore about losing a slave, and in no mood to stick up for Luisa or console her over the loss of her lover.

When the apothecary's man did marry another woman, Doña Ana's comment was, "I am sure it was Luisa's fault. She got what she deserves." She felt no pity for the girl's misery. She hated Luisa, even though she tried to hide her feelings and camouflaged them as moral indignation.

One day, after the will had been proved, Luisa herself came to see me. I was reading my breviary, sitting on a bench behind the parish house overlooking the cemetery. From time to time I looked up at the wooden crosses of the poor and the mausoleums of the rich, the final resting place of the dead and a fitting place to contemplate for a priest who must have no stake in this world. A ghost rose up, or so it appeared to me for a moment — a black figure, a silhouette backlit by the afternoon sun — but it was no ghost. It was Luisa coming through the wrought-iron gate of the graveyard. She was wearing her Sunday best: a white mantilla over her shoulders and a stiff skirt, newly starched, swaying from side to side as she walked. I thought she looked preoccupied and unusually sombre, or perhaps I had that impression only because we were surrounded by reminders of our mortality.

She greeted me, and I invited her to sit down beside me and asked for her news. She said she had left Doña Ana's house and had found employment in the barrio of Triana, the port lands.

"What kind of employment?" I asked.

"I am working for a woman who rents out rooms to bargemen and sailors," she said.

The port was not a good place for a young woman. The houses there were dens of iniquity. To call them "boarding houses" was a euphemism. They offered cheap rooms to sailors, but for the most part they served as places of assignation and were no better than brothels. A young, beautiful woman like Luisa would soon fall prey to flattery and the temptation of making easy money. Perhaps Luisa had already succumbed to that temptation and was in trouble now. That would explain her preoccupation, I thought.

"What kind of work are you doing there?" I asked Luisa.

"I help out with the cooking and cleaning, and I do the laundry. In return I am given room and board and paid a peso a day," she said.

I am trying to remember what exactly she told me, the street in Triana she named, but my poor head can no longer keep facts from fantasy. I cannot hold on to the words she spoke; they slip through my fingers, get lost in the fog of my childhood memories. Thinking of Triana, it seems to me that the walls of my cell in the hospice have opened up and the room is filled with the noise of cartwheels turning and a confusion of raucous voices. I am a boy again, walking with my father across the pontoon bridge over the Guadalquivir River, which leads to Triana and the port lands. The fleet had arrived that day from the Indies, and we walked along the public promenade and watched the wondrous treasures as they were unloaded by a great wooden crane, and later the carts pulled by teams of oxen, as they rolled across the pontoon bridge. What a marvel I thought it then, what excitement, the incessant movement of people, carts, coaches, and beasts of burden crossing over into the walled and turreted city and others being ferried across the river on barges. By the time I was a man, the pontoon bridge had become too narrow, so that another, broader bridge had to be built. But one thing never changed, despite all the laws being passed and penalties being threatened: the streets of the port were thronged by prostitutes and fouled with mountains of refuse. The air reeked with the noxious odours rising from the lagoons, and even the public promenade was edged with dung heaps. The householders were supposed to keep their street clean, but the law produced only a system of graft. The owners paid off the inspectors of sanitation. The gutters along the streets remained stagnant cesspools, and the prostitutes continued to ply their trade and parade their wares there.

But why am I thinking of the harbour now? Ah, yes, Luisa — she began working in Triana after she obtained her freedom. The lawyer had given her the document of manumission and paid out her inheritance, and being a girl with a great deal of common sense, she came to me and asked me to hold the money for her and keep her documents safe.

"I don't like keeping such a large sum at the rooming house, Father," she said to me. "The place is full of rough customers, sailors and their ..." She hesitated a little, but I knew what she meant.

"Their consorts?" I said. I was right to be suspicious of the place, and she herself knew that it was a house of sin.

"Yes, consorts," she said, her mouth turned down at the corners. "Theft is a common complaint in that house. You can't leave anything of value in your room. No matter how much care you take to hide it, the thieves will dig it out of your secret spot."

At least I think that was what she said, but now I wonder, because Luisa was a very silent woman. She never said much. Her animated eyes and full lips and the telltale movements of her body took the place of speech. The words I remember her saying may well have been my own, or what I read in her eyes, but one thing I know for sure: She gave me the money to safeguard and I promised to keep it for her in trust. She counted it out to me, taking the coins from a small leather purse, one by one. I put the money and the document of manumission, which she had neatly folded and tied with string, into the strongbox where I kept the alms, but thieves are everywhere, even in God's own house, and so on second thought I took the purse and the document out again and hid them in the niche behind the statue of Saint Mary in my own room. I asked the Virgin to guard the money and Luisa as well, to keep her from the temptations surrounding her in that evil house, but I also trusted in Luisa's own good sense and probity.

I didn't hear from her for almost a year, at which time she came to ask for her money back. I was relieved to see her looking happier than the last time I had seen her. She was neat and tidy in her blue cotton dress and white apron, and her hair was wrapped up in a scarf as colourful and exotic as the spice shops in Triana.

She came to me after Sunday mass. I was in the sacristy, putting away the embroidered mass clothes. She stood at the door, hesitant, modestly waiting to be asked in. I sent the altar boys on their way and dismissed the sacristan, to give us privacy.

"I am glad to see you so well, my dear," I said, taking off the liturgical vestments and folding the alb and chasuble into the drawers of the oak chest. "Are you still working in that rooming house?"

"No," she said, "I'm looking after an old couple now. They needed a girl of all work. I do the household chores for them, the shopping, cleaning, and cooking, and I tend to their ailments. It's more work and only half the pay, but I like their quiet little house a lot better than the rooming house, which was in turmoil day and night." She stopped and lowered her eyes. "I am content with my life, but a matter has come up on which I want your advice, Father."

Then she told me that a friend of hers had died in childbirth three months ago and she was looking after the baby, as she had promised the woman on her deathbed.

"The old couple have no objection to my keeping a cot in the kitchen for the little one. They are quite fond of him. But now I have received an offer of marriage."

I congratulated her, although I only half believed the story of the friend's baby and wondered whether I had been right in my surmise when I saw her the last time: that she was in a sombre mood because some man had gotten her into trouble. But perhaps he was doing the right thing now and proposing marriage.

"Is he a good man, and to your liking?" I said to Luisa and gave her a searching look. I did not mention love because when a young woman has lost her virginity, she must take what she can get and be satisfied. I assumed that it was a marriage of convenience, an arrangement serving the practical needs of both parties. She wanted to give the child a name. He wanted her money, and perhaps that was why she had come to me, to retrieve the money rather than to seek my advice.

"Jorge — that's the name of the man who wants to marry me — is a sailor," she said, "but he has grown tired of risking his life at sea. So now he has decided to seek his fortune in Mexico."

"Mexico!" I exclaimed. "And you are willing to leave your native land and go with him on such a dangerous journey?"

I myself had never travelled more than five miles beyond the city walls of Seville and could not imagine leaving my country behind and abandoning all that was familiar here, the church and the parish house and my congregation, which I loved despite their imperfections, but perhaps it was different for Luisa.

"My native land?" she said. "I don't know where that is. The Maghreb, someone told me. Morocco, Don Diego said. My

first memory is of a ship, its dark hold, and a shaking and rolling motion that would not allow me to stand up. That is how I
came here, and that is how I will go away, it seems."

I had never asked Luisa about her childhood and re-
proached myself for having taken so little interest in her. But
she was unlike the other household slaves in my parish, who
wearied my ears with their sad tales and made me feel impotent
because I could not comfort them or help them materially. I
could only offer prayers for them. Luisa was a woman of few
words and had never said anything to me about her childhood.
I had heard the wretched stories of the others, their violent
capture and abduction, the separation from their loved ones,
the beatings, the journey across the sea from North Africa to
Spain, chained in the hold of a ship, their attempts to escape,
fugitives drowning at sea: tales of endless woe that left me des-
pairing of my fellow men. How could Christians engage in
such cruel practices and treat other human beings like prey
taken in a hunt?

Luisa had always been very quiet and had never spoken
to me of her life. For all I knew, she too had suffered long
nights of tears and loneliness, hopelessness and bitter anguish.
Maybe that accounted for her good sense. Life had taught her
a lesson: how to keep her mouth shut and cope with adversity.
Even when she told me of the offer of marriage that she had
received, she said no more than was necessary and answered
my questions about her prospective groom with few words, but
her steady look told me that she was not sorry to leave Seville.

Yet I could not but wonder. "To cross the ocean and go to
the New World!" I exclaimed.

"There is good money to be made in silver mining, Jorge
says."

"But apart from the danger you incur, such a journey must be costly." What she had told me of her plans confirmed my belief that she had come to retrieve her money. The man was marrying her for her "dowry," the sum Diego had left her.

"The voyage itself is costly," she said, "and money is needed also for the overland journey to Zacatecas — that's what the mining town is called."

"And something also to start out with, once you are there," I said. "Does your suitor have sufficient money to cover all that?"

"My money, together with what he has laid by, will get us to the New World and help us set up in Zacatecas," she said.

We looked at each other silently. The light poured down from the stained-glass window into the sacristy. It lit up the holy vessels in their vitrines and made them glint mysteriously. The sweet, heavy scent of precious incense still hung in the air; a holy blessing, I hoped. We both knew how much could go wrong with Luisa's plan. The ship taking the couple to Mexico might founder in a storm or strike a reef and sink. She might not survive the journey. Her husband might die in an attack by Indians, or abandon her in Mexico for another woman.

And there was another stumbling block, she told me. "Jorge is willing to marry me," she said, "and I am willing to go with him to Mexico, but what will I do about the child? Jorge tells me to leave him here and board him with friends because the voyage is too dangerous for a newborn. He will surely die."

That might be so, but it also sounded as if the bridegroom was reluctant to take on a child and was using the hardships they would no doubt suffer as an argument to deter her from taking the child along. Presumably, he was not the father of the child. Perhaps the man who had courted Luisa earlier, the apothecary's helper, had gotten her with child. Or perhaps it was as Luisa had told me, and she was merely looking after the orphaned child of a friend. In any case, her prospective husband did not want to be burdened with the child.

"I don't have the heart to leave the little one behind after the promise I made to my friend," she said. There were tears in her eyes.

"The promise you made to your friend?" I repeated her words slowly to show her that I had my doubts about that story. She flinched under my probing look and lowered her eyes.

"If I take the baby along, I would be putting him in mortal danger because the voyage is rough even on men and women. I don't want to abandon him to the care of other people, but I couldn't live with myself if he died on the journey. It would be my fault for putting him in harm's way and no different from taking him to a plague house or putting him in the street to be run over by a cart. If I could leave him with trusted people and fetch him later, when we are established and he is older and better able to withstand the rigours of the journey ..." She trailed off and looked at me with pleading eyes. "Don't you know of anyone who would take good care of him for a few years? I am willing to pay for his board in advance, and Jorge would be content to marry me even if I brought him a smaller dowry and put some of the money toward the child being fostered."

"Do you trust this man Jorge?" I asked her.

She did not answer my question. Instead she said she was afraid there would be no other offer of marriage. No one wanted to take on a woman burdened with a child. She was right, I knew.

We stood in silence while I thought about her request. Then I told her I would speak to the Abbess of Saint Clare.

"If she agrees to foster the child, we will do everything in the right order," I said. "First you marry Jorge. I will perform the wedding ceremony myself. Then you give him your money less the cost of boarding the child with the Clares."

And that was how we managed it. To my surprise, Jorge turned out to be a white man. I had expected him to be one of her own race. He was quiet in manner, but rough in appearance, no longer quite young and not a man to attract a woman by his looks. He was tall, with the ropy, muscled arms of a worker, and he had grown a scruffy beard as if he wanted to make up for the sparse hair at the crown of his head. His face was like wood carved by wind and weather, his neck creased and cross-hatched, but he was able-bodied, at any rate, and his speech was respectful. On the whole, he made a decent impression on me. So perhaps it was all for the best.

I thought of what I had read in Bartolomé de las Casas's accounts of the New World, that there was such a dearth of female company that the men took up with Native heathen women who understood not a word of Spanish, and that they coupled with them in an unholy manner. So perhaps this man showed some foresight in bringing along a Christian wife who would bear him lawful progeny, tend to him lovingly, and bring him comfort in the wilderness. At any rate, the couple would have the blessing of the Church and be man and wife. Luisa had been no more than chattel to Diego. To this man, she might be a help- and soulmate.

I thought I would test the man with a question.

"Do you love Luisa?" I said to him and watched his face closely.

Would he say yes and mean it? Or was he in love with Luisa in the carnal way that Don Diego had loved her? Or would he tell a lie and say yes because that was expected of him, although he did not love her at all and was only after her money?

He answered well.

"I don't have much use for that word — love," he said. "We like each other. And we have interests in common."

"Luisa's money, you mean."

"And what if I mean that — it's as good a reason to get married as any other, and goodwill lasts longer than love."

I was reassured by his level-headed response and his blunt honesty; I liked it better than the polite lies I encountered so often in talking to my parishioners, the fog of pretense I fought continually and was unable to penetrate. I was impressed also by the man he brought along to be his witness to the wedding. He introduced him as Captain Juan Diaz, a man of fifty or so, with sharp and precise features and alert eyes that held your gaze steady as if to say: "My conscience is clear. I have nothing to be afraid of." His freshly brushed suit of clothes and his polished boots marked him out as a prosperous as well as tidy man.

Jorge had been on his crew and sailed with him for many years, the captain told me.

"We are both embarking on a new course," he said. "I intend to sell my ship and settle in Mexico. My brother-in-law has a large hacienda and a refinery in Zacatecas. I am getting too old for a life at sea, and he wants my help. His duties as mayor of the town do not leave him enough time to look after his business."

He was glad of Jorge's decision to join him in the New World, he said. He no longer thought of him as just one of the crew. They had become friends over the years.

Jorge had already told me that he had obtained a land grant in Zacatecas and intended to set up a mine, and the captain confirmed it.

"The area is rich in silver ore," he said. "Jorge has a good chance of success."

It all sounded promising to my ears, and I was glad on Luisa's behalf.

Meanwhile, the sacristan I had asked to be the second witness arrived and we began the solemn ceremony. It was a weekday afternoon. The church was deserted. We were the only people in the nave, with the sun slanting through the windows, bringing the statuary to life with a flicker of colour and illuming the painting above the altar, of Christ ascending to Heaven and God the Father on his throne.

I asked the couple to step up to the altar and join hands, to take the vows in the presence of God and promise to love each other until death parted them. Then I brought out the parish register and asked them to sign. Luisa drew an X beside her name, in the spot I pointed out to her. Jorge, to my surprise, signed his name in well-rounded letters. *There aren't many sailors who can read and write*, I thought. *Perhaps he is a better man than I thought and I should not have judged him by his appearance.* The captain, too, signed his name firmly beside that of the sacristan.

I had expected Luisa to bring her master and mistress along to witness this important day in her life, but they were too infirm to attend the ceremony, she said. It appeared she had made no other friends since leaving Don Diego's house and moving to the port lands. Or else she was ashamed of her acquaintances there.

I still think, though, that Luisa misled me about the child, that the baby was her own, begotten by Jordan, the apothecary's assistant. I did not question her further, however, because I was afraid of the complications that might arise from her answer. In retrospect, I think it was a mistake not to ask those questions. I was a coward. I should have persisted and dug deeper for the truth. A promise of marriage, such as she had received from Jordan, is a marriage once the promise has been consummated. That is the law of the Church. There were legal implications if Luisa had lain with the man and got pregnant by him. In letting that question go, and joining her in marriage to Jorge, I had neglected my duty as parish priest. I should have ascertained her status. I regret that omission now, but God is merciful and does not judge by human laws.

In any case, Luisa was right to invest her money in marriage. There might have been no love lost between her and Jorge, but they seemed to respect each other. Their feelings, I thought, might yet grow into affection, and affection was more durable than passion. I had seen some couples who married in a haze of romantic love and were at each other's throats within two years.

Mulling over Luisa's life, I doze off. When I open my eyes again, the shafts of the sunlight coming through the small window make the dust motes glitter. I am surprised to see that I am alone. I blink in confusion. I can still feel the pressure of Luisa's hand on mine, and realize that I quite forgot to ask her how she and Jorge fared in Mexico. Or did I ask her and can no longer remember the answer? She in turn never asked me about the child — or did she?

My thoughts begin to drift. I wonder who is looking after the garden in the parish house now, the pink and white oleander, the yellow mimosa, the purple jacaranda, the tiny pink and red hibiscus, and my pride, the yellow bee orchid. Ah, here is the boy, God bless him, weeding the beds and watering the flowers!

"Come, my son," I say, and he sits down by my side. He has memorized a passage from the gospel of Luke and is reciting it in his clear voice, which reminds me of Luisa's.

Luisa! She was here a moment ago, it seems to me. And there was something I was going to tell her. What was it again? Something of vital importance. Something about Don Diego's lawyer. What did Miguel Aguirre say to me one Sunday after mass?

It was a strange conversation, as I recall. And why did I think it strange? Slowly Aguirre's words are coming back to me and falling into place. He asked me if I knew whether Luisa had given birth to a child. I can't remember what I told him about the boy who may or may not be hers.

"I would have expected Luisa to contact me," Aguirre said. "It is a matter of great advantage to her, after all. Do you know where she lives?"

"She has gone to Mexico," I said.

I should have told Luisa to go and see the lawyer now that she is back. Or has my erring mind made up the whole story: the lawyer's questions and Luisa's return? Am I mixing up the boy in my garden with the baby left in the care of the nuns?

Dear God, take me to your bosom soon! I am no longer fit for this world.

3

Veracruz, Mexico, 1575:

Captain Juan Diaz, ship owner

JORGE AND LUISA. I CAN'T shake the feeling that they are in some kind of trouble. The words of my brother-in-law come back to me: "Half-castes are unpopular here," he said. That was one stroke against Luisa when she and Jorge moved to Zacatecas — and the fact that she has no talent for making friends. She is too reserved. A little like me, perhaps, but her case is worse than mine, because she doesn't talk, and how can you make friends without sharing your thoughts? Maybe she would have done better back in Seville, in familiar surroundings.

I have often asked myself whether I did the right thing when I persuaded Jorge to give up the sailor's life and settle in Mexico. I think I wanted to persuade myself more than him when I praised the advantages of beginning a new life in the

New World. I repeated to him a version of the advice Pedro, my brother-in-law, gave me almost ten years ago, when I lay at anchor in Veracruz.

We were sitting in a tavern fronting the pier, with every kind of life eddying around us, sailors who had come for a good time, girls looking for business, roughs looking for a fight, merchants celebrating a profit or drinking to forget their losses. The doors and windows were open to let in the evening air. It was salted with the ocean breezes and carried the din of the work going on in the port — the hammering and sawing, the low rumbling of carts, the voices of hawkers and brawlers, and the sharp commands of foremen.

I was in the tavern to pass the time, waiting for my ship to be loaded with merchandise before setting out again across the ocean. Pedro had come to Veracruz from Zacatecas to ensure the safety of a wagon train transporting his silver bars, because in addition to being the mayor and a haciendero, he also traded in ore. I don't know how he juggled it all, but he was a restless man and never happy unless engaged in some business dealings.

"I thought you hired soldiers to accompany the wagon train," I said to him. Surely a troop of soldiers offered better protection against robbers than Pedro — a middle-aged man with a flabby body and a paunch that betrayed his love of food. Sometimes I thought that food was his only true love.

"Someone has to guard the guardians," he said, opening his eyes wide and looking around, as if he wanted to root out any criminal lurking in the inn where we were drinking to his success. I suppose he was right. Those soldiers he had hired to protect the silver bars weren't above padding their pay by stealing from the paymaster.

Pedro had sold his silver to a merchant in Veracruz trading in precious metals. The transaction was to be completed the next day, and then those bars, too, would make the voyage from Mexico to Spain.

We had finished our dinner and were sitting idly, finishing off our mugs of ale — at any rate, *my* mind was idle, but Pedro had a plan. He had merely been waiting for the food and drink to get me into a mellow mood and make me receptive to his proposal.

"Let's face it, Juan," he said. "Sailing the ocean is a game of chance. You risk your life every time you set out, and you risk your profit as well. You have been reasonably lucky so far — reasonably, I say, because the last two runs weren't exactly profitable for you, I understand."

I nodded. "I didn't make much money, what with the fluctuations of the spice market, but I didn't lose money, either."

"You are getting too old to run such risks. You want my advice? Quit while you are ahead. Cash out and invest in something more solid."

"Such as?"

"Mining, or land."

My head told me that he was right, but my heart was pulling another way. I was fifty years old and knew very well that I challenged God's benevolence every time I sailed out of the harbour. But I loved the sea despite the rough treatment she gave me. I had no taste for land or precious ore, which struck me as nothing but a great weight around my neck, tying me down and taking away my freedom. I craved the salt air. I loved turning my face into the wind and looking out over the sea stretching to the horizon, with nothing to curtail my view, no walls to pen me in, no narrow streets to channel my path. At sea, I was a free man, setting my own course.

"Sell your ship to your partner," Pedro said. "Or if you like gambling, risk your money rather than your life, and be an investor like me."

"And where would I live if I gave up my ship?" I said.

"Why not settle in Zacatecas, where you have family? I'll tell you what," he continued, making it sound as if the idea had occurred to him that very moment, although I suspect he had met with me for the very purpose of presenting his proposal, "it would benefit us both.

"I'm in need of a manager for my hacienda. You can live comfortably there on your investment and on the salary I'm offering. The guy I have at present can't handle the workers. He knows it and is ready to move on. You'd be just the man for the job, a man who knows how to keep discipline. I won't be stingy with my offer because you are family, and because you are a capable man and trustworthy. That's worth gold these days."

I would be doing him and myself a favour, he said, looking at me with the eyes of a dog begging for table scraps. It made me leery of his offer. I would be close to my sister and my three nieces, he said. After all, they were the only blood relatives I had. He was offering me security and the affection only family can give.

I thought it curious that he put such emphasis on love and family when, in my estimation, he had no feel for either and understood only one thing: money. But he was clever that way. He adapted his expression to the situation at hand and chose his words with an eye to his advantage.

"I know you have reason on your side," I said, "but I'm an old sailor, and although my bones are beginning to creak, the very idea of settling so far from the ocean constricts my heart."

"Well, take your time to decide," he said, as we drained our mugs and rose from the table. "Sleep on it, and we'll talk again tomorrow morning before I go back to Zacatecas."

Think it over, he had said, and indeed I could not stop my thoughts from going round and round in my head and pondering what he had said. I slept poorly that night, tossing in my bed at the inn, turning Pedro's proposal over in my mind. His arguments were sound even if he was thinking of his own advantage, and what he had said about love and family was just empty talk. It meant nothing to him, but I had already asked myself: Who in the world cared for an old bachelor like me? My world had shrunk to the size of my ship, which I knew from bowsprit to aftercastle, and from top gallant to keel and sternpost. I knew every bit of rigging on the fore and main mast, the mizzen and bonaventure, and every flat piece and curve of planking, and I could read the ocean and the clouds like a book, certainly better than I could read human faces. Oh sure, I knew my crew and could guess a man's next move. I could gauge words and actions, but not feelings. That is a skill I have never mastered. Perhaps it was time to expand my ken and pay more attention to the hearts of my fellow beings if I did not want to find myself completely alone in old age.

My partner in business had remained just that, a commercial partner, and being always between ports, I had made no friends. I did not think it was wise to be too familiar with my sailors because they tended to be an unruly lot. I liked to run a tight ship and, to achieve that, you have to keep your distance and remain master of the crew. Jorge was the lone exception. I suppose I could call him a friend. He was the odd man out among the sailors, a sober fellow with a strict sense of honour and a disciplined mind, and he had been on my crew for four-teen years.

He came to me as a lad of sixteen, in my judgment almost too old to start as a cabin boy. I liked to hire them at thirteen or fourteen, at an age when they were malleable and not yet hardened by life or prey to vices, but my last hire hadn't worked out. I had misjudged the boy. He looked like a good lad and turned out a bad bargain — a thief, a liar, and a brawler. I had to let him go and was in a hurry to find a replacement because I was about to leave port and set out on another voyage. Jorge heard that I needed a cabin boy and applied for the job. He had a plain face and a habit of compressing his lips into a straight, unforgiving line that made him if not exactly ugly, certainly unprepossessing. He was tall and thin, a little too reedy for my taste, but when I put his strength to the trial, those stringy arms of his performed well. I hired him, and he justified my expectations. He was honest and loyal. He grew into a tough, wiry man — all muscle and tendons, with a body that served him well.

At the time I hired Jorge, he told me that he was born on a farm in Aljarafe. He was the youngest of twelve children and had to earn his keep as soon as he was old enough to lend a hand. He said he had been working in the harbour, helping the stevedores, but he wanted something more adventurous. *You'll get your adventure all right*, I thought; *more adventure perhaps than you bargain for*. I half expected him to quit after the first voyage, for we went through some rough weather on that pas-sage and almost ran out of food and drinking water, but he stuck to the job despite the hardship it entailed.

Much later, after we had become more comfortable with each other, he told me about his life before he hired on with me.

His parents decided that they needed to dedicate one of their brood to the Church to have an advocate in Heaven, and so at the age of twelve they sent him to the house of the Franciscans in Seville. There he was put to work helping out in the vineyard and the stable and giving a hand with any repairs needed in the house itself. For his service, the Brethren clothed and fed him at the least possible expense. He did, however, receive one gift from them: They taught him reading and writing and even a few bits of Latin. He had shown a talent that way, and they thought they might put him to work profitably in their archive, for the abbot took an interest in the history of our time and kept a record of events. He set Jorge to work copying out his notes and collecting them in a chronicle to be printed as a book and sold at a modest profit for the benefit of the monastery.

It was during a lull at sea that Jorge told me about his life with the Brethren. The waves undulated lazily, the sails hung slack, and a preternatural stillness prevailed. There wasn't a breath of wind. The ship swayed idly, rocking us as in a cradle and putting us into a trance and vacant reverie. We were sitting on the hatches, Jorge and I, drowsy and listless in the profound calm, looking out over the stagnant sea. To break the spell, we entertained each other with anecdotes, bits and pieces of our lives.

"Of course, the Brethren expected me to take the vows once I reached the age of sixteen," he said. "They tried to persuade me, depicting the cloistered life as a seventh heaven, but I could see for myself what it was like. The cloister was no better and no worse than the outside world. There were good monks among the Franciscans, who lived a pious life, and there were liars and gluttons and misers worse than any heathen."

The friars were bound by a triple vow of chastity, poverty, and obedience to their abbot, but many of them did not live up to their promise, he said. They lay with women, and men, too; they quarrelled with the abbot and each other; and they accepted money for saying special masses and prayers.

"But their sins did not concern me," he said. "That was between them and God. As for me, I did not want to take vows that I could not keep. I was willing to obey the abbot and do without worldly possessions, but I did not think I could keep the vow of chastity."

"You surprise me," I said. "I have always thought of you as a temperate man, but I suppose there is a difference between moderation and total abstinence."

"And a sixteen-year-old knows no moderation. I fell in love with the cook's daughter, who sometimes came to the cloister to help," he said. "When the two of us were caught mooning and holding hands, the abbot locked me in the root cellar and put me on a scant diet of bread and water. Then he gave me a choice: Take the vows or leave. I left."

Jorge laughed when he told me the story of his dismissal from the cloister, as if it had all been a joke, and perhaps it was amusing so many years later, but at the time it was no doubt a serious business to be cast out and find yourself without the means of putting food into your mouth.

"I left, but I was ashamed to go home and burden my parents again," he said. "That's how I ended up in the harbour, looking for work, and by God's good grace I ended up on your ship."

"I don't regret hiring you," I said. "You've proved a good sailor, and those writing skills the Brethren taught you have come in handy as well."

By that time, I had entrusted Jorge with keeping the ship's log, to record the weather and the distance covered, for he was quicker and more proficient at forming the letters than I. I also taught him the use of the astrolabe and the cross-staff to plot our course, so that he could relieve me at the tiller when needed. In a word, he had become my right-hand man.

Then, as we sat on deck, kept idle by the lull, I took my turn telling him my life story.

"I was one of three children," I said. "My father was a printer, and my older brother, Miguel, followed him in that trade. My sister, Maria, married a merchant banker, who had financed the Crown's expeditions in the New World and was rewarded for his services with a large tract of land in Mexico. He and Maria moved to the New World, while I apprenticed with an uncle who was a shipbuilder."

"Ah, your father was a printer," Jorge said. "That explains the books in your cabin, for I don't think sailors are in the habit of carrying books around with them. They are an inheritance, then?"

I nodded. "My father gave me the first one, a Bible, when I started my apprenticeship, and the second, *Lazarillo*, when I became a sailor, for he thought the story suited my adventurous life. The rest of his library went to my brother, who took over his print shop and who was a reading man himself. As for the third book, it's a keepsake. On my father's death, Miguel offered me the choice of a book to remember him by, and I picked out *In Praise of Folly* by the famous scholar, Erasmus of Rotterdam."

"A curious title," Jorge said. "Why would anyone praise stupidity?"

"I can't tell you," I said, "because the book is written in Latin, and I have never read it. But I remembered my father showing me the woodcut illustrations when I was a child. I was intrigued by them, especially one of a schoolmaster flogging a boy, and also the title page, which depicts a woman wearing a jester's cap. I laughed at those pictures and my father laughed at me. So I picked the book in memory of our mutual amusement."

"I wouldn't mind practising my reading skills on your books," Jorge said. "If I don't, I might lose them altogether."

"By all means, read the books. You won't be wearing them out," I said.

After that, he often came to my cabin at the end of the day and turned over a few pages in the books before sleep overwhelmed him. I believe that over the years, he read the whole of the Bible and halfway through *Lazarillo*, and once I found him poring over Erasmus's *In Praise of Folly*, but he admitted that the little Latin he had acquired did not allow him to make out more than a few words here and there.

We became close over time. Are we friends now? Perhaps so, but I think of Jorge more as the son I never had. He came to me as a young fellow. I feel I have had a hand in shaping his character and I take a certain pride in his accomplishments. He hasn't disappointed my expectations. He turned into a competent sailor, a reliable second-in-command. He is an upright man. Of course, whenever we lay at anchor, he carried on as all young sailors do when they are in port, consorting with loose women, drinking, and picking fights, but he never got into serious trouble, and he saved his money and placed it with a Jew in Seville to earn him interest. I thought he turned out well under my tutelage, although he never had a passion for sailing to match my own. He did his job well, no doubt about it, but I knew it was merely a job for him, a way of gaining a livelihood. That is my only regret: that I could not bequeath to him my love of the sea.

When I told him that I was going to give up the seafaring life and proposed that he join me, he was of course surprised.

"I would have thought you wanted to live and die on your ship," he said.

"If the *Marisa* went down in a storm, I'd want to go down with her," I said. "But I'm getting old. I don't know how much longer I can do the work of a captain. That's why I've decided to take up my brother-in-law's offer to manage his hacienda, which seems less strenuous and offers me greater security. So, what do you say? Will you come with me?"

"And what would I do there?" Jorge said.

I explained to him that Zacatecas was a prime spot for mining silver. I knew he had saved up a fair amount of money and told him that my brother-in-law might scout out a promising piece of land for him with mining rights that he could take over.

"Mining is hard work," I said, "but you are still young enough to do it and make a tidy profit from it."

Jorge thought it over for a few days and then decided to come along to Mexico.

"I'll do it," he said, "not least because I'll never find another captain like you."

I was glad to see that we had formed a mutual attachment, but he caught me by surprise when he said he wanted to marry before setting out for Mexico. He had never said a word to me about courting a woman.

"Then there is someone close to your heart?" I asked him.

"I don't know if that's the way to put it," he said, "but I have someone in mind. The question is will she have me?"

Then he told me that his intended was a mulatta from Seville. I didn't know what to say to that. I had reservations about such women. They seemed to me half-Christian, half-pagan, and although they might do for a night, I could not see why a man would want to marry one of them and be yoked to her for life.

I changed my mind, however, when he introduced Luisa to me. He took me to the house in the port lands where she was serving as a maid of all work, a shabby little cottage but spotlessly clean. As the owners were an old couple in the last stages of dotage, the neatness was obviously owing to Luisa's housekeeping. The moment I laid eyes on her, I thought Jorge had done the right thing after all. To begin with, she was beautiful. Her dark eyes drew me like a magnet, and she was full figured without being stout or corpulent. She moved with grace and had a pleasant smile. Her looks would certainly prejudice a man in her favour, but that must not be the deciding factor in choosing a wife. A bridegroom must first of all observe his prospective wife's character. In that respect, too, Luisa made a good impression on me. She seemed modest, keeping her eyes down and her mouth shut most of the time, at least when she was in my company. Silence and modesty are certainly desirable characteristics in a woman. Then there was the fact that she had money, as Jorge told me.

"But where did the money come from?" I asked him.

"An inheritance," he said.

I made inquiries on his behalf then, because I felt it was my duty to look into the matter, seeing that he was like a son to me and had asked me to be a witness to his marriage. In the course of my inquiries, circumstances came to light that did not reflect well on Luisa. The money had come from her late master. She had been the old man's lover and, what's worse, on his death, she had immediately taken another lover. At least, that was the information I obtained when I talked to the mistress at the house where she had served. She called her a lascivious girl, who had worked her charms on her husband and after his death had an affair with an apothecary's helper. Of course, I understood that the woman who gave me this information was none too pleased about having to pay her husband's mistress the money he had left her in his will. The provision might have come as a shock to her, and even if she was aware of her husband's affair with Luisa, the disclosure was an embarrassment to her, and the payment came out of her own share of the inheritance. I understood that she was disgruntled and resentful. Of course she would give Luisa a bad name, out of spite. But in addition there was the fact that Jorge had come to know Luisa at the hostel of La Vieja Negra, a house of ill repute, where she had been employed before she was hired by the old couple. Working at that boarding house cast another shadow on her reputation. And then, of course, there was the baby, a child out of wedlock. Against that damaging information, I weighed the testimony of her present employers. The couple was clearly very fond of Luisa, praised her highly to me, showed much appreciation for her care and industry, and lamented her decision to leave them. With two such contrasting reports, it was difficult to come to a satisfactory conclusion, except that the marriage was to Jorge's financial advantage.

My good impression of Luisa was confirmed, however, when I observed her on board ship as we crossed the Atlantic, and my respect for her changed to admiration when I witnessed her courage in Mexico later on and saw what a loving wife and good housekeeper she was to Jorge. I tried to befriend her then, but she remained a stranger to me — no, more than a stranger: an enigma. She was in the habit of saying very little, and

I am no good at reading minds or, for that matter, reading her eyes, which were downcast most of the time. But her singing! It mesmerized everyone on the ship. They gathered around her in the evening and listened as if in a trance. I kept away because to me her voice had something otherworldly and disturbing about it. It raised the hair on the back of my neck. Her melodic tune lingered in the air and slipped under the door of my cabin, wrangling over my soul. It seeped through the walls and made every other noise fade. Once or twice, I saw her dancing. It had the same effect on me. I looked on like one charmed. The movement of her body made the air around her undulate and turn into a shimmering mist. I tried to understand why her dancing unmoored me, but I was like a dog trying to understand a cat. I have always been a stranger to women. Why this is so, I cannot tell. After all, I had a mother once, and aunts, and I have a sister and three nieces, but I cannot penetrate the world of women. It remains as remote from my senses as the Isles of the Blessed.

Luisa confounded me, but then I was in a strange mood throughout that voyage, perhaps because I thought it was my last journey on the *Marisa*, or perhaps because of the people I had on board. I was carrying a hundred settlers, among whom was a group that kept to themselves most of the time. I gathered that they were fleeing Spain to avoid scrutiny by the Inquisition. They came together in the early morning, lifted up their arms and testified to God's greatness, raising their voices in his praise. To me it was a showy kind of piety they practised. I'm not a religious man myself. I do what's right and read my Bible once in a while, at Easter and Christmas, but I wouldn't call myself devout and I have no very high opinion of monks, priests, and the whole clerical order. From everything I have seen, the Church, like all large institutions, is corrupt. Nor did I waste much time thinking about the nature of God. I left that subject to the theologians — until I got talking to those strange passengers of mine. They were eager to explain it all to me. "You need no Bible," they said. "God's finger has written his message right into your heart. You need no priest, no middleman. Speak directly to God, and he will hear you, for he is all around you."

"Are you Lutherans, then?" I asked. "Or Calvinists?" I had heard of those heretics in Germany, France, and the Spanish Netherlands, who denied the need for confessing to a priest and did not recognize the Pope's authority. I had also heard that the Church condemned them and burned them at the stake together with their writings.

"No, we are no followers of men," they said, "although we think Luther and Calvin are good theologians and have a better understanding of God than the Pope and all his cardinals together."

"What are you, then?" I asked.

"We call ourselves *alumbrados* — illuminated," they said, "because we have seen the light of God."

"All the same," I said, "you will give offence if you are not more discreet in your devotions. And there is one man here on board — you may have noticed him making the rounds on deck; an austere fellow. He is an agent of the Inquisition and may cause trouble for you."

But they said they were not afraid of the judgment of men. So I let them be. As it was, the fellow — Alonso de Herrera, a lawyer for the Inquisition — left them alone as well. He almost got *me* into trouble, though, and backed off only because I humoured him, very unwillingly. He said that one of the books I kept in my cabin was heretical and made me discard it. I complied, knowing that I could not go against the authority of the Church. They wield power over you here on Earth and have power over you even in death. At least they want you to believe it's up to them whether you go to Heaven or be damned. Mind you, Don Alonso wasn't the worst of the lot. At least he didn't have a closed mind. He was willing to talk things over. He was a thoughtful fellow — "the Philosopher," I called him; not in his hearing, of course, only when I talked about him with Jorge. He too thought that Don Alonso was an exception to the rule of men working for the tribunal. He lacked their haughtiness, their aloofness and stony look, the aura of menace that characterized officers of the Inquisition. Yet he was a man of rank and authority and had been sent to Mexico to help with setting up a tribunal there. I wondered how the *alumbrados* would fare under the watchful eye of that court of justice once it started operating in Mexico — not much better, I warrant, than under the Spanish institution whose judgment they fled.

Our voyage across the Atlantic to Mexico — my last one, as I thought — began well enough. The sea was calm, the swell hardly large enough to break into billows, and the wind fair for most of our journey. I was already thanking my good fortune for the smooth passage, when we ran into a heavy gale that cost the life of one man and caused grave injury to another. After we had weathered that calamity, however, we made our way to Veracruz without further incident. There, with a heavy heart, I handed over my ship to the care of my partner, Andre Roldan. He was what I considered a youngish fellow, in his thirties. He came from a merchant family who owned trading posts along the coast of Mexico and invested in ships that carried goods across the Atlantic, thus increasing their share of profit in the trade beyond the markup on the goods he sold. I was only one in a stable of shipowners and factors with whom he engaged in business. He had a good mind for calculations and was shrewd in business matters, but I never warmed up to him even though he always had a ready smile — too ready, I thought, and not backed up by natural generosity or goodwill.

When I arrived in Veracruz that time, we drew up a contract, which gave him the use of the *Marisa* for eight months, or the time it took for a single crossing to Spain and back again to Mexico. He would invest his own money in the transport and get half the profits accruing from the two voyages. After that, I would decide whether to sell him the ship, remain a silent partner, or take the *Marisa* back and return to my former profession.

In this manner, my farewell to the ship was not quite as melancholic as it would have been had I let it go directly, without allowing for any change of heart. The arrangement gave me time to make up my mind and decide if I could bear to live out my days as a landlubber. It allowed me to determine whether I liked managing a hacienda and could be of use to Pedro, and if I enjoyed spending time with my family, seeing my nieces married and the generations continue. If, on the other hand, I felt regret or could not handle the business or did not get along with them, the arrangement would allow me to give up the land venture and resume my old life for however long I was able to carry on as captain.

Accordingly, the three of us — Jorge, Luisa, and me — disembarked in Veracruz. Over the next few days, they got together the gear they needed: a covered wagon and a pair of mules to transport their possessions, the tools required for mining, and the household goods needed to establish a home. I had brought along two horses, as they were in demand in Mexico and would have cost me a great deal more there than in Spain. I intended to ride one of them and use the other as a pack horse. Beyond that, I had brought only what I needed for the overland journey. Once in Zacatecas, I could rely on Pedro's help, I thought. He had undertaken to install and house me on his estate and equip me with everything necessary to take over the management of the *hacienda de minas*, as such operations were called — a combination of farm and refinery.

Together with a dozen families of settlers also headed for Zacatecas, we joined a caravan of wagons carrying lead and mercury, the metals needed to refine silver. The drivers of the wagon train were armed, and so were we. The road between Veracruz and Mexico City was well travelled and therefore offered us a degree of safety, but farther north, we entered a dreary stretch. The land did not look promising, at least in my estimation, although I cannot claim to be an expert in that sort of thing. At any rate, the soil seemed thin to me and the natural vegetation consisted of little more than shrubs, cacti, and rough grass. The land was as featureless and monotonous as the waves of the ocean during a lull. This place seemed to be in a permanent lull. The view remained unchanged throughout the journey. It was as if you were standing still and, by the day's end, had not moved at all.

An Indian at a supply post along the road told us that the land had looked very different in the time of his grandfather. There had been woods here and wildlife in abundance — hares, deer, and partridges — but now there was only the odd little wild palm tree. The forest had been cut down to feed the fires of the smelting furnaces. Now wood had to be brought in carts from ten leagues away and cost a great deal.

There was less traffic on the stretch between Mexico City and Zacatecas than in the south, although we did pass quite a number of carts going in the opposite direction, loaded with silver bars and heavily guarded by soldiers. The man in charge of our caravan told us that it had been a lonely stretch when he first began to ply his trade, but much had changed in the last decade. Ten years ago there had been constant wars between settlers and Native Indians and much destruction and loss of life, but the Native people had been pacified, he said. Indeed, they had settled along the road, as we could see for ourselves, and were employed on haciendas and as workers in the mines. A generation ago, our guide said, there had been few way stations or inns, and the road was in such poor condition that only two-wheeled *carretas*, light wagons, could pass. It had been widened and improved and was known now as the Camino Real, the royal road, although in my opinion it did not deserve that proud name whatever the improvements. Nevertheless, it was maintained in a condition that allowed heavy wagons to pass without breaking an axle. Keeping the road passable and safe was of the utmost concern to everyone, settlers and merchants alike. It was the talk at every inn where we stopped.

"What's the road like?" we asked of those coming from the north.

"How safe is the road around here?" we asked the innkeeper at the roadhouse where we passed what we hoped was the last night on our way to Zacatecas. It was a rustic place with rickety chairs and canting tables and cots with mattresses so thin that only exhaustion could guarantee a good night's sleep.

"Safe enough," our landlord said in answer to our questions. "Land grants have attracted settlers, and settlers in turn make the land more secure."

"Because there is safety in numbers?" I asked.

"Yes, it is good to have more people around here. As you may know, those who receive royal charters are obliged to render military service and defend the land." In fact, many of the estate owners were former military captains, he said, and had come to a mutual understanding with the Otomi and Chichimec Indians to keep the peace.

"They used to stage raids on the wagon trains and on estancias around Zacatecas, making off with silver bars and livestock. It was a constant worry, for they are a match for any Spaniard, both in bravery and in riding skills."

"But there is no more cause to worry?" I asked hopefully.

"I haven't seen a raid since I took over this inn two years ago."

"I couldn't help noticing, though, that your inn and all the other staging posts we passed are fortified like garrisons," I said. "I suppose that discourages attacks."

"That, and the fact that some of the supply posts are run by the Indians themselves. Others are managed by religious houses. Perhaps some of the credit for pacifying the Indians should go to the missionaries," he said.

"But the two monasteries I saw along the road also looked like fortresses," I said.

"Well, better safe than sorry," he said.

His words did not exactly put us at ease, and we soon found our apprehension justified.

The next morning, we set out at dawn, with Jorge driving his team of mules and Luisa on the seat beside him, for company. I rode behind their wagon, leading my pack horse and keeping a little distance so as not to swallow the dust churned up by their wheels. I believe now that I had a premonition of danger, but it was that nameless, shapeless kind of fear that arises from the haze of the early morning and is driven out by the first rays of the sun rising over the hilltops.

We hadn't gone far on the road before we heard the crack of shots, the shouts of men, and the pounding of galloping hooves. Almost immediately we were caught up in a fray between a band of Indians and a troop of soldiers in hot pursuit. The Indians swarmed past us on the outside of the road, using us and our wagons as shields against the bullets fired by the soldiers. They wore grotesque coverings of hide and fur that gave them the appearance of being fox-headed and they yelled like crazed animals, to frighten off their pursuers, perhaps. Their shouts did frighten the mules pulling Jorge's wagon. They shied and pulled sideways, so that the cart swayed dangerously. In the midst of this commotion, and before there was time to take any measures for our safety, one of the savages swooped down on Jorge's wagon. In one fluid movement and with the skill of a circus acrobat, he leaned out of the saddle, locked a muscular arm around Luisa's waist, wrenched her up, and carried her off on his horse. It was the work of a moment.

I let go of my pack horse and took off after the kidnapper. Jorge jumped down from the wagon, unhitched one of the mules, and took up the chase, but soon fell behind. Nothing could persuade the animal to increase its pace and do more than trot along. Nor could my horse match the pace of the Indian riders. The distance between us widened. Meanwhile, the troop of soldiers kept up the chase. I could see Luisa in the distance, struggling with her captor, her head appearing from time to time above his shoulder. As I galloped along, I silently prayed that she would not be caught in the crossfire between the raiders and the soldiers hunting them down, for they showed no concern for any loss of life and discharged their guns freely, aiming at the fleeing tribe. Soon one of the Indians fell out of the saddle, mortally wounded, while his horse dashed on. Another was captured together with his horse. The Indians had split into smaller parties to get away more easily, but the soldiers were closing in on the stragglers, those most heavily encumbered with booty. One of the pursuers managed to bring down the man carrying Luisa with a well-aimed shot. We saw his horse rear up and throw off the rider and his captive, then slow down and circle back to the two bodies on the ground.

When I came up to the scene and jumped off my horse, I saw Luisa lying half-buried under the Indian's body and heard a moan, or rather a keening, which seemed to come from the corpse itself. It was an eerie, harrowing sound, such as I had sometimes heard at sea, when the wind played in the riggings. I thought of it as an evil omen and feared a bad ending. Some of the soldiers gathered around now and heaved off the body of the Indian. As we shifted the dead man's weight and pulled Luisa out from under him, I was alarmed to see her covered in blood, which soaked the front of her dress and her hands, but as it turned out, it was the blood of her captor. Apart from bruises and abrasions, she was unhurt.

The soldier whose shot had brought down the Indian was already on the spot to secure the horse, his rightful booty and a considerable prize. But when we checked the body of the Indian, we saw that the soldier's bullet had only grazed his shoulder. It was a knife that had inflicted the mortal blow. A slash across his stomach was still bleeding profusely. I shuddered at the sight of his guts protruding through the gash, while Luisa stood beside me in silence, her shoulder drooping as if deeply saddened, while the soldier shouted in triumph.

The dead man was naked except for a loincloth and hides covering his shins. His long hair, reaching down to his thighs, was streaked with red paint not unlike blood. His face and his robust body were painted red as well, in a pattern resembling a tattoo. His staring eyes were open but the light had gone out of them.

In the meantime, Jorge had also reached the spot, jumped off the mule, and put a protective arm around his wife. She leaned into her husband without looking up, keeping her eyes on the dead man as if transfixed by the sight. In her hand, almost invisible, was a small, stiletto-type knife. She released her grip on it only when Jorge loosened her fingers one by one and spoke soothing words to her as to a child until she slumped into him, burying her face in his shoulder.

The rest of the soldiers had ended the chase and had turned back as well, carrying the silver bars they had recovered and leading two wounded Indians by ropes knotted around their necks, like the nooses of a hangman. The law of war gave the man who captured an Indian the right to make him his slave and sell him on the open market. We were told that they fetched a good price in Mexico City. The soldier whose bullet had grazed the kidnapper was disappointed to see his man dead, but laid claim to his horse. Jorge in turn claimed the horse on Luisa's behalf, because, he argued, it had been his wife who had killed the abductor. A dispute ensued, with the soldier countering that it was his shot that had stopped the horse.

"Let the woman state her claim," he demanded, "and I will answer her."

Luisa was hanging back, saying nothing.

"Perhaps *you* prefer fighting with a woman, but if you want the horse, you will have to deal with me," Jorge answered.

He left no doubt that he was prepared to stand his ground, and I moved to his side, ready to do my part if needed. But the case was decided by the captain of the troop, who spoke with authority and declared that the law was on Luisa's side. She had killed the Indian; therefore, his horse was her booty by right. The captain was in a hurry to get back to the road and make up for time lost. He was in no mood for negotiations. Thus, the soldier had no choice but to obey his superior's command and conceded the bounty, grumbling. We brought the horse back to the road with us and tied it to Jorge's wagon — the spoils of our "Indian War."

Luisa took her seat beside Jorge again and, after a while, began crooning in a low voice, to console or calm herself, I believe. It was clear that she was troubled by having killed the man, unlike the soldiers, for whom death was all in a day's work. I would have liked to say some comforting words to Luisa and perhaps also some words of esteem for her bravery, but Jorge thought it was best to leave her in peace.

I took my place again, riding behind the wagon. I could only admire Luisa's courage and the presence of mind with which she had defended herself and overcome her captor. At the same time I thought, not for the first time, that she remained a closed book to me. Her mind was beyond my ken. Perhaps it was because I had spent so many years at sea, surrounded by men, and it was that kind of life that made me lose touch with the other half of humanity — women — but Luisa was more difficult to read than anyone I had ever encountered before. Jorge seemed to understand her, however, or rather, there was a deep, mutual understanding between the two of them, which I envied. Seeing them together made me feel my own loneliness and led me to wonder whether living close to my sister and her family would make a difference and turn me into a more gregarious man.

We were on our final approach to Zacatecas by then, following the course of a stream the Spanish settlers called the Rio Grande, the great river. Yet I was told that it flowed only during the rainy season, from June to October, when frequent, violent rainstorms turned it into a roiling brown flood. It was December when we travelled up north, and the river was no more than a mud flat with a runnel of water in the middle. At any rate, it did provide enough irrigation for the surrounding fields of maize and beans, the only crops that could be grown profitably. We also saw cattle and sheep grazing in the distance.

By the end of the day we reached our final destination, Zacatecas. The main road into town was cramped, running between two hills, following a narrow valley carved by the river. The road was rocky and, we were told, prone to flash floods in the summer, but safe at this time of the year. A cold wind greeted us, for the city was situated at high altitude. I myself enjoyed the healthy breeze, which reminded me of the sea even though it did not carry its tang. The adobe houses along the road did not impress me. They were no more than low-slung huts. It was only when we came to the main plaza of the town that we saw several handsome houses, two stories high and built of stone, one of which was Pedro's.

The family had been expecting us. We were welcomed and offered shelter, but Jorge could barely be persuaded to accept their invitation to stay the night.

He was impatient to inspect the property he had bought on Pedro's recommendation. At least that was the reason he gave for his reluctance to accept my brother-in-law's invitation, but I believe he was also reluctant to impose on his hospitality. We both recognized the awkwardness of the situation. As alcalde, Pedro was a man of consequence in Zacatecas and his every look and gesture was one of command. My sister, too, liked to bask in the sun of her husband's glory, and the house reflected his standing. It was spacious, its rooms furnished with fine pieces imported from Spain and glowing with silver, the trademark of Zacatecas. The mirrors had broad and delicately worked silver frames. The massive candleholders adorning the table, the chandelier hanging above it, the ornaments on the sideboard, and the goblets in which we were offered a welcome drink of wine were all crafted of silver.

Although my sister made a tolerable show of welcoming Jorge and Luisa, it was apparent — to me, anyway — that she did not think the couple was quite of the class of people she liked to associate with. No doubt she would have relegated them to the servants' quarters if it had not been for me introducing them firmly as my friends.

At dinner, the talk turned to the usual questions about the condition and safety of the road. Pedro was alarmed when we told him of our encounter with the Indian raiders, even though it had had a lucky outcome.

"I've heard that such attacks are on the rise," he said. "I hope it isn't going to escalate into a full-scale war."

"Then the host of the inn, where we stayed last night, lied to us," I said. "He claimed the Indian tribes had been pacified, and we were safe."

"That's true of Zacatecas, which is a sizable community. Besides, the local Indians have become townspeople. They live and work here. We all thought the times of war were over, and we had come to an agreement with the Chichimeca, the most warlike of the tribes, to live together in peace. Or, rather, we thought we had bought peace by supplying them regularly with the goods they want. You could call their demands blackmail, but I myself accept the arrangement as a sort of toll payment for using the road. But some fools have lately provoked the Indians, leaving their way stations without paying for the food they consume or putting their horses and mules to pasture in the Indian cornfields."

And, I thought, mining the land without regard for any prior claim the Native people might have had on the territory.

"Those Indian raiders looked like formidable enemies," Jorge said. "They seemed superior to the professional soldiers guarding the wagon train, even though they had only primitive weapons, as far as I could see — bows and arrows, clubs, hatchets."

"The Chichimeca are indeed ferocious. Some people even accuse them of cannibalism," Pedro said.

"Surely that's a myth," I said.

"Oh, but they are cruel," Maria put in. "I've heard some dreadful stories. They torture their prisoners and hack them to pieces. They cut out their hearts and scalp their heads while they are still alive."

"That's enough, Maria," Pedro said with a meaningful look at Luisa, who sat staring down at her plate. She had barely touched her food. When Jorge then told the company of her ordeal and rescue, she did not contribute a single word to the story. She kept her eyes down, retreating into silence.

Now she looked up and asked to be excused. She was tired, she said.

"Oh, I'm so sorry," Maria said. "I didn't mean to upset you, my dear. Of course you must be tired after all you have been through. I'll take you to your room."

After the women had left the table, we men drank the rest of the sherry Pedro had brought up from his cellar "to round off the evening," as he said. The conversation turned back to the Indian raiders.

"I myself don't believe in the talk about cannibalism," Pedro said, "but I know as a matter of fact that one man was found with his genitals cut off and stuffed into his mouth. And they do carry the scalps of their victims around with them, attached to their belts."

We contemplated that bit of information in silence.

Then Pedro continued, "Their skill with bow and arrow is remarkable. The tips of the arrows are obsidian, you know. The stone is so hard that it penetrates metal and goes through layers of buckskin. I was told it pierced a horse's crownpiece made of leather and metal — went clear through the animal's head and had enough force left to injure the rider."

"They seem to be excellent marksmen," I said.

"And they can fire off volleys of arrows with incredible speed. Someone told me about seeing one of them show off his skills. He threw a fruit up into the air and kept it aloft, pummelling it rapidly with arrows until the weight of the shafts themselves brought it down to Earth again."

We had emptied the bottle of sherry by that time and Pedro offered to open another, but Jorge begged off. He was planning to leave the next morning as soon as the sun was up. He was eager to inspect the land he had acquired from the widow of a man who succumbed to a mysterious illness, or so he had been told.

"Not mysterious at all," Pedro said. "He died of mercury poisoning, the mercury used in smelting silver — well, if people are too stupid to take the necessary precautions, they can't be helped."

Jorge, changing the subject, asked where he could hire a man to help him dig the mine shaft.

"First you will have to repair the house, I reckon," Pedro said. "It has been sitting vacant for half a year. No doubt it has been damaged by the summer rains."

"Can you recommend a man to help with both tasks?" Jorge asked.

"You want an Indian," Pedro said. "They are better than the Blacks at taking the damp and cold in the mine shaft, but you have to keep after them because they are an indolent race."

He promised to send Jorge a young man, the grandson of a woman on his hacienda.

"His name is Chulo," he said. "He has shown some enterprise, at any rate. I would gladly retain him, but he wants to get away — from his grandmother, I suspect. She is an old hag who gives me the creeps. Since his mother is dead and he is the youngest of five sons and has no sisters, it has fallen to him to look after the old woman. That's one reason, I suppose, why he wants to leave the hacienda. He also thinks he can make better money in mining than on my fields, and he is right, especially because working in a mine gives him an opportunity to carry off some of the ore. So, watch out for thievery!"

Jorge thanked him for the warning, but I could see that he had taken the measure of my brother-in-law. Pedro was not inclined to give credit where credit was due and always believed the worst of any man, from an abundance of caution for his own interests.

"Mining is, for the most part, a lawless and transitory enterprise," he said now. "The men dig a shaft and work the mine for a few years. Once the yield falls below a certain amount, they abandon it and open up a new one. They are like nomads, moving from place to place. Some of them don't even bother with building a house. They live in tents by themselves or band together with others in work camps."

That was their own business, of course, Pedro said. He didn't care how they lived, but many of them neglected to pay the taxes they owed to the Crown and, being the mayor, he was blamed for the shortfall. From time to time, the authorities in Mexico City sent an inspector to rectify the situation and collect the outstanding dues.

"But after a few attempts, he realizes that it can't be done. And it's a dangerous business as well. He might get 'lost' in the hills, you know, and never come back. After a few unpleasant experiences, he smartens up and comes to understand what I'm up against. Then he decides it's easier to take the bribes offered and shut his eyes to the goings-on. He returns to Mexico City and makes his report, and the authorities leave me in peace for a few years, until another wise guy comes along, who thinks he can 'clean up' the mess."

By the time Pedro finished his story, it was past midnight. We thanked him for his hospitality and retired.

The next morning, we went our separate ways. Jorge and Luisa headed to their property, and I rode with Pedro to his *hacienda de minas*.

I could see at once that it was a large and prosperous enterprise. Pedro was greeted with deference by everyone and showed me around proudly.

First, he took me to the house where I would be lodged, a large cottage with a base of pink quarried stone up to the windowsills and timbered above. It was spacious enough to accommodate a family and well furnished, with solid pieces crafted by a master carpenter. The kitchen was well equipped with gleaming copper pots and pans, pewter dishes, and crockery. A Native woman was stirring a spicy-smelling stew in a pot over the fire. She was small in stature and dressed in a simple shift. Her black hair hung down her back in long braids. I could not guess her age. Her face looked old, but her movements were quick and agile. I asked her name, but could not make it out, either because she was bashful and whispered or because it was so foreign sounding. In any case, she barely dared to raise her eyes to me and ducked out as soon as Pedro gave her leave.

"If the woman isn't to your liking," he said after she had gone, "you can always buy yourself a Black slave or a mulatta, or if you want a Spanish servant, Maria may be able to recommend someone. I leave that up to you."

I said I was content with the present arrangement.

"Well, let me know if you need anything," he said. "I suggest we meet here once a week, and you can brief me on what's going on."

Then he showed me the property. It was situated close to the river, as water was needed not only for the fields but also for refining the ore. There was a tidy village of adobe houses, where the Native workers lived, and the threshing floor, where they beat out the grain. It was surrounded by storage sheds and barns. I saw corrals for horses and mules, sheep pens, and pens holding pigs of a kind I had never seen before, no larger than dogs and chocolate brown in colour. Farther on, I could see pasture land and fields of maize and millet that seemed vast to me.

"You need a great deal of land just to feed the cattle," Pedro said, "because the soil yields very little fodder for them. I breed about two hundred head of cattle, five hundred sheep, and a hundred mules and horses."

More than fifty Indian families and some thirty Black slaves worked the fields and looked after the livestock, he said, but it was hard to get any work out of them.

"Bad to have them, but much worse not to have them," he said. "I prefer the Indians myself, but they are restless at heart and will take off any time it suits them, even if you have a contract with them. The slaves are yours permanently, anyway, and even if they are slackers, they are a good investment. Buying and selling them can be a lucrative business if you watch the market carefully."

He also gave me a message for Jorge. "By the way, warn your friend: If he hires the Indian I mentioned yesterday, he should draw up what they call a *tequio*, a contract that obliges him to produce a specific amount of ore a day. And tell your friend to deduct the cost of feeding and housing the man in advance."

"I'll mention it to Jorge," I said, although I thought it was a cutthroat way of dealing with a worker. To my mind, at least, it was better to be generous and maintain a decent relationship with the men working for you.

"There is a fair amount of labour-poaching going on," Pedro said. "Especially if a man is good, another miner will lure him away with the promise of better pay. Jorge may have to lock the fellow up at night."

"Is that so?" I said. The idea struck me as preposterous, but then I thought, *Wasn't a ship a kind of prison for the sailors as well?* They could not quit work if they disliked their master — not until they were in the next port, and the practice of keeping them on board forcibly was not unknown in my line of business, although I myself had never had to resort to this dire method.

Pedro gave me a thoughtful look. "That mulatta wife of your friend — is she a freedwoman?"

"She is," I said. "Why are you asking?"

"Half-castes aren't very popular here," he said. "You know what people say about them, when they dress up all in white on a Sunday? 'Like a fly in milk.' I'm surprised he brought the woman all the way from Spain — although she is exceptionally good-looking, with a good set of teeth and a solid build. I'll say that much for her."

"I thank you for not talking about my friend's wife as if she were a commodity," I said sharply.

He gave me a sideways look and raised his eyebrows. "You'll change your tune once you start working with Blacks and half-castes," he said. "And I don't know why you are getting all steamed up. After all, we treated your friend and his wife very handsomely last night, considering."

I bit my lip, although I was angry. It was not an auspicious beginning for our collaboration. Pedro went on to tell me that all the men in his refinery were Spaniards. He wouldn't have it any other way, he said. That operation required real men.

He showed me the smelting furnace and the four mills grinding the ore, which were his pride. Each of the mills was driven by a pair of mules trotting in a circle and turning a wheel, which in turn lifted and lowered a block of iron — weighing seventy pounds, he told me. The iron crushed the ore spread out underneath. Next, the "meal," as he called it, was taken to a large yard paved with stone, where it was piled into heaps and watered until it became a thick slime. Then salt was added and mercury sprinkled on top and the whole paste was turned over with shovels, like a giant loaf of dough, until it was all thoroughly mixed.

"It's the paste that killed the man from whom Jorge bought the property. You must take care not to touch it or get it on your clothes," he said.

In the yard, he shook hands with a man whom he introduced as the "most important" man for the whole operation. He was the *azoguero*, who had the critical task of assessing when the mixture had reached the right consistency so that the greatest amount of silver could be extracted with the least amount of mercury, for that ingredient was expensive. The "meal" was then taken in barrows to washing vats, he explained. After the excess water was removed, it was packed into canvas bags to squeeze out and distill the remaining mercury. In the final process, the refined silver was melted down into bars of a standard size, ready to be transported in the wagon trains we had seen on our way to Zacatecas.

After that demonstration, we rode out into the fields to inspect the crops and back to the pens and corrals to look at the animals bred there. Everything on Pedro's hacienda was in good order.

It was an impressive operation, but it took only a few weeks for me to know that the task for which I had been hired did not suit me.

My apprenticeship as a youth in the shipyard had given me a certain familiarity with machinery, and I felt confident that I could handle the crew in charge of refining the ore. They seemed competent enough, but they were a rough and quarrelsome lot. A tease would lead to a bloody fist fight, or worse. This meant that I was called upon not only to supervise their work but also to settle disputes and (Pedro warned me) watch them closely so they would not steal any of the valuable metal.

At our first briefing, with the ledgers spread out before us on the table, I said to Pedro, "How can anyone hope to stay on top of all that and make sure the men don't cheat you and make off with some of the ore? You would be better off hiring decent and honest men in the first place."

"And where would I find these decent and honest men?" He laughed sarcastically and tapped the pages of the ledger with a finger. "All you can do is compare the figures and confront the men if there is too much of a discrepancy between what you got and what you expected to get."

Perhaps I could have remedied the situation over time and gotten together a more reliable crew, but I soon realized that my ignorance in agricultural matters was an insurmountable difficulty. When I made the rounds of the corrals, several men requested to be transferred to field work.

I asked Pedro about that matter at our next meeting, and he laughed.

"Ignore them," he said. "Of course they prefer to work in the fields. It pays better than looking after livestock."

"It would be a kind of promotion, then, for those who deserve it?" I asked.

"That would hardly be to our advantage," he said. "The best way to stop these constant requests for transfer is to lower the pay for the field workers and thus eliminate the demand. But that kind of move will work only if I can get the other haciendaros to do the same thing, or my workers will run off to those who offer better pay. There is another solution, however: work the field hands harder and save money that way."

He then put pressure on me to get more out of the field hands and try new and different methods of working the land. But I had no idea whether I could justly expect more of the workers, as

I was not familiar with planting or harvesting or stock breeding and, more crucially, could barely communicate with them. The men and women who did the field work and looked after the animals were Indians, most of whom did not speak the Spanish language. Sometimes I suspected that they did not want to learn Spanish and, even if they had acquired some knowledge of it, preferred not to speak what was, after all, the language of the conquistadors. When I asked the meaning of a word in their language, they could not help laughing at the way I pronounced it. Indeed I seemed unable to shape my lips or draw my breath so as to produce the correct sound, and gave it up altogether after a while. Otherwise, the hands seemed friendly enough and happy in the bosom of their families for, unlike the workers refining the ore, they lived with their wives and children and old parents in a tightly knit community. They seemed to have a good understanding of the Earth and its creatures, whereas I was like a blind man who discerned nothing — or, rather, like an idiot who saw everything but for whom nothing had a meaning.

Still, I thought I owed it to Pedro and myself to make an effort to master the responsibilities I had taken on. Six months later, however, I was still of the same mind. I wasn't the right man for the task. I didn't have enough knowledge and I didn't see eye to eye with Pedro on the treatment of his workers, his singlemindedness about squeezing more profit out of them. In a word, I knew I couldn't please him. I therefore gave Pedro notice of my intention to resign at the end of the eight-month trial period on which we had agreed. However, the experience had given me a better understanding of the tasks involved. I therefore counselled Pedro to divide up the work of the manager, to hire two men instead of one, putting one in charge of refining the ore with the other supervising the agricultural production. Jorge, I thought, might make a good manager of the agricultural sector, as he had grown up on a farm, and I certainly could vouch for his honesty.

Pedro thought the idea was a good one but doubted that Jorge would be interested in such a proposal.

"His mine has proved very productive," he said, "judging by the ore he brings to my mills and the money he has already banked with me. But if you can persuade him to work for me, I would certainly hire him."

"I'll talk to him, then," I said.

I was in the habit of visiting Jorge and Luisa from time to time and had been watching their steady progress over the months. The first time I went out to their homestead, it still had an abandoned look. The August rains had almost dissolved the adobe walls, but Jorge and Chulo, his Native helper, had already made a start on repairing them and making the place habitable. The next time I visited them, I saw that they had dug a new well and added a cistern to store rainwater. The two men worked together harmoniously, and Luisa too welcomed Chulo, in her quiet way. In turn, the lad seemed content to work with Jorge.

Although I did not approve of Pedro treating his workers like inanimate tools, I thought Jorge was going too far in the other direction. He treated Chulo like family. Being on such close terms with a hired man, and so fast, was not good. I told Jorge so, but he thought otherwise.

"I like the man, and so does Luisa," he said. "It is good to have company in such a lonely place, and especially someone who knows the land and the people."

Despite the reservations I had voiced, I was a little envious at the ease with which the three of them got along. Jorge had started out as my hire and turned into a friend, but it happened over time. It took me years to warm up to him, as I gradually came to know and appreciate his honesty and hard work. Chulo and Jorge had become friends almost overnight. Luisa treated the young man as if she was his mother or an older sister, and I must say, when I joined them for an evening and we sat on our hard, three-legged stools around the table, I felt more like a family member in their midst than I did at my sister's house. I looked around at the whitewashed adobe walls, solid now and pleasingly rounded at the doors and windows, and the earth floor covered with an Indian blanket. It was truly a home. I suppose some people are made for friendship, and Chulo was one of them. In his company, even Luisa opened up and contributed the odd bit to our conversation. She did not say much, but what she said stayed with me for a long time. On that occasion, she referred to herself as a *morena*, a "Brown" woman, and the way she said it! With a special emphasis, as if the colour of her skin set her apart from people like me. She had always puzzled me, but I attributed my lack of understanding to an inability to relate to women. When she spoke of herself as a *morena*, however, I sensed that she meant there was a different kind of barrier between us, one that went beyond the many other divisions in society by class, sex, education, or wealth, and I wondered how Jorge navigated those waters. The subject of her skin colour never came up again between us, but it stuck in my mind. I raised the matter once or twice in general company, proposing it as a kind of riddle. To my surprise, most people did not consider the question puzzling at all. They answered readily. They either brushed away the notion of any difference between us, with the pious assertion that we were all God's children, or else, like Pedro, they were quite sure that God had created a hierarchy among the races, and ours was superior to all others, Black or Brown or "Red," as they called the Indians. But the diversity of opinions among people only proved to me that a definitive answer to the question was elusive.

I wondered if Don Alonso, "the Philosopher," could have given me a cogent reply and, for that matter, how he was making out as lawyer for the Inquisition in Mexico City. Judging people in court, he would have had to deal with all sorts and all races there. In any case, all the people I approached with the question agreed that skin colour had nothing to do with understanding each other. That was merely a matter of personality and upbringing, they said. As for Luisa and I, we remained on the same terms of goodwill as ever. But goodwill is not the same as understanding.

Once the homestead Jorge had bought was repaired and fit for living in, he and Chulo started on the mine shaft. They dug deep into the hillside and began the operation of breaking up the ore-bearing rocks and bringing them to the surface. One day, Jorge took me to the mine to show off the work they had done. A path, or rather a mule track, led up from the road to the entrance of the mine. It was a steep climb and a considerable distance across the hills to reach the place.

"Your mine is rather remote and far from the road," I said. "You can't even use a cart here to transport the ore, can you?"

"No, I use mules as pack animals, and so does everyone else in these hills," he said.

He took me down into the mine then. The shaft they had cut through the rock descended steeply. We clambered over narrow ladders to a considerable depth. Every bit of the ore-bearing rock had to be carried up those ladders by the dim light of lanterns hanging from hooks in the walls. The air was cold and dank. The deeper I descended, the closer the air felt, so that I found myself breathing hard even without carrying a load. Groundwater was accumulating at the bottom of the shaft and had to be drained every day with a system of pulleys. It was a dismal place to work. I don't think I could have put up with the lack of light and air myself, but it was a way of making a living, and the mine was certainly lucrative.

"Chulo chose the right spot for digging," Jorge said. "He knows the earth and the rocks as if they had been his cradle."

As Pedro had predicted, Jorge was not interested in the offer to take charge of the agricultural enterprise on his hacienda. When I made the suggestion to him, he acknowledged that becoming Pedro's manager would mean a steady income. The work was easier and a surer thing than the yield from a mine, which would be exhausted sooner or later.

"But now that I have had a taste of being my own master," Jorge said, "I would not want to go back and work for another man. If the mine goes on producing for a few years as it does at present, I will do very well. When that vein is exhausted, Chulo and I will dig another mine elsewhere on my land."

It helped that Luisa was a frugal housewife and added to the couple's income by her handiwork. My sister soon discovered her skill in embroidering collars and cuffs, and Pedro discovered the potential of selling her wares in the City at a healthy markup. Luisa therefore had more orders than she could fill.

That was the situation when I left Zacatecas after eight months and took up my old life again on board the *Marisa*, crossing the ocean back and forth between Spain and Mexico. I inquired after the couple whenever I was in the port of Veracruz and met up with my brother-in-law or his agent. I thought of them and hoped for news of their well-being, when I sailed into port yesterday, thanking God for another safe crossing.

While the *Marisa* was being unloaded, I went to the office of the harbourmaster to settle my account with him and to pick up any letters left for me, for his premises also served as a deposit for messages.

His assistant, perched on a stool behind the rough-hewn counter, raised a hand to me in greeting.

"I'll let the master know you are here," he said. "He is busy just now."

The master's office was in back. I could hear voices raised in argument.

"Should I come back later?" I asked the clerk.

"No, he won't be long," he said and bent again over the lists in front of him.

I walked to the window, grimy with the soot of the oil lamps, and looked out at the pier. I watched the carters driving by, their wagons piled high with bales and bundles of merchandise. I saw a gang of Black slaves in ragged pantaloons clanking along, dragging their chains. They were being led to the market, like so many heads of cattle, to be exhibited and sold at the block.

The voices in the harbourmaster's office had died down. An angry-looking fellow rushed by me and out onto the pier. I could not imagine anyone getting into a fight with Master Samano. He was invariably calm, not to say lethargic. We were old acquaintances. Samano had held the post for more than twenty years. During that time, his appearance had hardly changed, but then he had always had an old look about him. The skin of his face was like a hide cured and preserved, his eyes were the colour of a rainy day, and his voice monotonous. He had only one topic: the rules governing the port.

He came out from behind the counter and beckoned me into his office, a corner partitioned off from the main room to provide a semblance of privacy. The shelves nailed to the walls were piled high with stacks of paper. The straw laid on the wooden floor soaked up the grease and dirt carried in by a steady stream of seamen.

After we had settled our accounts, he handed me two letters bearing the seal of the Holy Office of the Inquisition in Mexico City.

"The first one came for you more than two months ago," he said, "the second just the other day."

He watched me closely as I broke the seal of the first one. It was a summons to appear before the tribunal and attest to the marriage of Jorge and Luisa Abrego. The second letter told me that there was no more need for my testimony. The case had been settled.

"Bad news?" the harbourmaster asked, seeing my clouded face.

"More like puzzling news," I said and told him the contents of the letters. "I'd better find out what this is all about."

"If you want my opinion," he said, "do nothing. It's never a good thing to have business with the Inquisition. If they say your testimony is not required, leave it at that."

It was the most forceful remark I had ever heard him utter and the only time he went beyond the subject of the rules governing the port. I wondered whether he had any personal experience with the tribunal.

"You may be right," I said. "I met an inquisitor once — or rather, a lawyer for the Inquisition who booked passage with me nine years ago when they set up a tribunal in Mexico City. Our acquaintance was brief, but not entirely pleasant."

"Then you know what I mean," the master said. "In any case, you won't get an answer from them. The trials are conducted in secret. All you get to see are the poor sods who have been convicted and sentenced to an auto-da-fé, the public act of penance. You can watch them on a Sunday, marching around the main plaza barefoot and dressed in white penitential gowns that make them look like ghosts. I myself was present when they burned a witch. She stood on top of a pyre, tied to a post, and the people cheered when they saw her go up in flames."

"But you don't believe in witches?" I said, half-mockingly. He did not even break a smile.

"The less said the better," he said, his lips a thin line.

"All right," I said, "I'll take your advice and let it go."

I decided to write to my brother-in-law instead and find out what was going on with Jorge and Luisa. Three years ago, Luisa had given birth to a girl, and there had been talk about fetching her other child, the boy she had left behind in Seville. Jorge asked me to find a family of settlers willing to bring the boy with them once he had passed his eighth birthday. That was the term for which the nuns of Saint Clare had agreed to look after him and that was the age when they thought he might be strong enough to weather the journey. Luisa had paid for the first four years before she and Jorge set out for Mexico. As that term neared its end, she asked me to go to the convent in Seville when I put into the harbour next, and to pay for a second term of four years. I did so, handed the money to the abbess, and asked to see the child in order to report back to Luisa. The little boy looked healthy enough to me, but I was uneasy about the nun to whose care the abbess had entrusted him. She struck me as not quite right in her head. She made a great fuss when I asked to see the child because she had the fixed idea that I had come to take him away from her. The abbess and I reassured her on that point and calmed her down eventually, but what a dance she led us, howling and weeping! I said nothing about that to Luisa in my letter confirming that I had paid the money and seen the child. I did not want to disturb her unnecessarily. After all, what do I know about children? The little man looked happy enough to me, and perhaps at that age all they need is love. The crazy nun certainly loved him — perhaps too much.

A year later, Jorge wrote to say that their baby girl — in frail health from birth — had succumbed to a fever. They no longer wanted to stay in the place that held such grievous memories for them, for Luisa had had two miscarriages in earlier years. In that letter, he talked about selling up and returning to Spain. They had saved enough to allow them to start anew in Seville, he wrote. They might open a shop or a boarding house there. Then Luisa's little boy would have a proper family at last.

The second term for which I paid the boarding fees on Luisa's behalf must be up by now. I had expected another letter from Jorge with more concrete plans or instructions. Instead I held in my hands the two letters from the Inquisition. I could not imagine how Luisa and Jorge had become entangled with the tribunal.

"Is Pedro de Ahumada's agent in town?" I asked the harbourmaster. "I want to send a message to my brother-in-law."

He nodded. "You'll find his man in the usual place," he said.

He meant the Golden Shield, a popular tavern in the port.

I resolved to go to the tavern and give the man a message for Pedro, asking him to let me know what was going on with

Jorge and Luisa. But I was uneasy in my mind. It's the gospel truth: Man makes plans and God directs. Here I am, back at my old trade plying the sea, not knowing what will become of me in my old age. And Jorge? He was planning a life of prosperity for himself and Luisa. That may have come true, but his dream of a family has remained just that — a dream. And now, it seems, the Inquisition has opened a case against the couple. What could those good people have done to bring them before the tribunal?

4

Zacatecas, Mexico, 1575:

Alonso de Herrera, fiscal of the Inquisition

JORGE DEAD. LUISA IN PRISON. Who could have foretold this tragedy years ago, when I first met the couple on the deck of the *Marisa*, as the ship made her way across the Atlantic to Mexico?

I was braving the journey at the urgent request of my patron, Fernando de Valdés. He had been appointed to the post of Inquisitor General of Spain. In other words, he had reached the pinnacle of power after a distinguished career as archbishop of Seville and professor of law at the University of Salamanca. I could not deny the request of my old teacher after everything he had done for me.

Three years earlier, he had put me in charge of his foundation, the College of San Pelayo, a residence for law students. It was a task after my own heart: to look after the administration of the college and set up bursaries for twenty-five promising students whom Don Fernando himself had selected from a large number of applicants. He appointed me director of the institution, and I enjoyed the challenge. It was my task to look after the maintenance of the building, keep a watchful eye on the accounting, and ensure that the students observed the regulations governing their life in residence. I made sure that they followed the curriculum, enrolled in the required courses, and took the required examinations. It was a prestigious post and well remunerated. There was, of course, some grumbling about my appointment among the professors at the University of Salamanca. They would have preferred to see one of their own proteges selected for the post, but their official objection was to my age and standing. At twenty-eight, I was too young and inexperienced to take on such grave responsibilities, they said. Besides, it would have been wiser to appoint a cleric to the post rather than a layman, but I believe I served my patron well and vindicated his choice.

Thus, when he invited me to dinner, I expected only praise. Instead, he proposed ending my duties at the college and entrusting me with a different responsibility. I could not suppress the thought that the complaints of his colleagues had wearied him after all, and that he wanted to replace me with someone more in line with the general opinion: an older man and a cleric. But as I listened to his explanation, I realized that he had another reason for transferring me, a reason that was rather flattering. He wanted me to work in a sphere that was closer to his own heart, for he was an avid — not to say overzealous — guardian of the Catholic faith against its many enemies.

I joined him for dinner at his residence in the Inquisitor's Palace, an imposing building that looked like a fortress except for a few ornamental touches, a nod to its Moorish history. A grand portal broke up the plain stone facade. It was crowned with a broad arch and framed by a border artfully carved and embellished with arabesques, floral motifs of acanthus and grapevine, palmettes, and pine cones.

A servant showed me into the great hall. Under the vaulted ceiling adorned with a honeycomb pattern, the tiled floor spread out before my eyes like so many turquoise and red stars. Don Fernando himself welcomed me and led me to the dining room, where a feast awaited us, of delicious food and animated conversation. As always, my host began with teasing questions about my love life. Had I chosen a bride as yet, or at least settled on a lover, for despite his clerical profession, he was not above such banter. Indeed, he was a quirky old man full of contradictions, a militant defender of the faith but also devoted to scholarship; a stern taskmaster, but also a man of passion (and reputedly the father of an illegitimate child) — and, even in his old age, as vain as a peacock. I took note of the exquisite gold embroidery on his collar and the comb-over to conceal his incipient baldness, a manoeuvre that included three carefully arranged and rather ridiculous curls plastered to his forehead.

I smiled at his questions.

"I'm afraid I have no romantic tales to tell," I said. "I have not yet succumbed to the charms of any woman."

"You disappoint me," he said, "and, I suspect, your father as well."

After the death of my older brother two years before, I was my father's only hope of seeing his name perpetuated.

"I know I will not be able to hold on to my bachelor life much longer," I said. "On every visit home, I have to listen

to the pleas of my parents to provide them with progeny, but
none of the young ladies paraded for my benefit has raised my
heartbeat so far."

"Then you must be very hard to please," he said.

The women introduced to me by my mother and my well-
meaning aunts and cousins were most eligible as far as their
appearance and pedigree were concerned, as well as the dowry
their parents offered into the bargain. They were pleasant
enough company for an afternoon, but the thought of spending
the rest of my life with one of them, listening to their sweet but
insipid talk, looking into their eyes innocent of all knowledge:
that did not appeal to me at all.

As my host and I exchanged pleasantries about my love life,
or lack thereof, and congratulations about his recent advance-
ment, the servants poured wine into our crystal cups and served
the first course of the dinner — terrine of partridge with fig
sauce, which gave off the most tempting aroma.

Don Fernando changed the subject. He related the news
he had recently received from a man who was actively engaged
in the conquest of Peru. I soon realized, however, that my host
was not just entertaining me with anecdotes about encounters
with savages or adventures at sea. He had a more serious matter
on his mind: the purity of the faith.

He began talking about his responsibilities as Inquisitor
General, which he said would soon extend to the New World.

"It is not enough to purge Spain of all traces of heresy and
of the tainted blood of Jews and Moors," he said. "As we extend
our reach to the New World and harvest new wealth, as our
ships return laden with gold and silver, we in turn must bring
the precious metal of the true faith to the heathens there and
harvest new souls."

I had read the works of the missionary Bartolomé de las Casas, who related not only the work of converting the Native people to our faith but also their shameful treatment by the Spanish conquistadors and the plantation owners who used the Natives like slave labour.

"I understand that our missionaries have been quite successful in their efforts to convert the Natives," I said. "I only hope that those new Christians will be treated in a Christian manner."

"I share your hopes, of course," my host said. "At the same time, I fear that those new Christians will fall back on their pagan practices and, what's worse, contaminate the pure faith of the Spaniards living there."

Age had not mellowed Don Fernando. He was as forceful and determined as ever. Being a peaceful man myself, I wondered whether he meant to set in motion a new wave of persecutions and forced conversions among non-Catholics, and thus precipitate another crisis at a time that was already turbulent enough. After the conquest of Granada, the Moors had come under Christian rule. They resented the harsh enforcement of Catholic rites under King Philip. A few months ago, a bloody rebellion had broken out in the Alpujarra mountains and was repressed with equal cruelty by the royal troops. Neither side had any scruples about selling their captives into slavery. In addition, religious dissent had led to a war in our Dutch territories, where Calvinists rebelled against Philip's strict enforcement of the Catholic faith and seceded to form their own republic. Peace was nowhere in sight.

I felt that the warm glow of the candles on the magnificent chandelier above, the intricately designed wall hangings, the excellent dinner, and the old wine before us deserved a more pleasant conversation than the subject of enforcing orthodoxy. Instead, as the dessert was served, my host dropped all pretense of entertaining me and assumed a stern expression. Clearly his mind had turned from pleasure to business.

"King Philip is willing to provide funds to extend the arm of the Inquisition to Mexico," he said. "I have appointed a deputy to begin the work of establishing a tribunal in the City of Mexico, but he seems to have difficulties attracting qualified men to fill the positions of prosecutor and assessors. In particular, he writes, there is a dearth of qualified lawyers."

He paused. I could tell what was coming.

"I immediately thought of you," he said, "a man in the flower of his age, capable of bearing the hardship of a voyage to Mexico, and a man, I know, who will not refuse my plea or decline to do the work of God in the New World."

I very much wished to decline that work, even if Don Fernando meant to do me an honour. I was more than satisfied with my present sphere of work, which suited my temperament. I was a man who liked his comforts and had no taste for travel and adventure. Crossing the Atlantic struck me as a death-defying venture, but it was dangerous also to defy Don Fernando. I feebly objected to his proposal.

"You flatter me," I said. "Although I have a degree in both civil and Church law, I have no experience in the latter, and surely that is a requirement for a post in the Inquisition."

"A staunch adherence to the Church is the most important requirement," he said, "and on that point I have no doubts whatsoever that you are well qualified. Indeed you are the right man for the task, in my opinion."

"I would have thought that missionaries rather than lawyers are needed in Mexico at present," I said, desperately looking for a polite way of declining his invitation, but I realized that my chances of escape were small. I could see that Don Fernando had made up his mind and nothing could dissuade him from his plan to send me to Mexico and serve the Inquisition there.

"You are mistaken, Alonso," he said. "Now is the time to establish a tribunal in the New World to deal with the growing ills in the colony. Protestants and Jews have taken refuge there after we drove them from our fatherland. But there are worse enemies to our faith than these wretches. They at least believe in the Trinity, even if their beliefs are heretical. The threat posed by pagans is more serious by far. African slaves, mulattos, and Native Indians now constitute more than half the population in Mexico. They spread their superstitions among the Spaniards, infect them with their loose morals, and have created a quagmire of sin. It is the hope of the King, our most pious ruler, that the Inquisition might quell those evil spirits and recall the people to the respect they owe to the Church and to the faith they owe to God."

He signalled the servant to fill up my glass again, well aware that a drop of the sweet dessert wine might smooth over any arguments I could advance against him.

"A false belief is like the plague," he continued, "and now it has infected the pure body of the Catholic Church. Just as medical doctors are needed to cure the body, so the Inquisition is needed to cure the maladies of the soul and heal the congregation."

"Will you allow me to think about your proposal?" I said at last. "The hour is late and the wine too strong for my poor head."

He graciously let me off for the time being and returned to more general talk, but when it was time for me to leave, he walked with me into the hall, holding on to my sleeve as if he meant to arrest me then and there.

"I hope you will give my proposal serious thought, Alonso, and see the justification or the trust and expectation I place in you," he said before bidding me goodbye.

On the next day, he followed up with a letter, telling me again that my services as a jurist were urgently needed in Mexico, that I must aid the authorities in setting up the tribunal and assist in the procedures. I could see that he would not take a no for a no. He had couched his request in polite but ominous terms, letting me know that he would take it as a personal affront if I did not yield to his entreaties.

I showed the letter to my father, and he concurred. Of course he wanted me to stay in the country, of course he wanted to see me married in the near future and establish a household nearby, but it was not possible to deny Don Fernando. We had to put aside our own preferences, my discomfort at the thought of the journey, and his hopes for progeny. Accordingly, I accepted my appointment as *fiscal* — that is, prosecutor — of the Inquisition in Mexico.

I told myself that it was a worthy cause and to be content in the hope that God would reward me for advancing the business of the Church, although I wished that business involved less drastic methods. Thus I embarked on the journey, praying for His benevolent guidance.

The *Marisa*, a four-master, was carrying livestock and new settlers from Seville to Veracruz in Mexico. I hardly needed the captain's warning that I must put up with a rough life during the three months we expected to be at sea. He had, however, made special provisions for me and two other noble passengers. They were military men bound for Mexico to lead an expedition in the northern region, in quest of gold. A rather luxurious cabin had been erected on the lower deck of the *Marisa* to accommodate the three of us and a servant, but that arrangement was not to my liking. I asked the captain if I could share his cabin instead, and he graciously agreed to my request when I gave him my reasons. Although the two soldiers were men of standing and from good families, they were too rowdy for my taste and too violent in their temper and language. The servant employed by them was no better. Because space was at a premium on the ship, he was supposed to serve me as well, but I preferred to look after myself than have this coarse fellow around. The captain, by contrast, seemed a man of discipline, who kept his crew in good order. Whether it was a matter of discipline or fear of God, I do not know, but he absolutely forbade his sailors to swear, blaspheme, or tell lewd stories, and harshly punished any transgression. That was more than could be said of the two gentlemen, who carried on like common mercenaries. They seasoned their talk with curses and ogled every woman on board. More than once, they provoked angry exchanges with husbands who took issue with their lascivious tone. In one case, their harassment prompted a knife attack from a husband defending his honour, but they fought back and gave as good as they got, so that neither side escaped unharmed from the melee.

The captain gave the two soldiers black looks, but he was powerless in view of the wealth and standing of their families. Encouraged by plenty of drink, they laughed off all threats and continued with their provoking talk. Nor did they make any effort to preserve their own dignity and present an appearance in keeping with their noble standing. They looked unkempt, with their scruffy, untrimmed beards. They did not care how filthy their clothes were; they spat and broke wind. They shamelessly reached into their pants to relieve the itch in their nether parts and cracked lice between their fingernails for sport. I loathed the sight and sound of them.

By contrast, I quite liked the company of Captain Diaz. There was only one incident that made me uneasy, but the matter was soon cleared up. When I entered his cabin the first time, I was surprised to see books on his working table. I had not thought of seamen as readers. I was even more surprised when I examined the books. In addition to the Bible, which should of course be in the hands of every man, there was *El Lazarillo de Tormes*, a plausible choice for a man of adventure. The third, however, alarmed me greatly. It was Erasmus's *In Praise of Folly*.

"What do you think of the author?" I asked the captain.

"I know nothing about him other than that he is famous," he replied.

"*In*famous, you mean. And what do you think of his subject?"

"I can't speak to that. I have no knowledge of Latin and have never read the book. I do admire the illustrations, which I was told are by the renowned Dutch painter Hans Holbein."

In that case, I thought, I need not fear the worst.

"I'm glad to hear that you have not read the text," I said, "because it is on the Index of Forbidden Books."

The questioning look I saw in his eyes told me that he had never heard of the Index. It confirmed my impression that I was dealing with a case of ignorance rather than defiance of Church laws.

"Does that mean a Christian is not allowed to read this book?" he asked.

"Or even own it," I said. "I should tell you that Erasmus spoke disrespectfully of the clergy and voiced heretical opinions."

"I take your word for it," he said, "for as I told you, I do not read Latin."

"How did the book come into your possession?" I asked him.

It had come from the library of his late father, he said. His father, in turn, had received it as a present from his older brother, who was a learned man.

"Then it is likely that the book was acquired before the Church issued the Index. You, however, are in danger of being cited before the Inquisition for possessing a forbidden text."

"Then what do you counsel me to do?" he said.

"I suggest you destroy the book."

He sighed.

"It is a keepsake," he said, "and I would be sorry to lose it. But if it is an offence in the eyes of the Church, I will do as you say. Only tell me, are the illustrations heretical as well?"

"The Church condemned only Erasmus's words," I said, "not Holbein's images."

"Then, with your permission, I will cut out one or two of them and keep them in memory of my father, who I assure you was a pious man and would not have defied a command of the Church."

"No blame adheres to him if he obtained the book before it was placed on the Index," I said.

And so the captain took a knife to the pages, cut out two illustrations, and in my presence cast the book overboard. Later I saw that he had tacked the pictures to the wall above the table on which he kept the ship's log. His choice surprised me: One was of a jester in a dunce cap, the other of a schoolmaster flogging a boy. I did not find either of these pictures particularly edifying or doing justice to the fame of the artist.

Once the question of the books was resolved, the captain and I were on good terms. I had brought along my own books: a compendium of the canon law to support my new profession, and two slight volumes for my entertainment. First, my own copy of *Lazarillo de Tormes*, describing the comic adventures of a rogue and wisely published without the author's name. I do not know whether it is superior to Erasmus's *In Praise of Folly* as a piece of literature, but it was not on the Index, at any rate. I had also brought along the sonnets of Garcilaso de la Vega, the laments of a romantic lover, a gift from my dear mother who has a poetic vein. She was hoping perhaps to create a romantic mood in my heart as well, although Garcilaso's verses are rather melancholic.

I noticed that the captain's books were chained to the wall of his cabin. I had seen valuable books in monastic libraries chained up to keep readers from making off with them.

"Are you afraid of thieves here?" I asked the captain.

"I am indeed afraid of losing my books," he said, "but the only thief I fear is the sea. That is why I have chained them up: that they will not tumble off the table in a storm and end up on the floor, which tends to become waterlogged. I counsel you to do the same."

I took his advice and, with a gift of chains from the captain and the help of a passenger who had the necessary skills, my books were secured — a move that was necessary, as it turned out.

Thus I benefited from the captain's hospitality and shared the modest comforts of his cabin and the services of his cabin boy. The sailors and passengers — prospective settlers, for the most part — slept anywhere on deck that offered enough space to stretch out. In bad weather, they were obliged to huddle in the hold below, with the cargo and the livestock. It was hard for them to maintain any semblance of modesty, moreover. The deck offered no privacy. I myself kept a slop pail in the cabin. The sailors and common passengers had no choice but to relieve themselves in public, giving anyone around a free view of their most intimate body parts. They did not seem to mind, however, and really what could be more natural, when the arse figured so prominently in their language as well? "Lick my arse" was uttered as a common encouragement, and their sentences were punctuated with "shit" and "fuck." The women were more modest than their men and used pails set up in places somewhat shielded from view, but it seemed to me that it was more a show of modesty than the real thing, for they sat on those pails as comfortably as I sit in a barber's chair. Indeed, sharing space with the common people provided me with quite a few new insights. In particular, I was struck by the casual manner in which they confronted life and death, for I had occasion to witness both. A child's birth was no great reason for rejoicing, and natural death occasioned no more than a brief silence and, at most, a few tears. The family of the dead man, woman, or child went quietly about the sad task of sewing the body up in a length of canvas and tossing it overboard into the swell, saying a prayer. No Stoic philosopher could have been more accepting of fate than these simple people.

To my relief, I weathered life on board quite well. I did not suffer unduly from sea sickness, although for some days I was unsteady on my feet and tottered around like a drunkard. I had to lean against walls and hold on to ropes and spars to keep from falling, but after a while I learned to roll with the waves.

In the beginning, I was afraid also of tumbling out of my narrow berth at night, for the captain's cabin did not accommodate a wider bed. For the first few nights, I was kept awake by the discomfort of the hard mattress with straw poking through the ticking, the scrabbling of the rats, and the clicking of the omnipresent cockroaches, but I soon got used to the rhythm of life on board ship as well as to the poor diet we all shared, of necessity. It consisted of biscuits, wine, beans, rice, oil, salt meat, stockfish, and cheese: food stuffs that would not spoil on the long journey, for there was no opportunity to replenish them or to obtain any fresh fruit or vegetables. I had, however, taken along a sack of limes, on the advice of my doctor, and sucked on them every evening. I was told that this was essential to maintaining my health on board ship. I do not know whether his advice was based on science or merely on Moorish lore, but I did remain healthy throughout the ordeal of the voyage, through cold and wet and stormy days.

I had plenty of time on my hands during the journey to reflect on my appointment as prosecutor to the Mexican Inquisition and on the people I might encounter in that country, judging by the sample of settlers I met on board the ship. Don Fernando, my patron, had worried about the faith of the Spaniards there and spoken of applying the remedy of the Inquisition to ailing souls in Mexico, but in my opinion, it was more important to prevent the disease from taking root in the first place, by sending out good settlers. As it was, I heard more blaspheming than prayers among my fellow passengers, and on deck I met more rogues, who were bent on profit at any price — even if it meant stealing and cheating — than decent people like Jorge and Luisa. Indeed, there were very few like them: prudent, of good repute and sound conscience, and zealous for the Catholic faith. One little group, consisting of two brothers and their families, seemed to be devout, but there was something secretive about them and an unhealthy fervour about their morning prayers. I suspected them of being *alumbrados*, a sect that considers themselves chosen by God and under his direct inspiration. I hoped they would not begin to preach and proselytize and try to involve others in their unorthodox beliefs, or I might have to denounce them to the Inquisition. I was reluctant to take on this sad duty in advance of entering on my office, but denouncing heresy was the duty of every Christian, and once the tribunal had been set up, I was fully engaged in dealing with just that sort of unorthodox behaviour. How many times since then have I regretted coming to Mexico and indulging Don Fernando's wishes!

By comparison with those foolish people whom I suspected of being *alumbrados*, Luisa and Jorge struck me as eminently sensible. My attention was drawn to them first, however, not because of their good character, but because it is rare in Spain for a white man to take a mulatta as his wife. Apparently, the captain knew the husband well. Jorge had been on the crew of his ship for many years, he told me.

The captain and I often spent the end of the day talking in his cabin — or rather, with me asking questions and he answering them, each of us lying on his berth, with the words floating between us in the darkness, until I fell asleep.

"Jorge hired on with me at the age of sixteen, after running away from the Franciscan house in Seville," he told me.

"You mean he was going to enter the Church?" I asked, surprised, for Jorge's build, his muscular arms, and large, capable hands seemed to destine him for hard work rather than prayer.

"He was placed with the Order by his parents," the captain said. Jorge himself had had no vocation for the clergy and no taste for the cloistered life, he said, and therefore left without taking the vows, but the time he spent with the Brethren had been useful to him. At any rate, he was grateful to them for teaching him to read and write.

"Not a skill of much use to a sailor, I suppose," I said.

"But good training for his mind nevertheless," the captain said, "and a skill that made him more useful to me, for he could read maps and help me chart the course, and he kept the ship's log for me."

"He also seems to be a man of good character."

"Very much so. He has always been a rather serious man and not given to frivolities."

"Then you must have regretted his decision to exchange the life of a sailor for that of a settler."

"On the contrary," he said. "I welcomed his decision. I myself asked him to settle in Mexico together with me, for this is my last sea voyage. I am joining my brother-in-law in Zacatecas as manager of his *hacienda de minas*, and Jorge has bought land there as well. He intends to become a miner. The area is rich in silver, you know."

"Rich in silver and poor in other respects," I said. "I understand there is a shortage of women in the New World. Your man was wise to bring along a wife. It is rare, however, to see a white man married to a mulatta."

I must confess I wasn't just making idle talk. I raised the subject because I wanted to know more about Luisa. She exerted a strange fascination on me. I couldn't explain what drew me to her. She had beauty, but handsome mulattas were by no means a rare sight in Spain, yet I had never been particularly attracted to them. There was something special about Luisa. Her face had an aura of calmness that promised to dissolve all anxieties, worries, and uneasiness that might trouble a man. She had the face of a sacred icon, which stole into my soul. Looking at her, I trembled. I felt a novel sensation, as if I had heard my heart beat for the first time. I became aware of air entering my lungs and yet I had to tell myself to breathe. In other words, I was a man in love, a sinful kind of love, which burdened my conscience.

"They seem to be a good match," the captain was saying. "Luisa too is a serious woman, with a good head on her shoulders and hands that are never idle. I was a witness at their wedding and thought Jorge had chosen well."

After that we fell silent and I gave myself over to the rocking of the ship and my thoughts. I agreed with the captain's assessment that Jorge had indeed chosen well and that there was a gravity about Luisa, in her eyes and in her movements. I rarely had an opportunity to talk to her, and she was not given to talk. Yet I observed her closely. If anyone addressed her, she always smiled, and it was a memorably sweet smile. The few times we talked, every word she said struck a chord, left an echo in my heart, ran through my body like a tremor. I often sought the company of the couple because, as I told myself, it was a relief to be with decent people and to see Luisa's quiet dignity after I had witnessed so much loose and godless behaviour among others. In my heart, I knew that I was deceiving myself, that I enjoyed her company for reasons I ought to suppress. Luisa always looked neat and tidy, her black locks plaited in tight coils, her skirt and vest brushed clean. She was never without occupation, keeping a basket of knitting or embroidery at her side at all times. She was a woman of good character and habits, but I was more sensible of her other at-tractions, her potent aura. "Saintly," I chose to call it, although it was something more earthly that moved me, an attraction I knew I must not pursue because it was wholly inappropriate for a man in my position. It was a feeling that eddied within me like water disturbed by an undertow, and I was afraid it might turn into a riptide.

Others were attracted to Luisa's company as well because she had a heavenly singing voice, as soft as velvet. In the even-ing, she was therefore often surrounded by a knot of listeners, and sometimes she got up and took a few rhythmic steps as if she wanted to dance, but was too modest to do so and did not want to risk attracting the eyes of men by drawing their atten-tion to her body. Apart from singing, she was a silent woman. I myself do not agree with the common notion that silence is a virtue in a woman. But it became Luisa, and silence was more precious to me on board ship than it had been at home, because it was so difficult to attain. We were at all times surrounded by noise: the man-made noise of shouting and trampling boots and the ringing of bells to strike a change of watch or mark the mealtimes. In addition, there were the sounds of inani-mate things, which were no less disturbing: the wind whistling though halyards with an unearthly scream, the sails straining against the wind, the groan of bulkheads, and the thud and shudder of the steering gear.

In my more rational contemplations, I realized that Luisa was by no means a perfect icon. She had flaws, after all. She was inclined to superstition — as was to be expected in one of her class, I reminded myself. She was pious in that primitive way of ignorant people, who cling to externals and would rather per-form meaningless rites instead of examining their conscience.

She believed more readily in the power of candles and incense and the beads of her rosary than in prayer and inner faith, but perhaps that sort of ritual was excusable in the circumstances, for the sea is dangerous and we were caught in a horrendous storm during the last days of our voyage.

Most of our passage was tranquil. For weeks on end, a mere breath rippled the sea. It undulated in long swells around us, so that the ship sank gently into the trough of the waves and as gently moved up onto the crest, in endless repetition. We were only three days short of reaching the harbour of Veracruz, and I had already given thanks in my prayers to God's strong hand for protecting us, when a fierce and deadly storm blew up. It was my first encounter with a storm at sea, and I hope my last. The gale shook our ship with a wolfish howl, lifted it up on the crest of a giant wave, and dashed it down into the seething abyss again like a toy, tearing and ripping at the sails.

The waves washing over the deck sent one of the sailors tumbling overboard, without anyone being able to help him, for it was impossible to lower a boat. The captain could barely hold the course of the ship. The women and children sought refuge down in the hold. The crew and every able-bodied man among the passengers, me included, were desperately trying to beat down the sails. In this venture, I came to see people in a new light. The military men, for whom I had nothing but contempt, turned from louts into heroes before my eyes. They were in the forefront of the battle against the storm. The *alum-brados*, whom I expected to do nothing but surrender to the force of Heaven as they considered themselves God's chosen people, did not surrender at all, but exerted themselves to the utmost and leaned in to help wherever they were wanted. Jorge was conspicuous as well among those who took the initiative in helping others, but then I had expected nothing less from a man who was an experienced sailor.

A spar had snapped in two and was swinging this way and that, smashing everything in its sweeping path. With the greatest difficulty, we secured it at last. One man was caught underneath the broken beam, however. We dragged him out. His leg was shattered, the shinbone visible through the wound and rapidly draining his lifeblood. All his features announced death: the greying of his skin, the strained lines around his mouth. Death looked out at us from his eyes, even his voice was already like ashes, and yet he survived thanks to the help and diligent care he received from the *alumbrados*. While I and the other bystanders were inclined to give up on the man, one of the *alumbrados* took off his shirt, ripped it into strips and bandaged him, staunching the blood. Afterward, the women of his family watched over the man day and night with unselfish devotion, spoon-fed him and patiently held a cup to his lips when he barely had the strength to sip. They cared for him as for a babe until he was out of danger. When we arrived in Veracruz, they took the helpless cripple along to wherever it was they established their new home. It made me think that I had been quite wrong in my previous assessment, before the storm. They were good Christians after all. I sadly reflected, moreover, that the shared danger and the aspect of death united us more readily than our common faith. Sinners or devout believers, we all felt a sense of community in the face of hostile Nature. We were one people, regardless of race, profession, or standing in society.

During the storm, however, when we confronted the wild ocean and the uncertainty of our fate, I noticed that people resorted to all kinds of irregular practices — practices that might have landed them before the tribunal of the Inquisition at other times. Paradoxically, I found myself almost in sympathy with them, or at least with more understanding of what motivated them. They had neither the strength of mind nor the ability to draw on the texts of philosophers and historians, nor indeed on the wisdom of the Bible and the Church Fathers since they were, for the most part, illiterate. Where could the weaker spirits turn for comfort, after they had exhausted prayers, if not to the lore of the ages and to rituals? I no longer wondered that they succumbed to their fears and cried out to the devil and the saints alike, making extravagant promises if only they would come to their aid and helped them survive the ordeal. I heard them call on the stars and the moon and make promises impossible to fulfill: mountains of wax candles to the Virgin or a pilgrimage to the Holy Land, where they would kill a dozen Muslims, and other such nonsense, but their actions no longer shocked me. I emerged from the storm a new man — a man unsure of his purpose. My own mission — enforcing the articles of faith and the rules of the Church — suddenly seemed unimportant, a useless endeavour in the face of a wrathful God and the powers of Nature he had created. If I had had doubts before about my ability to live up to the expectations of my patron, I became increasingly convinced that I was unsuited to the task he wanted me to perform. I did not have the necessary determination or strength of conviction. I lacked certainty. I fluctuated between approval of primitive devotions which, after all, did no harm, and disapproval of the superstitions they involved. The uncertainty I experienced on that count did not bode well for my responsibilities as a prosecutor of the Inquisition, who must be firm in his judgment at all times and be able to tell right from wrong without a shadow of doubt. But the time was past when I could have refused to take the path my patron had laid out for me. I had embarked on the voyage and had to go forward now. I therefore tried to suppress all further thought of my future by concentrating on the action around me.

In the aftermath of the storm, the sailors were kept busy beyond their normal duties. Some worked their way around the rigging, checking for cracks in the spars; others manned the bilge pumps below deck. A sickening stench emanated from the open hatches, of excrement from the overturned slop pails and urine-soaked straw in the cattle hold. A few of the settlers braved the stench and joined the sailors in calming the lowing cattle and securing the loose casks, bales, and crates rolling and tumbling about in the hold. I confess I did not have the stamina. There wasn't enough headroom down there to stand upright so that we had to crouch and crawl, sweating in the foul air under the yellow light of the lanterns. I lasted no more than half an hour before abandoning the job, retching and shamefaced at my lack of manliness.

Some of the sailors had the unenviable task of repairing the damage to the outside of the ship. They breathed the open air, at least, but it was precarious work. They were suspended over the side on swaying rope ladders to patch holes and replace the broken or splintered boards. Others fixed the cracks in the deck and resealed them with oakum.

Our cabin had been flooded, of course, and I put it to order myself as best I could. The books, knocked off the table, dangled by their chains. They had been licked by the waves although not soaked. Our bedding had tumbled to the floor and was in need of rinsing out and drying. The smell of mildew, excrement, and decay was everywhere. My clothes clung to me, soaked with brine. My hair, like everyone else's, was heavy with salt, but my wooden, iron-banded chest had held tight, so I had a change of clothes at least.

It was a joyful morning a few days later, when we heard the shout "Land ahoy!" and our ship sailed into the harbour of Veracruz at last. A boat conveyed us from the ship to the inner port. I clambered onto the pier, unsteady on my feet at first. Still dazed by the experience of the last few days, I just stood there and observed the sights and smells of the harbour. I soon found my bearings, however, with the help of a local priest who had been notified of my arrival and took me to his house. The next day, he set me on the road to Mexico City, where I was to assist in the establishment of the Inquisition. I said farewell to the captain and those of the passengers I had come to know on the voyage. We parted, on the way to our various destinations. I watched Luisa and Jorge making their way along the pier and felt both regret and relief, for I had come to regard Luisa as a temptation and a danger to my soul. I little expected to see the couple again, and even less to see them in my capacity as an official of the Holy Office.

Soon, my mind was fully occupied with my new responsibilities. It took almost four years to set up the tribunal, to ready the buildings to be occupied by the representatives of the Inquisition — the living quarters, the courthouse, and the jail. During that time, my duties were light, consisting of looking after the accounts, inspecting the progress of the construction and the furnishing of the quarters. Dr. Moya, the principal inquisitor in charge of the judicial process in Mexico, meanwhile was busy assembling the staff of officers and clerks needed to begin operation.

On November 22 in the year of the Lord 1571, finally, the town crier made his way through the streets and plazas of the city, exhorting the inhabitants to attend Sunday mass and witness the ceremony initiating the Holy Office. I thought it was a shame that the people had to be encouraged in this manner, when one would expect them to attend in the course of their Christian duty and of their own desire.

The entrance to the cathedral was adorned with crimson banners and topped with an elaborate silver cross. The mayor and the city council awaited us, as we approached in festive procession: Dr. Moya, the chief inquisitor, myself in my capacity as prosecutor, the assessors, the notary, and the treasurer. We were accompanied by the secretaries, the servants of the newly built jail and the familiars — the "spies," as the people called them, who were to gather and investigate the reports of crimes against the Church and bring them to the attention of the court. At mass, a Franciscan brother gave a moving sermon, stirring the souls of the faithful, although in my opinion he described the sins liable to punishment by the Inquisition in terms that were unnecessarily vivid. Was it really necessary to go on so about prostitutes and unnatural practices such as bestiality, or to repeat the exact words of a blasphemer or the doubts of a man who questioned the virgin birth of Jesus? It seemed to me that those words were too suggestive and merely introduced sinful thoughts in the congregation.

After the sermon, the chief notary asked the people to raise their right hand and say in unison, "I swear to assist and defend our Holy Catholic faith and the Holy Inquisition, her officials and ministers, and not to hide heretics and enemies but to prosecute and denounce them."

Dr. Moya once more reminded the congregation of all the acts that were punishable offences: blaspheming, mocking the Church and its representatives, prostitution and procuring,

superstition and witchcraft, idolatry, Judaism, and the possession of heretical books. He adjured the people to come forward
if they had witnessed any such sinful practices and not to abet
them, on pain of excommunication. The effect of the priest's
sermon and Dr. Moya's admonitions was immediate. Right
after mass, many people approached him and the assessors and
divulged the sins of their neighbours and acquaintances. Some
even incriminated themselves.

I was immediately caught up in the work of the tribunal. We dealt with 256 cases that year, but contrary to my
expectation, there were few Judaizers and Protestant heretics
among those tried and sentenced. I suppose the crypto-Jews
were clever enough to pretend that they had been converted to
the true faith and, outwardly at least, adhered to the Catholic
practices. The Protestants, who tended to be openly defiant,
had fled inland, where they were out of our reach, at least for
the time being. The bulk of the cases concerned blasphemies
and superstitions and, to my surprise, bigamy. Looking back
at those cases now, I wonder whether they were an omen of
things to come — the unfortunate circumstances in which I
met Luisa again.

There were more than thirty cases of unlawful marriage
during my first year of serving as prosecutor. When I considered
the situation of the men and women called before the tribunal,
I realized why there were so many instances of bigamy. Many
Spaniards undertook the perilous journey to Mexico on their
own, leaving their families behind. Years of separation led to
alienation, and finally the men settled down with Indigenous
women and married them to escape the accusation of fornication raised against them by their neighbours. I remember my
first case, a man by the name of Marco de la Cruz, who excused

his ungodly behaviour: "I was dragged down by human weakness because I wanted the girl so much, and since she was a virgin, there was no other way to have her. Juana said she would love me only if we married. I was defeated by passion!"

What sort of excuse is that for a man to deceive the wife he had left behind in Spain and commit bigamy? Naturally I pressed for a verdict of guilty, but the punishment imposed by the judge — public shaming and a fine — was not enough to discourage others from doing the same. The guilty verdict was read out publicly in church. On the following Sunday, moreover, the bigamist and others like him were made to walk in a circle around the Plaza Mayor, wearing the penitential garb and holding burning candles. But he did not even have to suffer a dozen lashes, as the assessors had recommended.

Another sinner, one Maria de Sotomayor, who had been convicted of bigamy, defied the judgment imposed on her — to return to Spain and live with her first, lawful husband. When we discovered that she had remained in Mexico and continued living in a bigamist union, she was sentenced to a harsher punishment: to be stripped naked before the congregation and forced to kneel and hear mass in the cathedral, holding a burning candle in her hand. The second judgment against her included confiscation and loss of all her belongings and being placed forcibly on the next available ship bound for Spain. Did the punishment match her crime? I was uncertain. According to her sworn testimony, her first husband was a drunk who regularly beat her and their children. Is it any wonder that she had fled to escape such a marriage and did not want to go back to him?

The prevalence of bigamy was also the fault of the parish priests. They neglected their duty of inquiring properly into the marital status of the parties. They issued marriage licences carelessly, simply on the declaration of the bride and bridegroom that they were single, and without demanding any further proof or confirmation from witnesses. When I upbraided one of them for his negligence, he shrugged and said it was near impossible to ascertain whether anyone had been married before in Spain.

"No!" I said to him. "It is your indolence that has kept you from inquiring. After all, ships depart from Veracruz to Spain every day and an equal number return from there, so that it would take no more than three months for a letter to reach the home parish of a man, and the same time to receive a reply."

"Exactly," he said. "It takes too long to find out. In the meantime, the couples live in sin and those who are accused of bigamy languish in prison while their case is being investigated, and are forced to pay for their stay in prison out of their own pocket."

"And even if it took twice as long to verify the marital status of a person," I said, "it is essential to establish the facts before administering the sacrament of matrimony."

But I knew I had not convinced the man or answered his arguments. He, like the other parish priests, would be quite as careless again the next time a couple was in a hurry to get married.

At least bigamy could be verified, whereas a person's beliefs were another matter altogether. To my mind, many of those accused of idolatry and other false beliefs were no doubt heretical, but they would not confess to their sins, and we could not prove what was hidden in their minds. Thus, we often had to leave their punishment up to God. We could look only at the manifestations of sin in symbols or signs, and consider the words they had used in the presence of witnesses. In other cases, I had no difficulty identifying the nature of the sin committed or in obtaining a confession, but applying the law to the individual on trial weighed heavily on me. I could not bring my feelings into accord with my reason. I kept thinking of the *alumbrados* on board the *Marisa*, who had acted in such a Christian fashion, but would no doubt be condemned if brought before the tribunal. I looked with pity upon those who had succumbed to temptation even as I was duty bound to condemn them.

After three years of attending the court, I was not only unhappy about having to judge others, but also exhausted and discouraged by the horrendous thoughts and deeds I heard of every day. The flood of sins overwhelmed me. By far the worst of them was the case of a priest who, instead of being a missionary to his Indian flock, had shamefully abused and corrupted them. One of the youths who was summoned as a witness testified that the priest said to him, "Come and take my private parts into your hands and play with them because this is a service to God."

The youth answered, "Father, this is a very shameful thing you are asking me to do! Look, here on the altar is the sacred chalice, and you say such things in front of it."

But the missionary told him sharply not to preach at him. He heaped insults on the lad and challenged him, "Go and complain to the bishop or the inquisitor and I will have you burned alive."

"Then," the youth told us, "he placed his hands on my member and squeezed it with such force that it began to bleed and he did not release me until I was very much injured, and I'm still bruised."

The missionary was found guilty, of course, and although he fully deserved the punishment meted out to him and more, I found the spectacle of the auto-da-fé distasteful and distressing. It was repeated every Sunday, and I was forced to attend together with the other members of the tribunal. The penitents were displayed in their misery on the newly constructed scaffolds before the high altar, while a large number of monks took their seats opposite, on another platform. Then Dr. Moya issued lengthy indictments and announced the sentences, before parading the sinners in the square outside the church. There was no end to the processions of men and women wearing the penitential hat and gown inscribed with two red crosses. While I was dismayed, many people took an unholy interest in the proceedings. They would trek great distances to see the spectacle, especially in the first few months when it was still a novelty. The plaza was filled with eager onlookers, a large crowd who carried on as if they were at a country fair. Dogs barked, vendors hawked their wares, girls flirted shamelessly, children played tag. It had altogether the air of a carnival rather than a solemn rite.

I was seemingly alone in my distaste for these proceedings. My colleagues felt that the spectacle was instructive to the congregation, reminded them of the Church's power, and put before their eyes the dire consequences of sin and heresy. It was good for the people to see God's enemies punished and atoning for their sins, they said.

Occasionally, capital punishment was meted out. A few men were publicly garroted, half-a-dozen witches burned at the stake, while others were whipped and dragged off to the galleys. These frightful spectacles, far from serving as deterrents, seemed to be regarded as entertainment by the people.

I was deeply dissatisfied with my life and began to think with resentment of my patron who had inflicted this task on me. I had always looked up to Don Fernando as a man of authority and insight, a model to adopt and follow, but now I felt that he had used me ill. How would I ever find my way back to my former self after hearing those vile confessions and witnessing the spectacle of the sinners' punishments? They left me in a quagmire of conflicting emotions. How was I to recover from this misery and clear my head? I wished I had a loving wife with whom I could share my anguish. I felt the lack of a soothing voice, the comfort and closeness of a familiar companion. I wished I had chosen one of the prospective brides presented to me by my mother and my aunts, although the prospect of a forced move to Mexico might have given pause to those young women and their parents as well. Jorge, I thought, had done well to marry before he came to Mexico and had been fortunate to find a woman like Luisa. Thinking of the couple, I recalled my fascination with Luisa and was relieved to find that it had faded and was only a memory now. The name evoked no more than a slight ripple in my mind. I thought of the couple again when Dr. Moya sent me to Zacatecas in 1574.

The new assignment offered me a way out of my responsibilities on the tribunal or, at any rate, temporary relief. It had become clear that the Inquisition in Mexico City could not handle all the cases that were brought to its attention by parish priests in other communities. Accordingly, I was dispatched to Zacatecas as a commissioner to establish a branch of the Inquisition there, a subsidiary tribunal to deal with local cases and lesser crimes — superstition, moral offences, and disrespect to clerics.

I was determined, however, to obtain a transfer to Spain, once this objective had been achieved and the officials in

Zacatecas were ready to embark on their task and begin their operations. I had come to Mexico to oblige Don Fernando, but he passed away within a year of my appointment. "Not soon enough," as my father said in the letter informing me of my patron's demise, for he resented my forced departure as much as I. Don Fernando's death relieved me of any obligation, but unfortunately also of his patronage, so that I was no better off than before. My allegiance now was to Dr. Moya. My career was in his hands, and he was not inclined to send me back to Spain. He was short of experienced staff, he told me with a firmness containing a barely veiled threat. I could not expect a reference from him if I left my position without his approval. Indeed, he might be disgruntled enough to impede my career. I had no choice, therefore, but to await my chance, and in the meantime leave for my appointment in Zacatecas.

As I rode north with my small retinue, I passed from the fertile land surrounding Mexico City into the semi-desert, a drab plain with a natural vegetation of rough grass that barely supported cattle and sheep. On the third day, we arrived in Zacatecas. The town rose before us like a navel from a smooth belly. It was surrounded by hills so strangely shaped that one could almost guess they held within them something extraordinary and precious.

I expected to arrive at a town, and I suppose you could call it that, for there were a great number of dwellings, but they were shacks put together of adobe bricks and patched with mud. They were lined up with no discernible order or regular streets, so that the place looked more like a sprawling village than a town. And yet it had a large market, and I saw every kind of merchandise on display as we passed the stalls: hemp, linen, silk, and damask, wine, barrels of olives and figs, spices, hoes, whips, axles, tack, furniture, and artful ornaments. These goods had been transported all the way from the port of Veracruz — or, rather, all the way from Spain and indeed from as far away as China, for ships from all corners of the world arrived in Veracruz every day.

After passing a score of small and decrepit adobe houses, we finally came to the centre, which had a few larger two-storey buildings: the residence of the mayor, the seat of the municipal council, the jail, the monastery of the Franciscans, and, a little off to the side, a whitewashed church, Our Lady of Nativity; beside it was the parish priest's house.

It looked to me as if no one was planning on staying in Zacatecas for very long, and certainly not on making his life here. I suppose the owners of the hovels we saw were intent only on staking out a plot, digging into the hillside, and producing as much silver as possible in the shortest possible time. They were no better than nomads. After bringing to the surface whatever ore there was in one place, they moved on to the next. The yield was certainly astonishing if the reports I heard were true. Every hundred pounds of dirt, I was told, produced up to fifty pounds of pure silver. But perhaps my informants exaggerated, for there was a certain atmosphere of braggadocio in that town.

I preferred being in Zacatecas, however, to serving on the tribunal in Mexico City. While on my new assignment, I had to deal only with administrative matters rather than attend the court sessions that distressed me so greatly. Yet I soon discovered that even those administrative tasks brought a burden to my conscience. Dr. Moya had indicated to me, in not too subtle terms, that money was needed for the operation. The Mexican Inquisition received a yearly subsidy from the Spanish Crown, but it was hoped that the institution would eventually be self-supporting and able to finance its operations independently, out of the confiscated properties of the sinners. This had not been the case so far, and the fiscal authorities in Spain were becoming impatient. The problem was that many residents in Mexico City, and especially the Blacks and the Indians, were poor. Nothing much could be gained from confiscating their goods. The districts in the north, with their rich silver mines, were a more promising venue, Dr. Moya noted. In other words, he wanted me to ferret out *rich* sinners and send them to the City, or deal with them in Zacatecas as soon as the tribunal was set up.

The secretary in charge of the goods that were confiscated at the time of a culprit's arrest was obliged to inventory each item. He was supposed to keep any moneys received in a locked and armoured chest, but we had found a great deal of mismanagement in the City: incomplete lists, shortfalls of money, and suspected embezzlement. The secretary and jailor bolstered their salary by charging so-called fees, although they were no more than a demand for bribes in return for doing their job. I was afraid it would be no different when the proceedings started in Zacatecas. In addition, I found myself battling a money-grabbing and corrupt mayor. Pedro de Ahumada not only tried to enrich himself but also importuned me with invitations to his house. In other circumstances, I would have welcomed the company and the opportunity to become acquainted with local citizens, but he had ulterior motives. He was keen on presenting to me his youngest daughter, a sweet, innocent girl of sixteen, who talked to me at great length about the antics of her kitten and her dream to be taken to Mexico City and visit the shops there. No doubt she would make a fine wife to a local fellow one day, but she offered no comfort to someone like me, who longed to talk about things of the mind and soul and to ponder grave questions: What is the nature of good and evil? Was the proverb true: *ubi bene ibi patria*, "home is where the life is good," or was it the other way round, *ubi patria ibi bene*, "life is best in your home country"? And the most important question: Who am I? Not that I expected to find definitive answers. I wanted only a sympathetic ear, a woman asking herself the same questions. A girl of sixteen was no help to me other than to raise my body heat and make the blood course faster through my veins, but it was not difficult to find a cure for that — dousing myself with cold water or committing a venial sin, which was regrettable but preferable to making a mockery of the sacrament of marriage, which was a deadly sin. No, Don Pedro's daughter did not inspire me with love. Nor did I have a desire to be in any way associated with her mercenary father.

I had been looking forward to renewing my acquaintance with Captain Diaz who, I remembered, talked about becoming the manager of the mayor's hacienda. He was an honest and thoughtful man, but Don Pedro told me that the task had not been to the captain's liking. He had returned to his old profession and was once again plying the ocean. I also inquired about Jorge and Luisa, but was apprehensive about meeting them in case Luisa rekindled my misplaced interest in her. For after all these years, I could admit to myself that I had been as foolish as a schoolboy and somehow managed to fall in love with her, although I had evaded the dangerous tide of base passion or, at any rate, did not drown in it. Still, even if I had not acted on those feelings, they were hardly to my credit — a man of standing, with an excellent education, scholarly interests, and pretensions to moral authority falling in love with a common mulatta! I was relieved therefore to find that I was proof against Luisa's charms when I finally encountered her and Jorge one Sunday.

It was a pleasant day and the townspeople were out, milling around the main square, when I came face to face with the couple. We greeted each other, and I asked how they were doing. Jorge told me that his mine had turned out to be productive, and Luisa was making a name for herself as a skillful embroiderer. In turn, I told them about my assignment. The two of them looked well, although the years had not been kind to them. Jorge had turned into a gaunt man with a grizzled beard and a head as bald as an egg. Luisa too had lost her youthful bloom. She had the same gentle smile and placid expression that promised peace and that had first attracted me to her, but I no longer needed to fear for my soul.

It took nearly a year for me to set up a tribunal of inquisition in Zacatecas. Shortly before Christmas, it was inaugurated. The parish priest gave a sermon on the occasion and encouraged the congregation to come forward and denounce egregious sinners in their midst. The reports came pouring in. Luisa was among those who wished to give a deposition and, to my dismay, she denounced herself. She had gone to the parish priest first. He in turn sent her to me because he was overwhelmed by the magnitude and seriousness of her confession. Her sin, she said, was bigamy. I was astounded. When she told me the particulars, I did not think the circumstances warranted an accusation of bigamy and advised her to think no more about it. But Luisa insisted on incriminating herself, and the parish priest encouraged her feelings of guilt, declaring that she was in a state of mortal sin. I had no choice but to have Luisa sent to Mexico City, where I knew she would be imprisoned to await trial. Her personal property was confiscated to pay for her incarceration.

On a chilly morning in January, I sent her off together with two other wretched sinners, a woman who insisted that a certain statue of St. Mary in the parish church spoke to her and allowed her to predict the future and a man who uttered unspeakable blasphemies. He was allegedly possessed by demons, although I suspected that his demons were alcohol and a concoction of poisonous mushrooms, and that both he and the fortune teller needed a doctor rather than a judge to cure their diseased minds. But the parish priest had whipped up popular sentiment, and thus the two unfortunate fools and Luisa were loaded onto an open cart padded with straw, were paraded through the streets and subjected to mocking and jeers, then taken on the road to Mexico City. The open cart afforded them no protection against the inclement weather. I had taken care to provide them with blankets at my own cost and hoped they would be able to hold on to them for the duration of the journey at least, although I was afraid that the jailor in the City would immediately relieve them of any useful possessions they had on them.

Jorge was in a state of shock and disbelief. I too was shaken by the gravity of the situation. He came to my office to see what could be done, but the circumstances did not give me any leeway. Before becoming Jorge's wife, Luisa had exchanged a promise of marriage with another man. Strictly speaking, a promise of marriage, once consummated, constituted marriage, and clearly it had been consummated, since Luisa had given birth to a child. Thus she was a bigamist by the letter of the law. At least that had been the law until a few years ago, when a Church council re-examined the question and decided that a promise of marriage without witnesses was invalid. The question was whether Luisa had witnesses to the earlier promise and if not, did this recent amendment apply to her case retroactively and invalidate the promise? I assured Jorge that I would press for an early trial, at any rate, so that Luisa would not have to suffer in jail longer than necessary.

We were sitting across from each other in the new premises of the Inquisition, an absurdly cheerful-looking place. A wing had been added to the Franciscan monastery to provide a courtroom and quarters for the officers of the Inquisition. The white stucco walls and red floor tiles still had a sheen of newness about them. The windows looked out onto the inner court of the monastery, planted with shrubs in an artful geometric pattern of squares and triangles and kept as tidy as a garden.

In this absurdly neat place, I had to deal with the chaos of Jorge's life. For a time he refused to take a seat and stood before me like a humble petitioner. I in turn wished it was in my power to grant him favours. As it was, I could only explain the situation to him after he finally took his seat across from my desk.

"How can a promise Luisa exchanged with a man, who later jilted her, invalidate our marriage, which was blessed by a priest? How can that promise make her a bigamist?" he asked me.

"The matter hinges on a technicality," I said. "Such promises are, under certain circumstances, considered equivalent to a marriage."

"What circumstances?" he asked.

"Consummation of the promise."

"But the man jilted her and married another!"

"I quite agree with you," I said, "and wish the question had never been raised. But Luisa insists that she has committed a crime. In the circumstances, the only legal way out is to go through with the trial and appeal to a decision made a few years ago by a Church council, which seems to favour her case."

"What Church council? I don't understand."

"The Council of Trent, which declared that promises of marriage without witnesses are invalid. It might be possible to convince the tribunal that this was the case and that the council's decision should be applied to Luisa retroactively."

"Retroactively?" he asked, puzzled.

"I mean it should be applied as if it had already been in force at the time when Luisa made her promise," I explained. "It will count in her favour that the Church considers such promises invalid now."

"If you want my opinion," he said, "Luisa's insistence on incriminating herself has little or nothing to do with bigamy. Her feeling of guilt is caused by another matter altogether. She believes she has to atone for killing a man, although she killed him in self-defence. She wants to be punished, Don Alonso."

He then told me about an encounter they had had on their overland journey to Zacatecas. Their wagon train had been attacked by Chichimec Indians, and Luisa had killed one of the raiders. I had heard the story before at the mayor's house, and I agreed with Jorge that Luisa had no reason to accuse herself of murder. But the heart is a wilful thing, and the voice of conscience cannot be silenced by the arguments of a third party. Only Luisa could quiet that internal voice. Or perhaps she thought the judgment of the Church was the judgment of God, and if she was acquitted by the tribunal of the Inquisition, she would be absolved also in the eyes of God.

"Will you be the prosecutor in her case?" Jorge asked, for he had heard people refer to me as "fiscal of the Inquisition."

"I used to act as prosecutor in Mexico City," I said, "but as you know, I have been sent here to set up the local tribunal. That task is now completed, and I will shortly return to the City. I do not intend to resume my old post there. Indeed, I have in mind to return to Spain as soon as my superior is willing to release me from my duties. I promise you, however, to interest myself in Luisa's case and personally testify to her good character."

He thanked me and we shook hands on my pledge.

I had been a reluctant participant in the proceedings of the Inquisition before I was sent to Zacatecas. Luisa's case turned my reluctance to revulsion. I therefore determined to insist on my release after my return to Mexico City. I vowed to stay there no longer than it would take to see Luisa through her trial and, as I hoped, her acquittal. Thereafter, I would return to Seville, even if it meant losing Dr. Moya's goodwill and doing without his recommendation. I was willing to live with the consequences and work in some lowly post as a notary or estate lawyer, if necessary. My greatest wish — and indeed my greatest need — was to recover my peace of mind, to forget the years of my service in the Inquisition, and re-create my life instance by instance until I felt whole again.

The day of my departure from Zacatecas arrived. My servant had saddled my horse and was waiting for me in front of the Franciscan monastery. I was saying farewell to the abbot, thanking him for his hospitality, when I was stopped mid-sentence by the sight of a rider coming toward us at full gallop. He halted by our side and told us news that soon drew a knot of curious listeners.

"There has been an accident," he said. "Jorge Abrego's mine has collapsed and buried him and his helper. We dug through the rubble and found the body of the Indian."

The mine must have caved in some days ago, he said, because the body was black with rot and crawling with maggots.

"And Jorge?" I asked.

"Dead for sure," he said, "although we didn't dig any further. It was too dangerous to dislodge more rocks. The whole passage is unstable."

"May the two men rest in peace, then," I said, and crossed myself.

Mulling over the tragic news on my way out of town, I could only console myself that Jorge's death might serve one good purpose. The tribunal, I hoped, would take pity on the widow and dismiss the case. Indeed, one could make a legal case for her acquittal because, Jorge being dead, she was no longer a bigamist by any law, new or old.

5

Zacatecas, 1574:

Pedro de Ahumada, Alcalde

WHEN THE INQUISITION CAME TO town, I thought to myself, *Just what I need! More bloody officiousness and interfer-
ence! They'll stick their nose into everyone's business, including
mine!* But in the end it turned out to be a good deal, at least
for me.

Alonso de Herrera, the lawyer they sent up to organize the
tribunal, wanted to have an extension built to the Franciscan
monastery. The extra space was needed to house the officials
they were about to hire to run the tribunal. Luckily for me, the
man has no head for business, or else he doesn't care how much
he spends because he isn't spending his own money. I expected
him to haggle about the price when I tendered the contract for
the material needed and for the work the masons would do, but
he barely glanced at the figures before signing the order.

"Just get on with it," he said, "and finish everything as soon as possible."

He was in a hurry to get back to Mexico City. I suppose he is accustomed to a more luxurious life and the comforts of his own home, whereas here he had to lodge with the Franciscans in God knows what kind of austere surroundings. They have taken vows of poverty, so they have to live that way, but he hasn't taken any vows and wants the good things. I can't say I blame the man. Life is rough in Zacatecas, and Maria and the girls would move to Mexico City tomorrow, but here in this town is where I make my money, and if you have the means you don't lack comfort in Zacatecas. Don Alonso has the means — the Inquisition pays its officers well — so there is no reason why he couldn't have some fun here if he looked around. It's just a matter of finding congenial company. I immediately thought of him as a possible husband for my daughter, the youngest of the girls.

The oldest, Cecilia, is off my back and married to Antonio Montesinos, the manager of my hacienda, who is a lot more efficient than my brother-in-law, who was a bleeding heart. It's a very nice arrangement, if I may say so myself. Now that Antonio is family, he will keep a watchful eye on things. We share an interest in the success of the operation, after all. Teresa, my second daughter, did very well for herself. She snagged a merchant who did tolerably well here, but she never stopped talking about moving to Mexico City, until he gave in. It turned out to be a good move for both. She is happy, and he has set up a silk emporium there and is flourishing. The third one, Anna, has just turned sixteen, so it's time to take thought for her as well, as my wife never tires of reminding me. So, to oblige her, I invited Don Alonso for dinner a few times, but we can both see that nothing will come of it. The silly girl has notions of romantic love, of someone who will moon over her and write her love letters. Don Alonso is too dour for her taste. He is a cheerless man, all right. Nothing seems to interest him except books. He turns up his nose at business matters and has only high-flying talk about philosophy and morals, which doesn't exactly endear him to a young girl. Ah, well, he can afford to be philosophical. He has an excellent and assured income. The money comes to him whether he moves a finger or not. All he has to do is sit and elicit confessions from the poor sods who have been denounced to the Inquisition. Some of their stories must be *interesting*, let's say, seeing that he deals with prostitutes and bigamists and the like. There must be a few dirty laughs in it, but I've never heard that man laugh at a joke or tell a joke himself.

Maybe he is homesick. He hinted a few times that he intends to go back to Spain when his mission here is over. What is it with people wanting to go elsewhere? The girls all want to live in Mexico City — all right, I understand. They want to shop and gossip, and there are more opportunities there than here. My brother-in-law is another one. Up and left. I paid him a good salary to manage the hacienda, but, no, he "missed the sea." What is there to miss, I ask you? The storms? The lousy food? The high risk of losing your investment? Jorge, too. He and Luisa were planning to go back to Spain. Can you give me one good reason why? Zacatecas was full of bad memories for them, he said to me. That was after their baby died.

"For Heaven's sake, forget it already. Babies die all the time," I told him. "The two of you can make more babies and have a good life right here. You are making money hand over fist, digging up the ore." I know how much everybody makes and how much they lay by. I am the banker here, after all. And Jorge did very well. Luisa, too, could have made a flourishing business out of her embroidery. I told her: "Whatever you produce, I have a buyer for it." Of course, that was before she went and ruined her life.

Don Alonso was another one who had "reasons" to go back to Spain. What reasons? He didn't come right out with it, but I know: There isn't enough culture here for his taste. Oh, well, let him go back, then.

In any case, he can't complain that I didn't fulfill my part of the contract. It took only a little over a year to put up the addition and finish the offices. He brought a theologian up from Mexico City to be the judge of the tribunal and to make all the other appointments in turn, from prosecutor to jailer. Let's hope there is husband-material among the men hired, although most of them will be clerics, I expect. The assessors certainly will be Franciscans and Dominicans, but they need a lawyer or two as well — less dour than Don Alonso, I pray.

Once the construction was finished and the officers installed, the tribunal went to work in earnest and kept the parish priest busy in his confessional. The spies they planted did their part as well, reeling in sinners. Not that there is a dearth of sinners in Zacatecas. In no time at all, they rounded up two dozen blaspheming drunks and a few superstitious old women, witches and fortune tellers. They slapped fines on them and made them march through the streets barefoot. It made for quite a show and was enjoyed by all. The more serious cases were sent on to the City and the sinners jailed there. Of course, they lost their property as well. It was confiscated to pay for jail time and whatever fine they'll be clobbered with.

To get the whole thing going, the parish priest gave a fiery sermon on the first Sunday before the tribunal started in earnest. I bet you somebody else wrote that sermon for him, because the man is a simpleton and could never have come up with the words or the content — the cases he cited, which had been tried in the City. That was the best part of the sermon, if you ask me: the examples of sinful behaviour that got people into trouble. I haven't been so well entertained in church for a long time, not since the Sunday last year when someone let loose a goat and it scampered up to the altar, leaving dung in the aisle. That raised a laugh all right, but it was nothing compared to the stories the priest told us. That was pure entertainment, even if he meant to give us a proper scare and teach us to respect the Inquisition.

A certain Juan de Llanes, he said, appeared before the tribunal to complain about his mulatta wife. He said he couldn't live with her because she had committed adultery with many men and now he was afraid that she would kill him or have him killed.

"Do not make me live with her," he pleaded (or rather, the parish priest pleaded — I did not know he had such theatrical flair). The man said he couldn't control his wife because he was too weak. Age had exacted a toll on his body and left him dependent on her for support. She resented the doddering old man and often screamed at him, he said, and even bit him once, so hard that he bled profusely. She did it just because he had admonished her to do her marital duty by him. He said she grabbed his beard, knocked him to the ground, and punched him, leaving his arms paralyzed. Then she deserted him and, as he had heard, gave her body to anyone who paid for it. And to crown it all, she married another man, totally ignoring that she was still married to him. So she was arrested, thrown into jail, and tried for bigamy. But she denied the charges brought against her and said she had only pretended to be married because the neighbours had seen a man touching and kissing her and were making a big scandal of it. But when they tortured her, she confessed that the accusations were all true, and was punished accordingly.

A priceless story! It immediately put me in mind of Jorge's mulatta, and I was not surprised at all to hear that Luisa came forward and confessed that she, too, was a bigamist. When we had Don Alonso over for the farewell dinner, my wife tried to get more information out of him — after we had sent Anna out of the room, of course. We don't want our daughter's morals to be corrupted. But he kept mum and said he was not authorized to speak about the case.

"Indeed," he said. "I cannot believe that Luisa committed such a heinous crime. I believe she is too scrupulous and misinterprets what happened to her."

That's all we got out of him. I bet you Jorge slipped him a few bars of silver to make the case go away. But the accusation stuck — or, rather, the stupid woman stuck to her self-incrimination. The crime was too serious to be tried by the local tribunal, and she was sent to Mexico City together with a fortune teller, who had already been given a warning to cease her godless behaviour, and an old drunk, a sot with a dirty mouth, who habitually blasphemed against God and all the saints. Of course, all of Zacatecas assembled in the square to watch the spectacle of the three sinners being chained together and bundled into a two-wheeled cart. It must have been a bumpy ride for them. I guess they deserve what they get, if not for their sins, then for their stupidity in getting caught. Still, I was sorry to see Luisa go, just when I got my son-in-law in Mexico City interested in an order for embroidered collars and cuffs. Her embroidery was really exquisite. It's not likely I'll find another woman who can work such miracles with the needle. For both her and my sake, I hope the Inquisition lets her off the hook without too much delay. After all, Don Alonso said it was all a misunderstanding. Whatever the outcome, one thing is for sure: She'll have to pay. That's what it's all about, if you ask me — a way to make money for the Church. As if they didn't already make enough, what with the tithe they extract from us.

So, the people saw the sinners off with a great deal of hooting and jeering, but there was more excitement to come. Two days ago I was about to enter my house, when a messenger from Mexico City handed me a letter bearing the seal of the Inquisition.

"A summons for Juan Diaz," he said.

"He no longer lives here," I told him.

"I know," he said, "but this is his last known address, and you are his nearest relative. Presumably you have his current address and can send the letter on to him."

Why should I bear the cost of sending a letter on to Juan? But you don't argue with a servant of the Inquisition, so I took the letter from him. I had been looking forward to a dinner of lamb and a glass or two of the red I had bought the day before — full-bodied, with a hint of spice, the merchant promised me. The encounter with the messenger spoiled my appetite.

"Just what I need," I said to Maria, as we sat down to dinner, "a summons from the Holy Office in Mexico City, addressed to your brother. They knew that he no longer works for me, but they expect me to forward the letter to him. That man is nothing but trouble to me."

"I don't see why a summons addressed to Juan should trouble you," she said. "What's it about, anyway?"

"How should I know? The letter is sealed with the insignia of the ecclesiastical court. If it was the Crown's seal, I'd break it and have no qualms reading the letter, even if it is addressed to Juan. I am an officer of the Crown, after all, but the Church is another matter. They are after you like rabid dogs if you take a wrong step."

And the Church is worse than the Crown when it comes to putting out their hand and grasping at your hard-earned money and holding you down with the iron fist of their laws. Wasn't it enough to have the Inquisition in Mexico City? Did they have to send the fiscal here to set up a branch office and send his spies (sixteen of them, they say) to report on our sins?

"Not that they care about us going to hell," I said to Maria, "but there is money to be made from sins, indulgences to be sold, fines to be levied, property to be confiscated, officials to be appointed — paid out of our tithes and taxes, of course."

It was a wonderful racket, or would have been if they had reeled in some people of means, because they confiscate the sinners' property to pay for their own salaries and that of the jailer who guards them. As is, I'm not sure it was a good investment for the Church. They won't get anything out of that fortune teller or the old drunkard. Luisa, maybe, but I don't know if she has property of her own.

"I don't think you have reason to complain," Maria said. "You made your money off the Inquisition, didn't you? Don Alonso signed some lucrative contracts with you."

"And he might have signed off on a marriage contract as well if you had taught Anna to be more pleasing to him."

"I can't teach her to love a man who doesn't know how to court a girl. He never smiled and always had a preoccupied air. That's all very well for a lawyer meeting his client, but it won't do for a suitor trying to woo a girl. You might have given him a few hints on how to behave if you were so keen on him becoming your son-in-law."

"What do you mean — keen on him? I'm keen on getting a good deal for your daughter; the rest is your business. In any case, Don Alonso is done with his job here. He'll be returning to the City today or tomorrow, and good riddance to him. His departure doesn't bother me. What bothers me is the summons for Juan, which has come just in time to spoil my dinner."

"I suppose it concerns Luisa Abrego, the poor woman," Maria said. "I wish Don Alonso had done something for her. She didn't deserve to be dragged through town like that and sent to Mexico City."

I didn't say anything because the servant had placed the soup in front of me and the aroma wafting up from the chili beans was too tempting to wait another moment. Ah, life is not so bad after all, I thought, as I savoured the soup, good to the last drop.

But there was that blasted letter.

"You are probably right," I said to Maria. "It's something about Jorge's woman. Presumably they want your brother to give testimony before the tribunal. It was an evil day when Juan hired Jorge, and a worse idea to befriend that man. It is never good to be overly familiar with your workers, and I suppose the same goes for a captain and his sailors. But I don't see how they can hold him responsible for the mess Luisa is in."

"Exactly. Juan had nothing to do with her, other than back in the old country, witnessing the exchange of the wedding vows between Jorge and Luisa and signing his name in the church register. That isn't a crime, and I don't know why you are making such a fuss over this business. Juan is not to blame."

I had no intention of making a fuss while the maid served the lamb and refilled my glass of wine, which was indeed worth the price that old gouger charged me.

"Who is blaming Juan?" I said as I took a first bite of the meat, then reached for my glass to wash it down. "I said just now that he can't be held responsible for the mess."

"Then hand the summons on to Don Alonso and ask him to forward it to the harbourmaster in Veracruz, and when Juan's ship comes in, he can deal with the matter himself," she said. "And don't deny that you are blaming my brother!" she went on. "You are always quick to find fault with my family ..."

And so on and so forth, spoiling an excellent lamb roast. Eating never slows down the tongue of that woman. She won't shut her mouth as long as she can think of another word to add.

"Enough of this business," I said after a while, but it was too late. She had ruined the dessert for me as well. I told the servant to take the flan away and left the table, grumbling.

In a way, Maria was right, of course. I couldn't blame Juan. It was Jorge who should have made inquiries before he married Luisa. A marriage is not so different from a business deal, and if a man does not look into the securities before he signs a contract, he cannot complain if he is drawn into a bankruptcy. Why did he marry a half-caste in the first place? They are nothing but trouble. Maria thinks there is something special about Luisa. "What?" I ask her. "What's so special?" She can't say — something about her smile, something about her voice. She is a "soulful" woman. Nonsense. I say she brought Jorge some money, and so he didn't ask too many questions. As far as money matters are concerned, he did all right with her. And maybe in other matters as well. She is a handsome woman and knows how to move her body to attract a man's attention. She looks like a lively one in bed, unlike Maria, who turns into a slab of marble the moment we are under the blanket. There is no heat in that woman's body. That's probably why she presented me with three daughters and no son. That's three dowries I have to come up with. Those girls are costing me dear, and who will carry on my name? No one, I fear.

It's a weakness in the blood, the doctor said. It's a curse, I say. It runs in Maria's family. They have a surfeit of females. She herself was one of four girls, three of whom died, thus relieving their father from having to provide them with dowries. As for her brother, I'd be better off without him.

Juan was supposed to settle down here and help me run the hacienda. I need a reliable man in that place. The foreman I had at the time was a scoundrel, and it got too much for me to look after everything: keeping the smelter and the stamp mill in working order, seeing to the storage sheds, the workers' huts, and the corrals for the horses and burros, the sowing and harvesting, the breeding and pasturing of the cattle and sheep. I have enough to do with the business side of the enterprise, buying the ore, selling the silver, playing banker to the miners. That was the idea when Juan came here, that he would free up my time and look after the production side, but he lasted all of eight months. Thank God, I was able to get my son-in-law to take over from him. So all went well, but no thanks to Juan.

He can't help it, Maria says, the sea is in his blood. Nonsense. Shipping is an uncertain business, at least the shipping of merchandise, and in the last two years, I suspect, Juan has lost more than he has gained. He is getting too old for this business. I offered him a regular salary. He could have sold his ship to his partner and invested the money with me.

When he quit and said he wanted to go back to sea, I tried to talk sense into him, help him along.

"If you want to make a profit in shipping, Juan, you should acquire a licence to carry slaves."

He shrugged. He isn't one for accepting advice, but I tried again.

"The money to be made in transporting slaves is as good and better than engaging in the spice trade," I said to him, "and if the ship runs into a storm, a human cargo will fight to stay alive and help you and your crew keep the ship afloat, whereas the spice chests will sink without so much as a sigh, and with them your investment."

"I don't like the idea of keeping men locked up in the hold," he said. "They are human beings, after all, not cattle."

"They are, but lesser human beings. They are pagans," I told him.

"Many of them have been baptized and are Christians like us," he said. "Besides, what if a fire breaks out in the hold? They'll never make it out alive. Not to speak of the diseases that are likely to breed among them when you crowd so many people together. I have heard from traders that of a hundred slaves shipped, only seventy or eighty make it alive."

"So what," I said, "that's still a healthy profit."

But I could have saved my breath. The man doesn't listen. After years of crossing the Atlantic, sailing back and forth between Spain and Mexico, what does he have to show for his efforts? I'm not saying that he isn't a hard worker. We both work hard. The difference is that my work has durable results. I can look around with satisfaction. I live in a house built of stone with a second storey of solid wood, a substantial home unlike the miserable adobe houses you see all over town. Ten years ago, my home was only the third house of substance, besides the council house and the monastery of the Franciscans. That's because I had the foresight to acquire the quarry on the edge of town. And so the monks had to come to me when they built their monastery, and the city council had to place their orders with me as well, when the Crown finally subsidized the building of a courthouse and *cabildo*, and the Inquisition had to pay me as well for the stone that went into the new quarters for their local officers. Now we have a main plaza surrounded by respectable buildings — except for the jail, which is in poor shape and will stay that way until I can pry loose the necessary funds from the Crown and persuade them to give our town a percentage of the silver tax. We pay them enough, I think. Zacatecas is a prosperous mining town. It's high time Spain did something for us in turn.

In my letters to the Crown, I exaggerated the poor condition of the jail, of course, or they'd never part with even a peso. I talked of imminent collapse, although it's not that bad — yet. While they are dragging their feet about providing a building subsidy, I engaged a master mason, but I expect to be paid back with interest when that Crown subsidy finally materializes. The mason and his crew are patching up the adobe walls now, at least the part housing the offices and the quarters of the jailer. I don't care if the cells crumble and the torture chamber is a stinking hole. It's supposed to be a hellhole. And I doubt anyone on the ropes, with the pullies wrenching his arms out of their sockets, will worry about damp walls.

Anyway, I made my escape from the dinner table and was about to slip out the door when I was waylaid by my youngest daughter.

"Papa," she said, "I —"

I cut her off. "Not right now."

"But I meant to talk to you about —"

I waved her off. "I'm in a hurry, child. I need to catch Don Alonso before he departs."

I closed the door on her, but out in the street, I thought maybe I should have talked to her; perhaps it was about the town secretary, who has been slinking around here lately, mooning after her. He wouldn't be a bad son-in-law if she were inclined that way, or even if she weren't. But I was in a hurry — I could see Don Alonso coming out of the Franciscan monastery. I waved to flag him down as he was getting into the saddle, but at that moment a shout went up and all heads turned toward a rider galloping into the plaza. He pulled to a halt at Don Alonso's side and jumped off.

By the time I crossed to the other side of the plaza, a knot of people had formed around the two men, listening to the bad news.

Jorge's mine had collapsed, the rider said. An old Indian woman noticed that the entrance was blocked with fallen rock and ran down to the road for help. Half a dozen men then went to work with shovels and pickaxes to rescue the trapped miners.

"It was too dangerous to go straight in, so we dug a parallel ditch and cut across at the back of the mine, which looked still intact," the rider said. "We thought maybe Jorge and his man were able to take refuge there, but when we broke through, we were greeted by the stink of death and decay. I guess the collapse happened a few days ago without anyone passing close enough to notice."

"If Luisa had been here, she would have known something was wrong when the two men didn't come home. She would have looked for them right away," I said, and the others nodded.

They understood my meaning. I didn't have to spell it out. My remark was aimed at Don Alonso. Why the hell did Luisa have to be taken to the City? Why couldn't the whole affair be taken care of here in Zacatecas, now that the Inquisition had a branch office? It was a case of overreach — the authorities in the City were meddling with local affairs and trying to make some money in the process. It was Don Alonso's fault. He could have handled the matter here, discreetly. Jorge would have paid him whatever price he named, I'm sure. I've never seen a man so much in love with his wife as Jorge. I can understand a man losing his head and playing the fool during courtship and the first few months of his marriage, perhaps, but he and Luisa have been married for God knows how many years. And she hasn't even presented him with an heir — two or three miscarriages and a sickly child who died within a year. Their blood doesn't mix well. Sure, you can cross a horse with an ass, but all you get is a mule. As for Luisa's present situation, I blame Don Alonso.

He understood my meaning when I said "if Luisa had been home." He frowned, but he ignored the remark and turned to the rider instead.

"Did you bring out the bodies?" he asked.

"One of the men shone a lantern into the hole we hacked out. We could see Jorge's man lying there, dead, with his head smashed and crawling with maggots. We didn't think it was safe to go in and risk our lives just to bring out a corpse."

"And Jorge?" Don Alonso asked.

The man shrugged. "No sign of him and, if you ask me, no hope of finding him alive. As far as we can judge, the rest of the mine is completely ruined. He is buried under a mass of fallen rocks."

"May he rest in peace, then," Don Alonso said. "I will pray for him."

And we echoed his sentiments.

"It's a sad story," I said, "especially for Jorge's wife."

Don Alonso sighed. "It will fall to me to give her the dire news when I arrive in the City. A hard task, that." He looked almost sincere when he said it, but those fiscals are good at keeping face.

"And speaking of Luisa and the trial," I said to him, holding up the summons, "I received this letter addressed to my wife's brother. Juan no longer lives here, as you know. He has gone back to sea. You might send the summons on to the harbourmaster in Veracruz."

"Very well," he said. "I'll see to it."

I handed the letter to him and wished him a good journey to the City.

Good riddance, I thought as he rode off. My business being discharged, I went home and gave my wife the news of the disaster that cost Jorge and his helper their lives. It was by no means the first time that a mine had collapsed. Digging out the ore is dangerous business. Still, I was curious about what exactly had caused the disaster. After all, the mining business concerned me, and the more you know, the better you are equipped to deal with the financial fallout. A mine collapsed is a mine that profits no one.

The next morning, I rode out to see for myself what had happened.

The earth around the mine shaft was a churned-up, trampled mess. I hadn't expected to see anyone except maybe a few curious people like me, wandering around, but it looked like the rescue operation was still ongoing. At the entrance, three fellows, their faces streaked with dirt and dripping with sweat, were hacking away with pickaxes and shovels to remove the rock pile blocking the way. I saw that they had shored up the entrance to the tunnel with beams to keep it from collapsing on them as they worked their way in. A woman was sitting on the ground beside the entrance, an evil-looking, toothless old hag with a face like brown leather. She was singing or talking to herself in the Native language.

"Who is she?" I said to one of the onlookers, for I wasn't the only man who had come out, undeterred by the drizzle in the air, which left a moist sheen on our clothes like sweat.

"That's the old woman who first discovered that the entrance to the mine was blocked and went down to the road to fetch help. As far as I know, she is the grandmother of Jorge's helper. She said she 'heard the cries of the Earth' three days ago. Or at any rate that's according to the Indian who translated for us, because no one can understand her jabber."

"'Heard the cries of the Earth three days ago'? What's that supposed to mean?" I asked him.

He shrugged. "We understood that she found out about the collapse three days ago, but didn't or couldn't get help earlier."

"So why are they still digging? I thought they'd given up after they found the body of Jorge's helper."

"That's what I'd like to know, too," the man said.

"Hey, you!" I said to one of the fellows working away at the entrance to the mine. He gave me an irritated look and kept digging. You'd think he'd show a little more respect, if not to me personally, then to the office of the mayor.

"Come here," I said. "I have a few questions."

He wiped the sweat off his brow and stepped up to me, making a face as if he had better things to do. The drizzle had turned to rain, meanwhile, and hammered down on us.

"Why are you still digging?" I asked him. "Aren't you wasting your time, not to speak of incurring the danger of going deeper and having the whole thing fall on top of you?"

"I don't like it myself," he said, rain dripping off his sodden hair. "To tell you the truth, we keep going only because we are afraid of the old woman. When we told her that her grandson was dead, she started howling and pulling at our arms. She said there was another man in there, near the entrance of the mine, and he was alive. She could hear him cry for help. That's what the fellow who translated for her said."

"That's Indians for you," I said. "They are full of stories of demons and spirits crying out to them."

"Right," he said. "We also thought it was nonsense. But when we started packing up our gear, she took to cursing and raging, calling us murderers for not coming to the rescue of our own. Then we became afraid she'd put a hex on us — she does look like a witch, doesn't she? So, in the end, we humoured her —"

Before he could say more, there was a shout from one of the workers at the entrance. He raised his arms as if to command silence.

"Listen!" he said, wonder in his face. "I think I heard a voice!"

Everyone fell quiet and pressed as close to the entrance as they dared, and then I could hear it too: a kind of low moan.

The men fell to digging again, and people rushed to fetch tools from their saddle packs or, in their eagerness, used their bare hands to help remove the rubble.

After another two hours of joint work and in great fear that the whole thing would collapse and fall on our heads, a shout of joy went up, as the men in front pulled out Jorge and laid him on the ground.

His body was all in a heap and mangled, but there was no doubt: He was breathing, his eyelids flickered, his mouth was working, he was trying to say something, although nothing came out except the kind of sound a wounded animal makes. He was bruised and bloodied, he looked like an exhumed corpse, but he was alive.

The rain had tapered off and a pale, yellow sun moved through the clouds, as if the miraculous scene needed illuminating. The old woman had stopped keening and was prostrating herself on the ground, thanking God, it looked like — if those heathens have a god, that is. The men, meanwhile, laid Jorge on a plank. We could see spasms of pain running through his broken body. They had to tie him down before carrying him down to the road and putting him into a cart to take him home. We all stood back, but the old woman couldn't be fended off. She kept pressing close to Jorge's body, and so in the end, they took her along, too.

The rest of us stood around afterward, talking, wagging our heads, wondering how much longer Jorge would live. None of us gave him much of a chance. We all agreed that he looked like a dying man. I myself thought that the rescue operation had been a waste of time, and I still didn't have an answer to the one question of interest to me: What was the reason for the collapse of the mine, and how could it be avoided in future so as to safeguard a man's investment?

There was some speculation — a tremor, perhaps; shafts located too closely together or going down too deep; or that this particular hill was unstable — but no one had a good explanation and, as usual, it came down to "these things happen." After we had all had our say, I rode home.

When I told Maria of the rescue, she crossed herself three times. "A miracle!" she said, but she is inclined to believe in that sort of thing. Of course the rest of the household showed no more sense than Maria and made it sound as if God himself and all the angels had come down from Heaven to rescue Jorge.

Everybody was in a tizzy of joy. You'd think Jorge was their nearest and dearest friend. "So it's true! He is alive!" they kept saying.

"Barely," I said. "I doubt he'll live much longer."

That evening, at dinner, Maria said to me, "Maybe you should send a message to Don Alonso, letting him know that Jorge is alive. It will be a comfort to Luisa in her troubles. Such a soul of a woman. I always enjoyed her company. There was something calming about her, something that made you feel good. I do feel sorry for her. She doesn't deserve all that misfortune."

She went on in this vein. I said nothing, hoping she'd run out of words eventually, but no, she kept going.

"I know you are busy, Pedro, but it wouldn't take much of your time to write to Don Alonso," she said.

I finally had to cut her short.

"Will you let me eat in peace?" I said. "I'm trying to enjoy my dinner, and you come up with a hare-brained idea and spoil it for me. Why should I get involved? It costs money to send a letter, you know. Let Jorge send a messenger to the City."

"But you said he is in bad shape, that he is barely alive," she said. "He won't have the strength to dictate a letter."

"Well, is that my fault? Why do you worry about him and Luisa? It's none of our business. I have enough on my hands as it is, with that daughter of yours refusing to receive the town clerk's attentions just because he isn't a youngster anymore. Make it your business to talk some sense into the girl, and keep out of other people's lives. Give me one good reason why I should incur the expense of sending a message to Don Alonso. Besides, if you ask me, Jorge won't live much longer, so what's the use of getting up Luisa's hopes?"

"It's our duty as Christians —" she said, but I stopped her short.

"Don't lecture me, woman. I know my duty. I pay my tithe to the Church and the quinto to the state. I don't owe anything to Jorge or his wife. If you ask me, it would have been better if he had died. What kind of life can a cripple have?"

6

Zacatecas, 1575:

Jorge Abrego, miner

THEY SAY THAT WHEN YOU are close to death, the whole of your life passes before your eyes, but when the mine shaft collapsed and I was buried under the rocks, I never thought about the past. It lay behind me like a long, foggy road. My mind was drifting.

I didn't know how much time had passed in that blind darkness when I woke to a fierce, stabbing pain in my shoulder and left arm, a deep ache in my bones. My throat was dry, but I had nothing to quench my thirst or still my hunger pangs. I raised my head, thumped against wood and sank back again. I couldn't shift my body or straighten my legs, but I was able to move my right hand to explore my surroundings. I felt a wooden barrier mere inches away and realized that a toppled beam was hemming me in, running along the whole length of my body. It had pinned me down but also protected me from the falling rocks and was forming a hollow space around me that allowed me to breathe.

I had been working close to the mouth of the mine when the shaft collapsed, and the fact that I was now surrounded by darkness told me that the way out was blocked. Not even a ray of light could penetrate to the spot where I lay. I was shut up in the mine like in a tomb. The silence surrounding me was complete, except for the ghostly rumbling of shifting rocks somewhere in the depths of the mine and gravel raining down on the beam above me.

After what seemed like many hours, I heard more rumbling and saw a glimmer of light. The new rockslide had opened up a crack no wider than my hand. However close I was to the surface, it did not help me because I was trapped by the beam and could not move even an inch toward the source of light. At least I would not die a wretched death of suffocation, I thought. That tiny gap assured me a fresh supply of air.

Then it occurred to me to call out in case Chulo, my helper, could hear me — if he was still alive. I did not know how far my voice might carry from where I lay, wedged under the beam, but there was no answer to my calls. No sound reached my ears except the ominous cracking of the shifting rock. I had hired Chulo to help me dig the mine. Later he worked with me underground, breaking up the rock with hammer and crowbar and carrying the ore to the surface in hide bags. He was a young fellow, but possessed of such amazing strength that he could shoulder loads of fifty pounds at a time, clamber up the narrow ladders from the bottom of the mine to the entrance, and carry on long after I was spent and had to rest.

It was my hope that Chulo had been spared, that only the front section of the mine had collapsed and he was safe on the far side. The disaster had struck at the end of our workday, when Chulo was picking up his *pepena*, as he called the bag of ore I allowed him to collect in addition to his pay, as a reward for good work. I myself had been at the front end of the mine, near the entrance, emptying the buckets of groundwater we brought up from the bottom with a system of rigged chains and whims.

When the ground beneath me began to rock and the walls gave way, the pail of water I had lifted off the chain tipped over and spilled, drenching my shirt. Now, with an infinite effort, I manoeuvred my hand up to my chest so that I could gather the folds of my shirt and bring them to my parched lips. I sucked at the fabric, but the liquid was barely enough to wet my lips and tongue. Time had passed while I lay unconscious; how much time, I could not tell — perhaps a whole night; perhaps another day— but enough that even in the cold, dank mine, my shirt was no longer sopping wet. It was merely moist to the touch. I tore off a bit of the fabric with my teeth and chewed it and, after sucking out as much liquid as it would yield, swallowed the mash. The fibre, I hoped, would calm my growling stomach even if it provided no nourishment. How long would it take for anyone to miss the two of us? There was no one waiting for me at the house, and Chulo was a single lad. His family lived on the mayor's hacienda at the edge of town. He slept at my house during the week and visited them only on Sundays. They would not miss him for days. And Luisa, my poor Luisa, was far away, but her image sustained me in the darkness, and I realized that I had been wrong all these years when I thought love was a meaningless word, no more than romantic nonsense. There was no love between men and women, I thought, only self-interest or lust or, at best, companionship. But the memory of Luisa's sweet voice settled on me like balm, and I realized that love did exist and had bound me to her all along.

After a while I was too lethargic to think at all. I no longer feared death or cherished hopes of being rescued. I no longer felt any pain. My body was going numb, a harbinger of death. It was the apathy of a body turning into a carcass, I thought, as I slipped into unconsciousness once more.

I woke to what sounded like the clattering of steel against stone and the voices of men. Was it a hallucination? Was my starving brain playing tricks on me, or was someone near and coming to my rescue? After a while, I became convinced that it was no figment of my imagination. Help had arrived. Someone was cutting through the rubble with shovels and pickaxes. I called out — or rather, meant to call out, but my dry throat gave off no more than a moan and a rasping sound, as I gasped for air.

Did the past flash before my mind? No, when I lay helpless in the darkness of the ruined mine, I never thought about my past life. Those memories came much later, during the months I spent in bed unable to move, when my life was hanging by a thread. It was then that I thought how lucky I had been to meet Luisa. The memory of her voice was more potent than any medicine.

A crew of miners dragged me out and carried me home and laid me down in my own bed. Chulo's grandmother came and tended me, perhaps to assuage her own grief, because she could not do this labour of love for her grandson, whose body lay buried under a ton of rock. The doctor almost gave me up for lost when he saw the shape I was in. I must have been buried for two or three days, he reckoned. He said it was a miracle I had not died of my wounds. The pressure of the fallen beam and my own body weight on the injured arm had kept me from bleeding out. Of course, there was still the danger of gangrene setting in. In that case, he would have to saw off my arm. And even if there was no gangrene, my bones were broken in so many places and my shoulder so mangled that I would never be able to use my left arm again.

Chulo's grandmother spoke no Spanish and did not understand the doctor's dire prognosis. Nor could she talk to me, except to make clucking noises and stroke my head, but she comforted me even without words. I listened to her soft murmur, as she diligently washed my broken arm and dressed it with a poultice of native herbs.

"Pipiltzintzintli," she said to the doctor, showing him the mash of herbs and smiling wisely, but he only frowned.

"I wish I could tell that old hag to keep her mouth shut," he said, "or the inquisitor will be after her. They are suspicious of the Indians using herbs. The churchmen call it black magic and witchcraft, although I myself believe that those plants have natural healing powers or, at any rate, a sedative effect. Still, it's wise not to make a ritual of it, as that old woman does."

I sank into a dreamless sleep, slept away the days in exhaustion, and awoke only when Chulo's grandmother laid a gentle hand on my cheek and sat down by the side of my bed to feed me. People said she was a witch, or so the doctor told me, but we are all afraid of what we don't understand. Her eyes were deep with a knowledge foreign to us. She did not speak our language. Her words were like the soughing of the wind or the rushing of the water or something that might come out of the beak or maw of an animal, but I knew she was a gentle soul. She patiently spooned broth into my mouth and held the lip of an earthen jug to my lips or changed the rags in which she had swaddled my lower body. All the while she was singing to me or to herself, or perhaps it was her way of talking, a gentle singsong that had as much healing power, I think, as any of the herbs she applied to my wounds.

One day I asked her name. I pointed to myself and said "Jorge," then pointed to her and raised my brows in a gesture of questioning.

She smiled her toothless smile and said, "Madre." Perhaps she had heard other Spaniards address her as "mother." In any case, that's what I called her from that time on: Madre.

It took weeks before I came out of my thick stupor and could sit up and save Madre at least the bother of cleaning up my shit and piss. She changed the dressing of my wound patiently, day after day. She poked at the sores that had formed around the split skin and clucked over the ragged edges oozing pus. I quivered at her touch and turned my head away, shuddering with pain and revolted by the sight and smell of my own body.

Weeks passed until the wounds dried and formed scabs and the swelling in my arm went down sufficiently for me to wiggle the thumb and forefinger of my left hand. The doctor thought that was as good a result as could be expected, even though I wasn't able to move the rest of my fingers or raise the injured arm. It hung down by my side, uselessly. In time I was able to sit up and feed myself awkwardly with my right hand.

Finally, one day, I got out of bed, leaning heavily on Madre's bowed shoulder and crooked arms, and made a few tottering steps. We must have been a laughable sight, a cripple supported by an ancient crone. Like a child, I had to be dressed in the morning, waiting for Madre to slip a shirt over my emaciated body and pull a pair of pants over my stick legs, while she sang a healing song with many twitterings, like a bird in spring, glad of the season changing. And yet, I thought, she could not be happy to see my powers reviving without feeling sad that she could not revive Chulo. I had lost a helper and friend. She had lost someone even closer, someone linked to her by blood.

The captain once warned me to think twice before befriending a worker. He might take advantage of you or disappoint you or abandon you, he said. By those rules, you could not trust anyone. You could not be close to any man or woman. But I would rather put up with disappointment and loss than never enjoy friendship at all. Chulo was a friendly lad, easygoing, with eyes that asked to be trusted and a mouth quirking up at the corners, ready to smile at you. We made friends quickly. Luisa took to him as well and treated him like a son. She lavished on him the motherly love that filled her breast to overflowing because she could not give it to her own boy, left behind in Spain.

During the long time of my recovery, my thoughts most often turned to Luisa. How I wished she was my nurse and stroked my head tenderly, but her fate was uncertain — or at least remained uncertain in my mind, which was clouded in those first weeks after my rescue. I hardly knew how to ask questions. The recent past was a blur, barely reaching the surface of my consciousness, but one scene rose up from the depths and came to me clearly: Luisa and I returning from church one Sunday. I wasn't much of churchgoer, but it was a special occasion that got everyone's attention and aroused my curiosity as well. It was the inauguration of the Inquisition in Zacatecas. The parish priest gave a rousing sermon, to drum up business for the tribunal, I suppose. He talked in great detail about the cases that had come before the court in Mexico City: fornicators, witches, and the curious case of a man who had left his wife and children behind in Spain and then, pretending to be a bachelor, remarried in Mexico. Luisa listened with rapt attention. On the way home, she seemed withdrawn and deep in thought.

"That sermon got to you, didn't it?" I said when we arrived back at the house.

She didn't answer and went into the house as if in a trance, walking stiffly and without turning her head.

She took off her shawl and said without facing me, speaking to the wall, "I am a bigamist."

I was thunderstruck.

"Luisa!" I said. "What's come over you?"

I stepped up to her and put my hand on her shoulder to turn her toward me.

"Look at me, Luisa," I said, but she shrugged me off.

"Don't touch me," she said. "I am a sinner. I am one of the damned."

I couldn't remember what else she said and what happened next because my mind was in a fog during those first weeks after my rescue. I only knew that they had taken her away. The recent past came back to me in faded and smudged images, yet things that had happened long ago were as vivid in my mind as if they had occurred yesterday.

I clearly remembered the day I first saw Luisa at the boarding house of La Vieja Negra in the harbour of Seville. She caught my eye because she was unlike the other women there — slatterns, all of them. She wore a modest dress that didn't show the tops of her breasts to draw the eyes and hands of men, an invitation to spend their hard-earned money rutting with one of them.

Luisa's smile was different from theirs, as well: not a leer or a smirk or a come-on. Her eyes were charcoal black and luminous, her lips full, almost too generous in proportion to her face.

Her skin, the colour of honey, was smooth and clean, and I don't mean just scrubbed clean of dirt, but clean all the way down to her soul. She was a rare sight. I couldn't stop looking at her, although my taste did not usually run to mulattas. But it turned out that the bagginess of her dress wasn't modesty. It covered up her pregnant belly. She wasn't so innocent after all, I thought.

After I had seen her belly, I averted my eyes and no longer looked at her. I still listened to her voice, though; I couldn't help it. The sound captivated me. It was unlike the voices of the other women in the house, who brayed and shrieked. It was unlike the voice of any woman I had ever heard. Luisa was quiet, but when she spoke it was with a softness that spread peace. And when she sang, I don't know what it was, but she touched my heart. I hungered for her voice. Most of the time she was silent, though. She saved up her words and let her eyes speak instead. Dark eyes, lit from within. I told myself not to be a fool, to pay her no more attention and seek my pleasure elsewhere.

Two weeks later, I was back on board the *Marisa*, on my way to Mexico, and the work of rigging and hoisting and the stormy sea itself kept me from thinking very much about anything beyond the necessities of eating, drinking, sleeping, and staying alive. But half a year later, when we lay at anchor again before Seville and I had lugged my canvas bag once more to La Vieja Negra, I looked for Luisa, and not finding her among the servants, asked the owner herself. She laughed her toothless, spittled laugh.

"You noticed that one, did you? You and fifty others. She could have had them all, but she was a proud one. She wanted nothing to do with louts like you."

"She was pregnant, wasn't she?" I said.

"Got a good look at her, did you?" She showed me her toothless gums. "Yes, she had a boy three months ago, dropped him like a puppy, and is already back at work."

"So where is she?" I asked.

"No longer working here. You'll have to get on with one of the others — they're all good at their job, you know."

She wouldn't tell me more, but one of the girls, when I slipped her a coin, told me that Luisa was working not far away, looking after an old couple.

"They are a good match," she said. "The old folks have no money to pay her. She has a suckling baby and can't make any demands. So now they have a servant to help them for free, and she and her little brat have a roof over their heads and food to keep them from starving."

I went to the house she pointed out to me, a poor, ramshackle place with a patched roof and rags covering the windows. I hung around until I saw Luisa leave the house to do the shopping. She was wearing the same loose shift I had seen her in when she was pregnant, well worn by now and faded from much washing, but with a flowery apron strapped over it, which showed her shapely figure. She was as handsome a woman and as neat and tidy as I remembered her.

I walked alongside and greeted her.

"I saw you at La Vieja Negra's house the last time I was ashore," I said.

She gave me only a quick look and walked on briskly.

I kept up with her. "They tell me you are not working there anymore."

She gave me another sideways glance and slowly shook her head. I already knew she wasn't one for talking, that I would have to carry on all by myself. So I did and kept at her.

"You were with child when I saw you last," I said.

"I have a son now," she said, her lips barely parting.

"And does he have a father? Or was it the Holy Ghost who got you pregnant?"

She did not even break a smile.

"His father is dead," she said. "May God bless his soul."

"I'm sorry to hear it," I said, but her answer told me nothing, really. Was she widowed or had she been duped and jilted by a lover? I probed a little deeper. "And did he leave you anything besides a child?"

"He did." She stopped and faced me. "And now you've asked me enough questions and I thank you for not following me around like a thief on the prowl."

It was the most I had heard her say in one breath, and her eyes were hard like enamel now, flashing me a warning.

I nodded and dropped back, but I was far from discouraged. Indeed, I was very much encouraged by the way she had faced me and much taken by her forthrightness. Besides, she was as lovely as ever, a sight for sore eyes. I decided to press on, even though I had my doubts about how much the father of the child had left her, given her shabby dress and the beggarly look of the weathered house where she worked. I needed a woman who could pull her weight and wouldn't expect me to support her. That was my way of thinking about marriage then, and it was not unreasonable, except that I forgot to add the value of her person into my calculations. That can't be counted in pesos and ducats, and yet it can make or ruin a man's life.

The next day, I waited for her again.

"Don't be angry with me," I said, trotting along beside her like a dog. "I meant no disrespect. It's just that I'm a plain-spoken fellow and don't have soft words, like some men. If I've hurt your feelings, I am sorry."

She only nodded and kept her eyes forward, but I could tell that she had accepted my explanation and was no longer angry at me for asking questions I had no business asking unless I was serious. So, I told her my name and a bit about myself, while we were walking on: that I was a sailor, but tired of the business of sailing; that I had saved up some money and was thinking of going to Mexico; that I intended to join a friend who had family in Mexico and had arranged for me to buy a plot of land and stake a claim in that place, which was called Zacatecas. I knew for sure that money could be made in the silver mines there, I said, and now I was also thinking of finding myself a wife who would go with me and stay by my side to cheer me up.

I wasn't so much talking to her as thinking my own thoughts out loud. She never said a word in response to encourage me, until we got to the market. Then she turned to me, locking her eyes onto my face as if to make a careful assessment.

"Why are you telling me all this, Jorge, and why are you following me around?" she said.

I took it as a good sign that she had used my name, so I spoke up boldly.

"Because I like you a great deal, Luisa."

"My looks, you mean. Because that's all you know about me."

"That's not my fault," I said. "You haven't told me anything about yourself."

"What do you want to know, then?"

"If you are looking for a fellow to marry and if what you said is true, that the father of your child is dead but has left you something —"

She interrupted me. "You want to know how much money I have, is that it?"

"It's no good talking about marriage if you don't have anything to live on," I said. "I have saved up enough to get myself to Mexico and set up there, and I want a woman like you to keep me company, but I can't afford it unless she can look after her share of the passage."

Then she threw her head back and laughed. "You are a strange fellow," she said. "It's as you said: You have no soft words and don't know how to court."

"True," I said. "I'm not good at that sort of thing. So what's your answer?"

"What's your question?"

"Do you want to come with me to Mexico, as my wife? But first I need to know whether you have enough money to pay for your own passage."

"And the baby?"

"You will have to leave him behind. It would be murder to take him along. A newborn will never survive the journey to Mexico."

She looked away. When she turned back, there were tears in her eyes, and she shook her head as if to say she couldn't do that.

"You wouldn't be the first woman to have her child fostered by others," I said. It was done all the time. Families who had more offspring than they could feed farmed them out to relatives or took them to religious houses and other charitable places. "I don't mean that you should abandon your child. Perhaps the people you live with can look after him for you."

"They are old. They can't even look after themselves," she said.

"Someone else, then. Don't you have friends or relatives who could take him in?"

We were standing at the entrance to the market. People were dodging around us. That was as far as I had walked with her before, but I didn't want to go away now that we were in the middle of a serious talk, and she still hadn't answered my two questions: Was she willing to marry me and did she have the money to book passage?

We stood there, looking at each other silently.

"Ask me again in three days," she said. "I have to think about it."

It wasn't much of a courtship, I admit. I didn't have time for niceties. I did not have a mother or father to carry on negotiations for me. My parents were dead. I was past the age when men usually marry, but I knew my mind. I knew what I wanted in a woman. But so far, I had never met anyone who matched my ideas. Now I was absolutely certain: Luisa was that match.

Three days later, I stood at the door of that ramshackle house she called her home and knocked on the door.

She came out onto the steps and greeted me but said nothing further.

I asked her again to be my wife, provided she had the money, and this time she spoke to me.

"Let's go into the backyard," she said, waving me toward a narrow path between the house and the hovel next door. I noticed her well-shaped hands and long fingers, but did not want to indulge in any thoughts of holding them or touching her, while I was still waiting for her answer.

There was a patch of brown, trampled grass in the back and a henhouse, as well as a bench consisting of a plank laid across two tree stumps. There we sat, side by side, and first of all she confessed to having told a lie: She had told the old folks that the boy was the son of a friend who had died in childbirth, and that she had promised to look after him. I suppose she had been trying to guard her reputation with that lie, but she couldn't palm it off on me because I had seen her pregnant. In any case, she said, she had consulted her parish priest and he had made arrangements for the child to be fostered by the nuns of Saint Clare until he was old enough to join us in Mexico. Of course the nuns expected to be paid for their trouble, but she still had eighty ducats to offer me as her dowry.

I couldn't believe my ears. It was a substantial sum.

"I'm certainly content with that," I told her. "It's more than I expected."

In fact, I was amazed. I was going to work for my passage and was hoping that Luisa had enough to pay for hers, but I had been besotted enough to consider taking her even if she had no money to offer me, as long as she found someone to take care of the child. And now marrying her turned out to be a good bargain.

I did not give much thought to children then and did not understand what a sacrifice I was asking of Luisa. I had never seen her baby. He was a cipher in my mind, a complication, an obstacle to my immediate plans. Would I have been moved if I had seen the child in her arms? I doubt it. I had no feeling for children, then. I considered them merely a nuisance, a responsibility, and an expense. Nor did I give much thought to Luisa's boy joining us eventually in Mexico, when he was old enough. I looked only to the visible horizon. The distant future was too uncertain to add into my calculations. A great deal could happen between now and then. The boy might die in childhood; the ship carrying him might be wrecked in a storm; indeed, the sea might swallow up Luisa and me, or we might die in Mexico of the cholera or the poisonous sting of a scorpion. There were so many ways in which life could go wrong and disaster strike. It was useless to plan for the distant future. We were puppets on God's stage. I concerned myself only with our immediate needs — the money to pay for the passage, for the necessary tools and household goods once we arrived in Mexico, and for a wagon and mules to take us inland to Zacatecas, where I had obtained a piece of land. If we put our money together, we had more than enough to see us through.

When I asked the captain to be a witness at our wedding, he hesitated at first. He was not sure that I had chosen well. He made inquiries about Luisa, "to protect my interests," he said. I thought he should have left that business to me and trusted my judgment, or rather my feelings. I thought of the marriages my parents had arranged for my older siblings. They were hardly consulted, and certainly no one mentioned love. What mattered was the character of the chosen woman and her dowry. That was considered a good enough foundation for a lasting union. By contrast, I had the luxury of choosing my own wife and, yes, I was in love with her! In the end, even the captain was satisfied that I had made the right choice.

So Luisa and I got married, the nuns of Saint Clare took in the child, and we sailed to Mexico. We were in luck, or God looked kindly upon us. We got to Veracruz safe and sound after coming through a terrible storm. Even Luisa, who felt unhappy and guilty leaving her boy behind, admitted that it had been necessary. A tender babe would hardly have survived that ordeal.

In Veracruz, we spent the night in an inn at the port before setting out for Zacatecas. It was the first time we were on our own, lying in our nakedness on the narrow bed. The darkness of the room was made transparent by the light of a full moon. I put my arms around Luisa and thanked God for giving me such a wife. She was a woman after my taste. I knew that much, although I could not say what it was that gave me such satisfaction. Sometimes I wished Luisa would talk to me more so I could know her better and understand: What did *she* see in me and why had she agreed to become my wife? But Luisa grew up as a slave. They are trained to keep silent, and perhaps words are not made to describe such things, in any case. I will have to accept her love as a mystery.

The captain was generous to us after he had satisfied himself as to Luisa's character. He made us a present of the passage to Mexico, but I thought it was only fair to do my work as a sailor one last time. Indeed, to me it would have felt odd and pretentious to play the role of a passenger and stand by idly, watching my crewmates go about their work.

Throughout the journey, the captain was unfailingly kind and respectful to Luisa, but I think he retained certain reservations about her because she is a mulatta. That came out much later, when Luisa referred to herself as a *morena*, throwing it out as a challenge: *Yes, my skin is brown!*

It happened at an inn on our overland journey to Zacatecas, when some men at the table spoke with disdain about the Native Indians, calling them savages hardly better than animals.

The inn itself was of the most primitive kind, resembling a military outpost more than a lodging for travellers. We ate our meal in the place where it was being prepared for us by a slovenly woman, who busied herself at the stew pots. The room had a low ceiling and smoke-blackened walls. The hearth was at one end, the large rough table where we sat at the other. The fire blazing under the iron pots and two wall sconces with tallow candles served as our only source of light and heat. Under our feet was an uneven stone floor, where two mongrels scavenged for table scraps. The inn offered a few private rooms, no doubt as dismal and filthy as the common room, but most of us preferred to sleep in our wagons, which we had brought into the walled yard, for the inn was protected by a stockade, like a fort.

We had passed an Indian post earlier in the evening, which looked more inviting, but our guide spurned it. He was an old soldier, a veteran of Indian wars, and reminisced about them often. That night, too, he regaled the table with stories of his derring-do and pulled up his shirt to show us his battle scars. Sometimes his stories were greeted with applause; at other times, they prompted heckling, and he was called a braggart and a liar.

"Those Indians are heathens," he was saying in conclusion of one of his stories. "They know nothing and have nothing and live like animals, from one day to the next."

"Except that they know the land and also know how to kill," another man at the table said.

"Know how to lie in ambush, you mean, and raid wagon trains. They are just marauders. Let them face soldiers like me. Let them come out in the open and match us in an honest battle, and we'll see who knows best how to kill."

We had heard similar talk from soldiers guarding the silver transports on the road. Fighting was the essence of their life, and they despised their enemies, perhaps to keep from fearing them.

Our guide was well into his drink and rambled on, "Dressing in hides and painting their faces and bodies red! Do they think the colour of their skin will scare us?"

"Does it?" Luisa said. "Because sometimes I wonder whether the fact that I am a *morena* scares people."

There was a momentary hush around the table, because it was rare for a woman to speak up in that rough company. Then the men broke into boisterous laughter.

"Try me," the guide said. "I'm not scared of tumbling with you, girl," but I stopped his lascivious talk, tossing my pot of ale into his face. I got up from my seat to defend Luisa's honour with my fists if necessary, and the captain rose as well, but the landlord, seeing a melee coming and fearing perhaps for his rickety furniture, put a heavy hand on my shoulder to hold me back.

"How about a round of ale, on the house?" he called out, a suggestion that was met with roaring approval.

Our guide, sodden with drink inside and out, was the first to hold up his mug to be refilled. He had already forgotten his insulting words injuring Luisa's honour. I had not, but my anger was no longer red hot and had given way to reason. I knew it was not wise to fight our guide and risk the crowd coming to his defence, for he was a well-known character. It was better to get Luisa out of the room quietly.

While the roistering continued, I took Luisa by the hand. The captain kept close behind us, and the three of us made our escape into the yard. Luisa climbed into the wagon, but the captain and I stayed out under the clear sky a little longer, talking quietly about the turn the conversation had taken. I was glad that we had to spend only two more nights in the guide's company.

"Luisa speaks up so rarely," the captain said. "She must feel strongly about the point she made — being brown like the Indians. What do you make of it?"

"I believe she meant to say that it isn't a man's skin colour that makes him a marauder or determines his actions one way or another. But you should ask *her*, if you want to know what she meant."

"All right," the captain said, "I will do that if an occasion presents itself."

There was a pause, and I was about to suggest turning in, when he added,

"But I do find Luisa puzzling. Do you think the difference in skin colour makes an understanding between people more difficult?"

The question cut too close to my own feelings. I was not inclined to speak to the captain or anyone else about my difficulties in understanding Luisa. It was a matter to be settled between the two of us.

"I can't talk about people in general," I said, avoiding a definite answer to the captain's question. "A marriage is between two particular people. If they understand each other, that's all that matters."

The captain nodded and let the matter go, but his question left me unsettled. Did I find it difficult to understand Luisa *because* the colour of her skin was different from mine? I pondered the matter as I bedded down beside her until sleep overcame me. Even after waking up with a clear head and putting all my thought into it, I wasn't able to settle that question.

We spent the next night in more comfortable quarters. The talk once again turned to the Indians, but it was about the safety of the road ahead, the last leg of our journey. The host reassured us: The war with the Indians was a thing of the past. No hostilities had been reported in a long time.

He was wrong, however. The next morning we were attacked by raiders.

I myself can look back on that attack now as an adventure that turned out lucky for us, a heroic encounter in which Luisa killed an Indian and gained a prize horse, but for her it was different. The incident turned into a nightmare that haunted her for years. She came away from the Indian attack seemingly unscathed, but with a wound festering inside her.

It was visible only in the depths of her eyes, where I glimpsed it sometimes. She finally talked to me about it one day, when we had already been in Zacatecas for almost two years and were comfortable in our homestead — or so I thought.

We were sitting together in front of a fire burning low in the hearth. It had been a long working day for me, and I was ready to go to bed, but she said she would stay up a little longer, doing her embroidery. But wanting to finish that piece of work wasn't the only reason for her reluctance to go to bed.

She got up and put another log on the fire.

"I'm afraid of closing my eyes," she said. "I'm afraid of going to sleep and dreaming of the man I killed."

She had visions of walking through a dark alley full of shadows rising up, of menacing voices twirling around her, of her hands streaming with his blood, she said. She couldn't wash it off. It burned on her skin, ate through her flesh, and hollowed her out. Worse, God was withholding the blessing of children from her because she had killed a man.

She stared at the walls. "I cannot give birth because the dead man's mother is crying out to God for revenge. She doesn't want me to have children now that she has lost her son."

I had whitewashed the walls to brighten up the room. But when I saw the despair in Luisa's face, the white colour suddenly looked ghostly to me. I put my arms around her and kissed her sad face.

"You mustn't blame yourself for the man's death, Luisa," I said. "You acted in self-defence. That incident has nothing to do with your miscarriages. They happen. Very few couples are spared those tears."

I cradled her in my arms and held her tight, but I could not console her. Her dreams remained full of sinister omens. She woke up crying in anguish and told me of seeing dark skies raining blood, hearing thunder that made her shudder, feeling the presence of the dead man stealing into her soul. She firmly believed that God was punishing her for taking the man's life. For a long time she suffered and had no peace of mind.

The nightmares faded only when she gave birth to a baby girl. Then at last the spectres vanished, Luisa's face became placid again, and her tender smile returned, as she held our newborn child in her arms.

"God has forgiven me at last," she said.

But our happiness was short-lived. The child was sickly and did not live to see her first birthday. For months the poor little thing languished in her crib, with Luisa hovering over her, anxious, tearful, and exhausted by her sad vigils. No medicine suggested by the doctor, no home-made remedies offered by Pedro de Ahumada's wife, no loving care could save the child.

"God is still angry with me," Luisa said, as she prepared the little body for burial. She was done with the sobbing that had shaken her body during the night, but her face was haggard with grief and her eyes shimmered with tears.

I tried to reason with her. "Think about it, Luisa. How many children are born who reach adulthood? One in three dies in infancy. There is no connection between our misfortune and the death of that Indian raider."

"There is," she said. "I am cursed."

There was no comforting Luisa, and her sadness became mine as well.

As we wept over the little coffin, the priest had nothing more to offer us than a trite bit of wisdom: "The Lord giveth, and the Lord taketh away." A better way to console ourselves, I thought, was to bring Luisa's boy over to live with us as soon as possible. In our evening conversations, I turned our talk to the future to keep Luisa from thinking about the past that disturbed her so greatly. I told her all the things we would do as a family; the life we would lead once we had her boy with us. I built up a whole new world for her, in which everything was wonderful. I made a great effort. I did not know I had that many words in me. I talked until my tales of a happy life took hold and warmed the room, until the simple chairs on which we sat softened, the candles gave off a scent of home, and Luisa's face brightened. I became hopeful. I thought I had found a remedy for her sadness — looking to the future — but her fears rose up again and got the better of her.

After we had lived in Zacatecas for four years and the period ended for which she had paid the nuns in Seville to look after the boy, she did not dare to bring him over. She was afraid the stormy sea would swallow him if he undertook the journey.

"God will not protect him," she said, "because I have not yet atoned sufficiently for the murder of the Indian."

"Why would God punish you for defending your own life?" I asked. "And even if you had done wrong, why would he refuse to protect an innocent child and punish him for something you did?"

"It's written in the Bible," she said. "The sins of the parents are visited on their children."

Nothing could convince her to trust in God's benevolence. Instead, she asked me to write to the captain and beg a favour of him. When he was in Seville next, would he go to the nuns on her behalf and pay them to take care of the boy for another four years? I wrote the letter, and she sent along a silver cup as a present for the child. Before sending it off, she filled the cup with water from our well and drank it worshipfully.

"It's like kissing my boy," she said, "for his lips will touch the rim of this cup in turn."

She wept over the cup and held it tight for a moment before handing it over to Pedro de Ahumada, who was going to meet the captain in Veracruz. She wept again six months later when the captain reported back that the boy was well and seemed happy.

"May God spare him," she said.

We were standing in our clean-swept yard, which Luisa had beautified with potted cacti and yucca plants dug out of the arid earth and with cuttings from Pedro's garden, a welcome gift when we first arrived. Pedro had ridden over to give us the captain's letter. We were talking in the yard because he declined my invitation to come in and join us for a glass of wine. He was too busy, he said. Yet, he took the time to give me his opinion about Luisa after she had gone into the house. Her fears were nonsense and superstition, he said.

"If you want my advice, take a firmer stand with her," he said. "Don't be a fool for love. People won't respect you if you allow a woman to ride you."

I did not think Luisa was "riding" me or, for that matter, that it would do me any good to be firmer with her. If I was a fool for love, so be it. I was, however, inclined to agree with Pedro that Luisa's fears were superstition. Yet when I held Luisa in my arms and felt her inward trembling, I knew I was powerless to help her. Her dread was deeply rooted, an innate awe of things that cannot be explained. It was part of her nature, which I saw I must accept even if I could not understand it. Oddly enough, my helper, Chulo, young as he was, seemed to have a better understanding of it than I did.

When we came home from the mine in the evening and had fed and watered the burros, we often lingered in the yard, sitting on upturned pails, talking and enjoying the clear sky after breathing the dank air in the shaft all day. We talked idly about many things — the mine, my childless marriage, his large family, how they managed to get along, what we each wanted from life, how to obtain it and be happy.

"I wish I could persuade Luisa that the death of our baby wasn't her fault," I said, "that this kind of misfortune has nothing to do with the raid in which she killed a man. It was self-defence, but she says even if it was, she is guilty of causing his death."

"That's the sort of thing my grandmother would say," Chulo said. "Maybe it's a woman's way of thinking. She says when the Earth receives a man's body, his blood calls out. It calls for revenge if his death was murder, and for a blessing if it was a sacrifice. The Earth listens to the call of blood."

She and all the women of her generation worshipped the Earth like a goddess, he said.

"The old women think that the Earth tends to us as we tend to her. We sow the seeds and water them. She rewards us with harvests, but she also punishes those who are ungrateful to her and strikes them with torrential rains and hail and with fires that ravage forests and devour houses. That's my grandmother's way of looking at nature, and she does not approve of my working in your mine, either. She says digging into the hills is an insult to the Earth and carrying away her treasures is theft, and I will be punished for it."

"And do you believe her?" I asked.

He shrugged and said no, he did not share his grandmother's views, but because he loved her, he left room for her words in his heart.

"You have to humour the women," he said. "They believe in the old lore."

•

And now it seems that his grandmother's prediction has come true. Nature took her revenge on us. Chulo is dead, and I am crippled. His death has added to my own pain. It weighs me down and presses on me like a reproach, as if I misled him into doing wrong. Yet I cannot get myself to accept the old Indian lore.

I don't know if Luisa's fear of God was part of the same ancient dread. It was certainly superstition when she said that seven years must pass before God's wrath would be appeased and we could venture to bring her boy to Mexico. I myself looked at that time span rationally and thought he would be old enough by then to deal with the rigours of a voyage across the Atlantic. I went as far as writing to the captain to see if he could arrange for the boy's passage. In the end, however, we thought it was preferable to leave the country that had brought us so much sadness, more sadness than could be compensated by all the money I made in mining. It was better, we decided, to return to Spain and live there as a family with the boy.

And now the Earth has swallowed Chulo, and the plans Luisa and I made seem like castles in the air. All my hopes have come down to one thing: living together with Luisa somewhere, sometime.

That was what went through my mind as I lay on my bed helpless like a child, with nothing to do but think of Luisa. I tried to allow only the good memories to surface and to keep the bad ones at bay — the Indian raid, the miscarriages, the death of our baby girl; I did not dare speak the child's name. I wanted to erase the image of her, so still in death, like a wax figure, and Luisa's tears, her drawn face. The death of that child turned her hair grey.

"No!" I cried out aloud to chase away those thoughts as I lay on my bed, but I could not repress the memory completely even as I tried to cover it up with good things. There aren't enough good memories to do the trick. Those good memories are too thin and threadbare to cover up the broad expanse of sadness. Indeed, memories pain me more now than ever because Luisa is so far away, and suffering in a jail I do not want to imagine, yet cannot help seeing in my mind — damp walls, a filthy cot, the company of lunatics, ruffians, and heretics. My sweet Luisa, my love! I cannot bear thinking of her in jail. I try instead to picture her sitting tranquilly in our yard, doing her embroidery; I try to hear in my head her pure voice singing, the melodies filling my heart. I think of the first year of our life together, starting out in Zacatecas: the little adobe house, shabby but our own; the new roof of wood shingles I put on; the comfortable, whitewashed room I added; the new well in the yard; a cistern for rainwater; and a shelter for the mules. There were times when we were happy together in our new home. But I cannot make that picture of peace cover up the vision of Luisa weeping over the coffin of our baby. It is a bad omen to think of her in tears, as if I myself were dead and she a widow already.

As my body healed, my mind too became stronger, and I dared to turn my thoughts to the future again. Now that I am a cripple and can no longer carry on with mining, it is time to think of a different life. *When Luisa regains her freedom ...* I repeat that line to myself many times every day to make it stick and come true. When Luisa returns, we will start over again. I have saved up a good amount of money. We can go back to the old country and open a shop or a boarding house and have her boy with us. Let us leave Zacatecas and forget. The captain left Zacatecas because he remembered. He missed the sea and the seafaring world. I never did. I think of those years on board the *Marisa* as an apprenticeship in the art of survival, as a way of making a living for a man like me who has learned no trade. I think of the tedium, the clanking bell that marked the watches and the hours of the days and nights, the unceasing sameness of our work, unless there was a lull or a storm. There was camaraderie among the sailors, but for the most part, they were a rough lot. I don't miss their company. Even while I was still a sailor, I wanted gentler company, the company of a woman — not for a night but for life. There is little gentility to be found in a port, however; Luisa was a rare flower blossoming in that barren earth. Sometimes I miss the feeling of homecoming when we sailed into the harbour of Seville. I enjoyed the bustle of the port and the variety of life awaiting me there. Luisa, too, said she missed the closeness of neighbours in Seville, the familiar traditions, the well-known faces and houses; indeed, the trees and flowers and shrubs whose names she had learned as a child. In a word, we both wanted to be in a place where we understood the world around us.

In Zacatecas, after all these years, we still felt like new-comers. Everything beyond our house seemed foreign — the bald landscape, the nomadic miners who had no neighbourly feelings. The Indians kept mostly to their own communities. Pedro and the other officials and merchants in the City kept to their own class as well. There were few homesteaders like Luisa and me, so that Zacatecas remained foreign, and after the death of our baby girl, became bleak as well. It was only when I lost a child of my own that I realized the enormity, the cruelty of my demand, of asking Luisa to leave her boy behind in Seville. Now at last I understand the heartache I caused her, even if the separation from her boy was not the long goodbye we said to our baby girl, and even if Luisa's sacrifice was for the child's sake as well, to protect him from the dangers of the sea voyage. I will make it up to Luisa, I have promised myself — when I see her again. We'll sell up and go back to the old country, when she is released from prison, when she comes back to me. We will have the boy with us and be a family. I will be his father and treat him the way Juan Diaz treated me, for a father lives again in his son. That is what we will do when Luisa returns: We will be happy together, she, I, and the boy.

How much longer will I have to wait? I thought. *How much longer will she be held in prison? How will it all end — with a guilty verdict, or an acquittal?* As soon as my health allows, I decided, I will travel to Mexico City and find out for myself. Let it all turn out well, I prayed fervently to God — a God I do not know and have never understood, a vengeful God, it seems to me.

The last time the doctor visited, I asked him whether he had heard any news of Luisa. He waggled his head and said no, he had heard nothing, but he avoided looking into my eyes. I suspected that he knew something but did not want to tell me. Fear crept into my heart then.

"How long is it that I have been lying here, doctor?" I asked him. "I have lost all sense of time."

"Some five months," he said. "They pulled you out of the mine in March."

"And what is today's date?"

"The fifteenth of August," he said.

"Doctor," I asked him, "is my mind playing me a trick or was Alonso de Herrera here on the day Luisa was taken to Mexico City?"

"I wouldn't know," he said.

"When was it that they took Luisa to the City?"

"I can't give you the exact date, Jorge, but I know it was early January. In spite of the cold, a lot of people came to see the prisoners off. I don't recall seeing you, though."

"I wasn't there," I said. "I could not bear to say farewell to Luisa in public or hear people jeer at her — they love other people's misery, you know."

I could not have put up with that. I was afraid I'd go mad and turn violent if I heard them mock Luisa. It wouldn't have done her any good if they had thrown me into jail as well. So we said goodbye here, in the privacy of our house.

"I seem to remember that Don Alonso was kind enough to come and accompany her to the transport," I said. "Is my memory correct, doctor?"

"I have no reason to think that your mind or your memory is impaired," he said. "You were confused in the first days after your rescue, but that was only natural. As your body recovered, so did your mind."

"Can you find out for me what has happened to Luisa since January?" I asked him.

"Dealing with that question may be too strenuous for you in your present condition," he said.

"Then you think I'm in for bad news?"

He shuffled his feet. "I'm not in the know, Jorge," he said, "but if you wish, I will send a message to Don Alonso on your behalf. That way you will have reliable news, at any rate, although it may take a few weeks or even months to receive an answer from him. He is a man of importance, as you know."

"And I am nothing, you mean."

He sighed. "Jorge, you know the world as well as I do."

He left to send the message, and I mulled over the day Don Alonso had come to the house to fetch Luisa. While she was getting together her bundle of clothes and a few provisions, the fiscal and I talked about her prospects in court and the help he might be able to give us. Don Alonso was an unusual man. The captain had nicknamed him "the Philosopher." I myself would say he was a Christian, not only sprinkled with the water of baptism, but a true Christian. Among all the great gentlemen and all the officials I have met in my life, he was the only one who retained his humanity and did not stand on ceremony. Although he was an officer of the Inquisition, I had a sense that he did not entirely approve of the procedures and the laws governing them. He was oddly apologetic the day he came to escort Luisa, almost as if he had been responsible for her troubles. I cannot tell what role, if any, he played in Luisa's arrest. The Inquisition and all its actions are shrouded in secrecy. Later, he explained the legal circumstances to me and promised to exert himself on Luisa's behalf, so that her wait in jail would be as brief as possible. We shook hands on his promise.

I was powerless then, and I am even more powerless in my present condition. Thinking of my troubles, I was once again reduced to memories, hopes, and strange dreams. I dreamed that Luisa was the Earth, giving birth to life, or giving me back my life. An aura of light surrounded her as if she were a saint or a goddess. I think it was the old woman, Madre, who put that dream into my head with her strange singsong voice. She always prayed over the food and drink before she handed it to me, cooing and looking up to the ceiling and bending down to the floor, as if to give thanks to the sky above and the Earth below. When I was a sailor, I encountered the same sort of superstitious reverence for nature among my fellows. They worshipped the sea like a goddess to make her more benevolent. There were those who believed that the sea demanded respect and was wrathful if you withheld your prayers, that she warned those who worshipped her faithfully and signalled dangers to them with certain signs.

And now I too have dreams of the divine power of nature, but they are only dreams. In my waking hours I cling to reason and wish I could condemn those superstitions with greater conviction and certainty. After all, isn't the God of whom we read in the Bible a mystery, so that we need prophets to read his signs? And isn't the Earth his creation? Perhaps God and his creation are one, and the old woman was right to worship Earth like a goddess. But what am I thinking! If I ever said that aloud, I would be condemned as a heretic.

7

Mexico City, 1575:

The minutes of the trial of Luisa Abrego, as recorded by Juan de Altamiro, secretary of the Inquisition

IN THE CITY OF MEXICO, in the chamber of the Holy Office, on this second day of August, 1575, Luisa Abrego, a freed woman, appeared before His Reverence Don Francisco de Zumarraga and the members of the tribunal after denouncing herself for the crime of bigamy. The oath was administered to her, and she promised to tell the truth in answer to the questions posed to her.

Before the interrogation began, however, Alonso de Herrera approached the inquisitor and asked to speak to the accused in private. His request was denied, the inquisitor saying that he would give Don Alonso permission if he were here in his official capacity as fiscal, but as he had been called in the capacity of a witness, he was not permitted to engage in conversation with the accused according to the law, of which he was no doubt cognizant. The inquisitor then proceeded with questioning the accused:

Asked what was her name and where she was from, she said she was called Luisa Abrego and was from Seville, but for the past eight years or so had been a resident of Zacatecas.

Asked who were her parents and where did they hail from, she said she had no memory of her parents, that she had been brought to Seville as a child and had worked as a slave in the household of Diego de Rodriguez until she was freed under the provisions of his will.

Asked if she understood why she was called before the tribunal, she said that it was because she suspected that she had committed bigamy and had denounced herself to ease her conscience before God.

Asked when she had conceived of this suspicion, she said that a year ago or so she had listened to a sermon preached by Father Curiel, the parish priest of Zacatecas, in which he had condemned promises of marriage without witnesses. He said a Church council whose name she has forgotten decreed that a marriage must take place in the presence of the parish priest and two or three witnesses. She did not know whether that was true, but his words had made her uneasy.

The inquisitor said the words of a parish priest were always true and she must not doubt them. He meant the Council of Trent, which had indeed published a decree forbidding clandestine marriages.

Asked if she now believed in the decree, she said yes. The parish priest had reminded the congregation: "If anyone knows of a case where a couple has exchanged a promise of marriage in secret and thereafter married another, they are bound by the laws of the Church to denounce them, on pain of excommunication, because they have committed bigamy, which is a grave sin." Those were his words, and when she heard them, she was terrified because it was exactly what had happened to her. She had exchanged a promise of marriage with a man, but he had jilted her and married another, and later she herself married Jorge Abrego.

Asked if she had confessed her sin as soon as she had become aware of it, she said that yes, she had told the parish priest of her fears and he told her that she was indeed a bigamist and must immediately separate from Jorge Abrego and not share his bed again. Father Curiel said her marriage to Jorge Abrego was a plot of the devil and a mortal sin. Those words of his, when she heard them, were like thunder in her ears.

Asked if she had followed the instructions of her parish priest, she said she had done so for two weeks but then in a moment of weakness, she had yielded to her husband's entreaties. Her husband said that they should send to Seville and find out first if the man with whom she had exchanged promises there was still alive. If he was dead, there was no bigamy. So she had yielded and they spent the night together. The next day, however, she was afraid again and resolved to go to Don Alonso de Herrera, who was in Zacatecas at the time, and denounce herself to him for bigamy and ask for his judgment in the matter. Then Don Alonso said this was a matter for the tribunal to decide and sent her here, where she was imprisoned to await trial.

Asked where and to whom she had made the first promise of marriage, she said she had done so in Seville, to Jordan Bui, an apothecary's helper who had been given permission to court her by her mistress and who had asked her to be his woman and lawful wife.

Asked if she had consummated the said promised marriage with Jordan Bui and copulated with him, she said no: she had met with him only three or four times, always in the house of her mistress, and nothing had happened between them except holding hands, kissing, and embracing.

Asked again whether she had copulated with the said Jordan Bui and warned to consider her answer carefully since she was under oath, she repeated that she had done no more than exchange kisses, since there was no place to do anything more. She had no room of her own and there were always people around.

Asked why she had not taken the said Jordan Bui as her husband in a formal church ceremony before God, she said that after a while, Jordan no longer came to visit her. He was angry because he had asked Doña Ana, her mistress, for permission to take her to his home, and she had refused. Then, some women she knew told her that he was about to marry another and they advised her to go to the church and disrupt the wedding and declare that he had made an earlier promise of marriage to her. At first she had thought she would do so, but then she did not because she had no witness and no proof of his promise of marriage to her.

Asked whether she had told anyone of Jordan's promise to her, she said her mistress was the only person who knew about it. She had not told anyone else.

Asked when and where she had married Jorge Abrego, she said that about a year after she had been jilted by Jordan, she was married to Jorge after the due publication of banns and was united with him with the Church's blessing by her parish priest in the presence of two witnesses, Captain Juan Diaz and the sacristan of the church.

The witnesses to her marriage to Jorge Abrego were to be called next. I informed the inquisitor that in response to my inquiries, I had received a letter from Seville informing the court that the marriage between Luisa and Jorge Abrego had taken place on the fifteenth day of September 1567 and was duly entered into the parish register, but the sacristan who had witnessed it had since passed away. The other witness, Captain Juan Diaz, to whom the Holy Office had sent a summons, was presently at sea and could not be reached.

The inquisitor then called on Alonso de Herrera to come forward and take the oath.

Asked whether he had observed the accused in a marital relationship with Jorge Abrego, Don Alonso answered in the affirmative.

Asked on what occasion or occasions he had observed their co-habitation, he said that he had come to Mexico more than eight years ago, on the same ship as the couple, and had seen them also in Zacatecas, when he was in that town for the purpose of setting up a tribunal. Both on board ship and in Zacatecas, they had shared quarters and were known as husband and wife. He then said he had additional information that he would like to bring to the attention of the court and that would affect the outcome of the present trial.

Asked what that information was, Don Alonso said it was a sad piece of news that had come to his attention. He had asked the court earlier to speak to Luisa Abrego in private because he was loath to give out this piece of information without prior warning to her, since it was certain to distress her greatly.

Asked to proceed with the information he had, he stated that Jorge Abrego had died in a mine accident, so that Luisa was in fact no longer a bigamist.

On hearing this information, the accused cried out and fell to the floor like one dead, so that the inquisitor ordered the servants of the court to assist her. When she was able to stand up again, the inquisitor proceeded with questioning the witness, Don Alonso.

Asked whether his information about Jorge Abrego's death was first-hand, he said that he had not seen the body of the dead man himself. One of the miners in Zacatecas had informed him that it was impossible to enter the collapsed mine and too dangerous to retrieve the bodies of the men buried under the rubble. However, he understood that their death was certain, since in all likelihood several days had passed before the collapse of the mine was discovered, so that the said Jorge Abrego would have perished if not of his injuries, then certainly from lack of water and air.

The court then recessed to deliberate about the verdict. The inquisitor said that the accusation of bigamy being moot with the death of Jorge Abrego, he proposed to dismiss the case, but the prosecutor said that the accused had nevertheless sinned and must be punished by having her goods confiscated and by undergoing public shaming. She should be obliged to walk in an auto-da-fé barefoot and wearing the penitential sanbenito. One of the assessors then asked for a list of the confiscated goods. They were, to wit:

- Two pieces of cloth from Holland
- Eight pillows
- One bedspread, embroidered, and four other bed coverings
- One Native blanket
- Four bedsheets
- Three long-sleeved cotton chemises, three kirtles, and three aprons
- One cape
- Two small wooden boxes embossed with gold
- Twelve silver buttons
- Three large tablecloths
- One pound of thread and a sewing kit with six needles
- One pair of silver scissors

- Two cotton mantles and three scarves
- One tortoiseshell comb
- One amber rosary
- One small red carpet
- One large wooden chest with iron bands and a lock and key
- One red silk bag
- One mirror with silver frame
- Two hats: one of straw, the other of wool
- A set of silver earrings

These goods were sold at public auction.

After discussing the case further, a vote was taken among the seven members of the tribunal sitting in council. Five of them wanted the case dismissed and the accused set free immediately. Two of them wanted to see her punished by walking in an auto-da-fé and having the price of her confiscated goods applied to the cost of her incarceration.

The final sentence, decided and pronounced by the inquisitor, stated:

In consideration of Luisa Abrego's remorse and repentance of her error as seen by the fact that she denounced herself, and in consideration of being told that Jorge Abrego, with whom she had formed a bigamous union, has died, so that Luisa Abrego is no longer living in sin, we resolve to impose on her a penalty as follows for the sins she committed: One half of the amount fetched for her confiscated goods will be returned to her. The other half will be used to defray the cost of her trial and other

costs associated with her being held in jail, the sum to be paid
to the treasurer before she may leave the said jail.

Recorded by me, Juan de Altamira, secretary to the Holy
Inquisition, Mexico City.

•

I copied the minutes out in good, signed and sanded the
paper, and filed it away. Of course, the minutes leave a lot
unsaid — or perhaps I should say that the accused, Luisa
Abrego, left a lot of things unsaid. Usually the women, and
especially mulattas, carry on a great deal, weeping and shaking and wringing their hands, trying to win the sympathy
of the court, but this one was different. She stood there un-
moving, like a statue. Like the statue of a saint, I should say,
because a kind of benediction went out from her, a calming,
as if she did not want to disturb the peace and therefore kept
her words to a minimum. There was an eerie stillness about
the court, as if everyone, even the prosecutor, was reluctant
to speak and move the air in the room. All through the trial,
she was composed and dry-eyed until she heard the news of
her husband's death. I was glad that Don Alonso had come
to speak on her behalf and that they acquitted her, because
all the way through the trial, I was convinced that she was
innocent.

Afterward, I talked to Don Alonso.

"That woman deserved to be acquitted," I said. "I've never
seen anyone more blameless. You had only to look into her eyes
to know that she was innocence herself."

"But the law is an ass," he said. "And she wanted to be punished."

"Punished for what?" I said, astonished.

Then he told me that she had killed a man in self-defence and was haunted by the deed. He hoped that her suffering in jail and the formal acquittal of the court would give her peace of mind at last.

"She certainly has atoned for any sins she might have committed," he said, and I agreed.

8

Mexico City, 1575:

Martin Acevedo, lawyer and notary

HERE IS A STORY FOR a man with a talent for writing up tales
of wonder and drawing a moral from them.

Some time ago, Alonso de Herrera, the fiscal of the Holy
Office, came to me in the company of a mulatta. He introduced her as Luisa, widow of Jorge Abrego, lately of Zacatecas,
and formerly of Seville. She was about thirty years old, neatly
dressed and moving with a certain grace. She had the smooth
brown skin that characterizes half-castes and a pleasant round
face and full lips that hinted at former beauty, although it was
marred now by sorrow. The woman struck me as rather shy.
She greeted me only with a smile, then hung back behind Don
Alonso, as if she wanted to efface herself. When I offered her
a chair, she took it hesitantly, holding on tightly to the satchel
in her lap, ready to bolt in case anyone said a loud word to

her — that was the impression she gave me. She kept her eyes down, while Don Alonso explained the purpose of their call at my office.

Luisa wished to return to Spain and had booked passage with a merchant sailing for Seville within a week. Don Alonso had advanced her the funds for the purchase of the passage, although he considered her hasty departure ill advised.

And advancing the woman money was just as ill advised, I thought. Good luck getting it back! Indeed, I wondered what his relationship to the woman was, what kind of fascination she had worked on him, for he seemed to be taking a great deal of trouble over someone who looked like a simpleton and had no standing. I was surprised because I had met him on other occasions when I had business with the Inquisition, and he struck me as a rather proud and aloof man. Now he was all concern and consideration. The woman had obviously worked her magic on him, although I myself could see no charm in her.

"I counselled Luisa to return to Zacatecas," he said, "and to settle her affairs there before sailing for Spain." She had inherited a house from her husband, Jorge Abrego, he said, which must be sold since she wished to leave Mexico, and there was also the land that he had been mining. In addition, an application must be made for the release of the moneys her late husband had invested with the alcalde, one Pedro de Ahumada. It was a considerable sum, as he understood.

Ah, I thought, thus his generosity. The woman has money and property, or is entitled to it, at any rate. He is sure to get his money back then, with interest.

"I concur with Don Alonso's advice," I said to the woman. "It would be better to sell the property and redeem the investment before you leave for Spain."

She only looked up briefly and shook her head silently.

"I have argued that point with Luisa," Don Alonso said, "but she tells me that she has no close friends in Zacatecas and no family and no desire to revisit the town, which now holds only sad memories for her."

"You have family in Seville?" I asked her.

She looked at Don Alonso as if she needed his permission to speak. In fact, I began to wonder whether she was mute, but then she whispered, "A son."

She immediately looked down into her lap again, so that Don Alonso had to explain the rest.

"The boy was left in the care of the Sisters of Saint Clare in Seville," he said. "He was an infant at the time of her departure for Mexico — too frail to be exposed to the dangers of the long journey across the Atlantic. Luisa is eager to be united with the boy now."

"And what can I do for you in this matter?" I asked, addressing myself to both, as I was not sure I could get an answer from the woman.

"Since Luisa does not wish to return to Zacatecas to settle the estate," Don Alonso said, "I advised her to put the matter into the hands of a capable lawyer, and that is why we have come to you."

"Very well," I said, "but if there is real estate to be disposed of and funds to be divested, it is not a simple matter. It will certainly take months, if not a year, to put everything in order, and additional time to send the proceeds to Spain." I did not think it necessary to mention that there would also be substantial fees to be paid for my services.

Don Alonso, at least, understood my meaning. If he had not pointed it out to the woman, she could see for herself that

I was no hack or pettifogger. Everything in my office — the spacious oak desk, the chairs with the smoothly turned legs, the ledgers on the shelves lined up with military precision, the very cleanliness of the floor and the freshly washed windowpanes — must tell her that I am well established in my profession and therefore not cheap.

"I have explained the matter to Luisa," Don Alonso said. "She is aware of the delay and the costs."

"Then, if you are ready to entrust the business to me, I need first of all two documents," I said, turning to the silent widow. "A paper showing that you are a free woman, and a confirmation from the priest in your parish that you were lawfully wedded to Jorge Abrego."

"We have already sent for the latter information," Don Alonso said. "A letter of the parish priest confirming Luisa's marriage is in my records."

"Then perhaps you will ask your secretary to copy it out for me, with your signature confirming that it is a true copy of the original."

To my surprise, the widow spoke up of her own accord then, honouring me with a whole sentence.

"And I have the letter of manumission with me," she said. Her voice was as clear as a bell and as lovely as a song. It would be only to her advantage if she used it more often, I thought, for no man could resist the charm of that voice.

She reached into her satchel and brought out two sheets of paper, folded over into a small square and tied with a thread of wool. She handed the packet to me.

I untied it and flattened the sheets out with the palm of my hand. I recognized the first page as the standard form of manumission, properly signed, sealed, and dated.

"Very good," I said, read through it, and went on to the second sheet, the contents of which took my breath away. I looked at the mulatta's placid face.

"Do you understand the instructions on this second sheet, Doña Luisa?" I said, holding it up. I added the honorific "Doña" to her name because from the information on that sheet, she fully merited it. A respectable sum of money was mentioned in the document.

"I cannot read what is written there," she said. "Is it not part of the manumission?"

"Did the lawyer who drew up these documents not explain their contents to you?"

She raised her eyes and looked at me without understanding. "He said to take good care of the documents and to keep him informed of my whereabouts," she said.

"And did you keep him informed?"

"I had no means of communicating with him," she said, her voice sunk to a whisper. Then she looked down to the floor again, as if she had given me all the information I could possibly desire and she did not have the strength to say more.

I had many more questions for her but thought it best to begin with an explanation instead.

"Well, then, let me explain the contents of the second document, Doña Luisa," I said. "If I understand you correctly, you gave birth to a son in Seville?"

She nodded.

"When was he born?"

"I cannot name the day, but it was in the month of July, the year after my master's death and my manumission."

"That would be seven months after your master's death, then?"

She nodded and coloured slightly.

"Is the age of the child of significance?" Don Alonso asked, a trifle impatiently.

"Of the greatest significance," I said. "With your leave, Doña Luisa, I will read and explain to you the terms laid out in this document, but perhaps you would like me to do so in privacy?"

Don Alonso immediately rose from his seat and offered to leave the room, but Doña Luisa stretched out her arms to him and begged him to stay. And so I read and explained the contents to both of them. In addition to setting Luisa free, her master had given separate instructions to his lawyer, to wit: to sell off land in his possession to the value of three thousand ducats. If Luisa gave birth to a child within nine months of his death, the interest from the three thousand ducats was to be paid to her every year on St. Martin's Day and used for the upbringing and education of the child. The capital was to be paid out in full when the child reached the age of eighteen if he was a boy, and paid out as a dowry upon marriage if the child was a girl. If the child did not live to see his or her eighteenth birthday, Luisa was to receive three hundred ducats, with the rest of the funds going to the hospital of San Raphael in Seville, as a donation in memoriam of her master, Diego Rodriguez.

Don Alonso was thunderstruck — as I had been on first reading through the document. Doña Luisa looked dazed, so that I repeated to her the instructions more slowly, explaining each clause in detail, until she said, "I see," and wiped tears from her eyes. Tears of joy, I expected, but they looked more like tears of sorrow. I was quite at a loss how to explain her reaction. What was there to be sad about, for Heaven's sake! But who can understand these half-castes?

I looked at Don Alonso with raised eyebrows. He did not seem surprised at all, however. I suppose he sees all sorts of strange behaviour, sitting on the tribunal of the Inquisition.

He took Doña Luisa's arm and said, "The ways of the Lord are inscrutable. We mortals cannot hope to fathom them," and she nodded as if she understood his meaning.

I then impressed upon her the importance of getting in touch with her late master's lawyer on her return to Seville.

"Indeed, I suggest you allow me to inform him at once of your whereabouts and your intention to return to Seville, since you are by now owed a considerable sum of money out of your late master's bequest — that is, more than eight years of interest on the capital set aside for your son."

Don Alonso agreed with my suggestion and counselled Luisa to entrust me with this task at once. "That way," he said, "the money will be ready when you arrive, and you will have enough funds to begin your new life together with your son."

Thus, I had my assistant copy out Doña Luisa's letter of manumission and had her sign — or rather, put her cross to — the instructions that put me in charge of settling the inheritance from her late husband and her former master. As agreed, I wrote a letter to the lawyer in Spain, one Miguel Aguirre, telling him that my client was on her way to Seville, and that she had a claim to the money set aside by her master as she had given birth to a son seven months after his death. She would see him about this matter on arrival in Seville and take the necessary steps to supply a baptismal certificate for the child and any other documents necessary to verify her claim.

I left nothing to chance, as was my duty, and expedited the business as much as possible. Indeed, I went down to the Viceroy's palace myself the next morning and entrusted the letter to a messenger of the royal court, who was to depart for the harbour in Veracruz within the hour and would sail to Spain from there on a fast dispatch boat. Because money was no object, I did not haggle over the outrageous sum he demanded for his service, although I thought he was rather impertinent. Then I rushed on to the inn where Doña Luisa was staying to get a copy of the letter to her, knowing that she too was about to set out for Veracruz. I wanted to hand the copy to her personally, since that would allow me to bill for the delivery myself.

I did arrive just in time, as the ostler was loading up the luggage and hitching the horses to the wagon that would take Doña Luisa and three other passengers to Veracruz. She was making her goodbyes to Don Alonso. The two of them were in the courtyard of the inn, standing rather close together, I thought, deeply immersed in confidential talk.

There was a great deal of bustle and noise in the yard, a press of people coming and going, luggage being carried into and out of the house, so that they did not immediately see me. As I came up to them, I overheard an intriguing bit of conversation.

Don Alonso was saying, "In my opinion, you have never been guilty. The provisions of the Council of Trent apply to your case. A promise of marriage without witnesses is invalid, and that is why they acquitted you."

She shook her head and said, "I don't exactly know what you mean, Don Alonso. I am sure they acquitted me because Jorge is dead." At that moment, she looked up and caught sight of me.

The fiscal turned around when he saw the look in her eyes.

"Ah, Don Martin," he said, "what brings you here?" He was clearly uncomfortable and looked like someone who had been caught out doing or saying something he should not have done or said.

"I was on the lookout for Doña Luisa," I said. "I knew she was due to depart today and thought I'd personally deliver a copy of the letter I have written to the lawyer in Seville on her behalf. I sent the original off by a royal messenger who will travel to Spain on a dispatch ship." I turned to Doña Luisa. "The royal ships are very fast and will reach Seville two or three weeks before you do. I am glad I found you in time rather than having to send the copy after you and bill you extra."

Then I wished Doña Luisa a good journey, emphasizing once more the importance of seeing the lawyer in Seville immediately upon her arrival to collect the money she was owed.

From what I overheard, Don Alonso spoke to her with more feeling than a professional or disinterested relationship warranted. And what was that conversation about her being acquitted — acquitted of what? I could not imagine that woman being guilty of any crime. I had never seen a more simple and innocent soul. She did not strike me as being capable of even a venial sin. Conversely, I cannot believe that the fiscal acted out of purely Christian and altruistic motives when he was so protective of her. My guess is that he was in love with the woman, or that he had been when she was younger, and that he was assisting her now out of gallantry and in memory of former times. Whatever his motives, they were none of my business, however, and I shrugged off the thought.

The next day I composed another letter on Doña Luisa's behalf, addressed to Pedro de Ahumada, the alcalde of Zacatecas. I informed him that I had been charged with settling Luisa Abrego's affairs and requested that he pay out Jorge Abrego's investment. I did not entrust that letter to a messenger, however. I had it delivered in person by my son, whom I am training to become my successor in due time. I told him to go to Zacatecas, inspect Doña Luisa's property, and set in motion the sale of the house and the mining lot. I also told him to keep reminding the alcalde of the need to pay out the funds the late Jorge Abrego had invested with him because I know what those men are like who play bankers and hold money for the miners. They are never prompt to pay out. They like to procrastinate and hang on to the funds as long as possible, as they understand the principle "money begets money." No doubt the mayor was one of them and would need to be poked and prodded to pay out.

Then the story took an amazing turn. My son returned from Zacatecas a week later with the news that Jorge Abrego was alive.

"How can that be?" I said. Don Alonso was not a man to make up stories, unless, unless … I wondered whether he was in cahoots with the so-called widow, but my son had a ready explanation for the confusion.

Jorge Abrego had been buried under rubble when his mine collapsed.

"They gave him up for dead when they found the body of his helper mangled and already decaying, as several days had passed before the accident was discovered. They gave the news of Jorge Abrego's presumed death to Don Alonso just as he left for Mexico City, and he in turn gave the information to Doña Luisa and the court of the Inquisition, where she had been accused of bigamy."

"Bigamy!" I exclaimed.

He shrugged. "That's what they told me, but apparently she was acquitted of the charge. In any case, no one bothered to inform Don Alonso or the woman that the news of Abrego's death had been false, or premature, at any rate. The day after Don Alonso left, the man was pulled out of the rubble, miraculously alive, but gravely injured. And he is still alive, though barely."

"You would have thought that he or someone on his behalf would have had the sense to convey the good news to his wife."

"That's what I said to the mayor, but he said it was none of his business, and at the time he thought Abrego might not live. Then I thought I'd better visit the sick man in person and see for myself what condition he is in."

"And what's your impression?"

"I saw that he was being cared for by an old Native woman. He is still in bad shape and was too weak to talk to me at any length. I guess he was shocked when I told him my business. Apparently he didn't know that his wife had departed for Spain. I couldn't get anything out of the old woman, his nurse. She looked like a witch and didn't speak a word of Spanish. On the way out I ran into the doctor and so I asked him what was going on. But you know what doctors are like. They never give you a straight answer. He was hedging his bets. He said it was likely that the man would survive, but he couldn't say for sure. You never knew in such cases."

"Then we shall have to await the outcome," I said. "If he survives, it will be an awkward business for us. We can't bill Doña Luisa for handling the estate if there is none to handle."

"You are right. It doesn't look good for us. In the circumstances, I did not think it was useful for me to wait around as the man might languish for another week or another month before dying. Or he may survive after all. So, why stay on at the inn and throw good money after bad?"

No doubt, my son had assessed the situation correctly. The boy has a good head on his shoulders and will carry on my business successfully. I quite agreed with him and was pleased with his decision to return. It made no sense to waste any more of our funds on handling Doña Luisa's case, when there might not be a case.

The whole business was certainly troublesome. How was I to recover my expenses — the money I had paid out in good faith to the royal messenger, the time I spent composing letters, the expense of my son's journey to Zacatecas? If the man died, all was well. I would simply deduct my expenses and fee from the moneys the mayor held in trust for the miner, but if he lived, he would no doubt refuse to pay me, and with justification, since he had not hired my services. Nor could I deduct my fee from the proceeds of the sale when there would be no sale of property and no handling of funds. Of course there was the money coming to Doña Luisa from her late master, but both she and the money were far away. I had little hope therefore of ever collecting my fees or being reimbursed for my expenses.

I did look up Don Alonso to consult with him. He was a co-sufferer, after all, for he too would be out of the money he had advanced to Doña Luisa. But I can't figure him out. Like me, he had just been informed of Jorge Abrego's survival through a letter from the man's doctor. Unlike me, he seemed to rejoice at the news. He was more concerned with getting the information to Doña Luisa as fast as possible than with recovering the money he had loaned her. Whatever his relationship to the woman, he strikes me as surprisingly offhand about money. It was not at all what I would have expected from a prosecutor of the Inquisition. I suppose he is wealthy enough to absorb the loss without worrying too much about it. Still, it was careless of him. At any rate, I declined to incur further expenses at this point.

"If you notify Doña Luisa," I said, "may I ask you to present my bill to her at the same time."

He agreed to do so, but with ill grace. He seemed to think it was in bad taste to send my bill at this time.

"On second thought," I said, "perhaps we should wait a little until we know whether the man will live or die. If he dies, there is no need to complicate matters, is there? And you can save yourself the cost of sending a message to Spain."

But he disagreed with me on that point. I suppose he was hoping against hope that she would repay his loan if he did her this additional favour and was the bearer of good news, however temporary.

"I only wish Luisa had taken my advice and delayed her return to Spain!" he said.

"Indeed," I said. "As it is, neither of us has much chance of recovering the money we spent on her behalf."

9

Seville, 1575:

The Abbess of Saint Clare

BAD NEWS COMES IN THREES.

First, some idle fellow starts a rumour that our most precious relic, a tooth of Saint Clare, is a fraud to trick the faithful into making donations to us. It was nothing but a piece of porcelain, he claimed. If that story gets around, all devotions will stop. No one will pay us even a copper coin for a private viewing of the miracle-working tooth or to place the relic against his cheek to avoid a toothache. They will all defect to the Discalced Nuns, who own a sliver of the Holy Cross, which is said to cure all diseases — rheumatism, rickets, syphilis, fevers, even the plague. A touch of the Holy Cross will cure it — for a price, of course.

It would be a great loss if our followers defected to the Discalced Nuns. I have invested a considerable sum of money into the little chapel where we display our relic. The precious tooth rests inside a beautiful vessel shaped like a woman's head, artfully crafted in silver. The face, which is said to resemble Saint Clare, is enamelled and the hair on the head gilded and adorned with pearls and rubies. In place of the mouth there is a small glass window through which the tooth can be glimpsed. The vessel sits on the marble altar in the chapel, on top of an embroidered cloth with golden fringes, which I ordered a few months ago. In a word, I have spared no expense, and have received many compliments on this elegant arrangement. Let us hope that it will elicit generous donations and that the income will justify the expense and prove my calculations right.

On the feast day of Saint Clare, the reliquary is carried through the streets of Seville in procession. Four choirboys swinging censers and perfuming the air with myrrh start off the procession. Next comes the float with the reliquary carried on the shoulders of four young men dressed in white tunics, then our nuns, walking in pairs, clothed in their black habits and white wimples, and finally a representative of the bishop in his finery, blessing the onlookers on the right and left of the street and sprinkling them with holy water. The spectacle always draws a great number of faithful to our chapel, where the procession ends and the reliquary is replaced on the altar. A long line forms at the door of the chapel, of old and young, hale and crippled, men and women, penitents in coarse wool and women in finery. Usually, the line is so long that it snakes down the street and around the block. When it's their turn, the people shuffle up to the altar on their knees and say a prayer to the saint. There are so many of them that we have to employ an usher to keep them moving past the reliquary, or they would kneel there and gawk all day, blocking the line. We do not even charge admission — unlike the Discalced Nuns — but a sacristan stands at the door with a basket to make sure no one leaves without making a donation. I hired the man because he has just the right look of disapprobation, a steep frown and unforgiving eyes that will shame even the most brazen visitor into leaving a coin. Just last year, I refurbished the chapel at great cost, installing a new wrought-iron gate to protect the reliquary from thieves and grubby hands reaching out to touch the saint's head. I also ordered a new upholstered bench to kneel on for visitors willing to pay extra for permission to stay an hour and pray a whole rosary.

The donations have turned into an important source of income for us. It would be disastrous for our budget if the number of visitors declined because some yokel casts doubt on the authenticity of the relic. I may have to offer that slanderer a bribe to leave off talking about the tooth of Saint Clare and start a counter-rumour about the holy sliver of the Discalced Nuns instead.

That was the first piece of bad news. Next, we received a visit from an emissary of the bishop, sent to check our compliance with the regulations of the Council of Trent. He comes every three years or so, when the bishop is short of money and wants to find a reason to slap a fine on us. I already know the man's routine. He goes around every cell and interviews every one of my nuns in private, to elicit complaints. There are always a few simple souls who can't keep their mouths shut and others who aren't simple-minded at all, but want to make trouble for me. Someone complained that I lavish expensive gifts on my friends. They don't understand that potential donors need to be flattered, cajoled, wined, and dined. Another complained that I speak curtly — for Heaven's sake, what does she mean by "curtly"? That I don't coax her into doing her duty? "She treats us as if we were children who need to be muzzled," she told the inspector. "She thinks we are worthless, that we have been hauled out of the muck." And another one was spiteful enough to say that I talk too long with the workmen, behind closed doors — as if those coarse men could hold any attraction for me! And what if I took pleasure in the firm body of a strapping young carpenter? It isn't a sin to look at a man. And was there any need to tattle about someone cavorting with her confessor, or two nuns being too friendly with each other, "like fools in love, flinging their arms around each other's neck, and walking hand in hand in the garden when they think no one sees them"? Was it necessary to snitch to the inspector about such things? And there were other petty complaints about nuns not concentrating on their singing and prayer, about expensive candles in the choir when a few tapers would do, and someone having too many visitors or too lowly visitors. "If a dog came off the street, she'd be friends with it in a second," the complainant said. And the most ridiculous of all the grumblings: that someone picked lice out of her hair and smeared them on the armrest of a chair in the refectory! I had to offer a "donation" to the inspector so he would cut certain remarks from his report to the bishop. It was cheaper to bribe him, I calculated, than pay the bishop's fine for our so-called irregularities. But before I got rid of the man, he made us all listen to a reading of the reforms promulgated by the Council of Trent: Observe solitude more strictly, sing more attentively, pray more privately, work more diligently, dress more modestly, be more charitable, obey more speedily, etc., etc.

The third stroke of bad luck was a letter from a lawyer delivered to me this morning. I could hardly believe my eyes when I read it.

*"Reverend Mother Superior, I understand that
my client, Luisa Abrego, left a male child in your
care before embarking on a voyage to Mexico in
the month of September, in the year of 1567. She
paid you twenty ducats in specie to look after the
child for four years and at the end of that period
sent you another twenty ducats by the hand of
Captain Juan Diaz. She holds a letter to that effect signed by the said Juan Diaz, but has received
no acknowledgement from you to date for the
above transaction. Luisa Abrego is, at the time
of my writing, on her way back from Mexico and
expected to arrive in Seville within ten weeks. She
will then fetch the boy and has authorized me to
pay any arrears for the care of the child. Thus if
you will send in your account,"* etc., etc.

Well, I'll be! I swear the devil has a hand in this. I'd better
gather my wits and see how I can best manage this unfortunate situation. If the news had come half a year earlier, there
would have been no problem at all: just spruce up the child
and charge interest on the payment missed, since it's now some
months past the eight years I contracted with the mother. But
as it is, I no longer have the boy. What bad luck! I need to get
him back at once, in time for the mother's return and with a
few weeks to spare — enough time to fatten him up a bit and
scare him enough so he'll keep to himself everything that has
happened, at least until the mother has paid up. But what am
I going to do about his face! Why didn't Don Francisco warn
me that the mother is coming? That's what you get for dealing
with a simpleton like him. That man has no business sense.

He is plagued by a thousand scruples and has a head stuffed with charitable ideas. He wants to do right by every one of his parishioners, and right also by God. But you cannot be a servant to ten different masters! No, Don Francisco was more unworldly than becomes a parish priest — always preaching at his congregation, waving the Bible at them, quoting it in and out of season. And look what he got for his troubles: a narrow cot in a bare cell and the thin gruel and hard bread they serve their patients at the hospice, and if he is lucky, a piece of cheese and boiled mutton once in a while.

There were enough rich men in his parish willing to patronize him, to assure him an annuity and a comfortable life in his old age if only he had shown himself a little more understanding and sympathetic to their weaknesses. Or else, if he absolutely had to play the severe guardian of their virtue, he should have done it right and scared them into generosity. He should have threatened them with brimstone and hellfire and pressed them for money to atone for their sins. He should have exhorted them to assure their place in Heaven by being generous to God's representative on Earth. But Don Francisco is a simpleton and a fool. So, after a life of toiling for the good of the Church, he is left with nothing to comfort him in his old age. Like a pauper, he depends on the crumbs that fall from the rich man's table — or rather, on the goodwill of the nuns at the hospice, who keep the poorest of the poor from starvation and allow them to live in misery a little longer.

Well, for all I know, he is no longer suffering and has already departed this world, or he would presumably have told me that the mother wants the child back. As it is, I had no warning that she was going to come in person to fetch him. What a bother to be caught out by a surprise like that!

I just hope I'm done with bad luck now that it has "come in threes" — the slanderer, the inspector, and the lawyer, all at once. Is it a punishment from Heaven? No, I have done nothing to offend God. I know what I owe to the Lord and have never been negligent in my prayers or in attending mass, but neither have I neglected my own interests, and it's no sin to look after yourself. Indeed, it's a good thing not to end up like Don Francisco, a burden to others because of his own lack of foresight.

I made mistakes when I was young, yes, but I learned from them. When I was sixteen, I was too conceited to accept the offers of marriage I received. No suitor was good enough for me, and I defied my guardian's wishes. My first suitor, a man of substantial means, was too old for my taste. His paunch and his double chin disgusted me. The second was not quite as rich but of an old and respected family. He was young and had a handsome, manly face and thick, curly hair, but he limped — and so I rejected him, too. Then came two offers from men whose means were too modest to support me in style. I turned up my nose at them and sent them away.

If my parents had been alive, they might have talked some sense into me or been wise enough to ignore my objections and betroth me to a man of their choice. I might have come to see in time that it was more important to look at a man's standing and his possessions than at his person. Good looks will fade; a large estate will support you all your life. Besides, my parents would have pointed out to me that I myself was no great beauty, that my haughtiness put men off, and that I did not have enough money to balance my shortcomings. My guardian did not care one way or another. He wanted to fulfill his duty with the least inconvenience to himself. He could not be bothered to argue with me. When I reached a certain age, he told me in so many words that the cloister was my only choice, and indeed the best investment for my remaining funds.

It was a frightful thought that I would have to spend the rest of my days immured behind the walls of a convent. I pictured myself living in a sombre cell or even forced to share it with another poor wretch, obliged to sleep on a thin straw mattress, dressed in a baggy habit and ordered around by the abbess. I had visions of having to do menial work every day of my life, washing the floors, dusting the books in the library, and tending to the kitchen garden. I saw myself kneeling on the cold flagstones of the church and praying at all times of the day and night, eating the bread of poverty and being starved during Lent.

Thank God it didn't turn out that way. At the convent of Saint Clare, we are all brides of Jesus, but those of us who brought Christ a handsome dowry live a good life, very different from what I had pictured in my fearful mind. And so my guardian was right after all in advising me to join the Clares.

On my nineteenth birthday, he called me into his study and said, "My dear girl, the time has come for me to discharge the duty I have assumed in deference to your late father's wishes. You have not been inclined to listen to my advice when I counselled you to accept one of the two excellent marriage offers tendered to you. You rejected them as you did the others, even though they were by no means unsuitable. And now you have reached an age when it is unlikely that you will receive further offers, since the money your father left you is unfortunately not sufficient to attract much interest. Nor is it sufficient to set up a household of your own."

He paused to allow me to absorb these unpleasant facts, moving his hands across the shiny mahogany surface of his desk as if to sweep away any objections I might voice. But I could hardly gather my thoughts on hearing his words. They jarred my ears and felt like stabs to my brain.

"Not enough to set up a household of my own!" I cried. "Then what am I to do?"

"I will give you one more piece of advice, dear girl, but if you are as unwilling to accept it as you were to accept the marriage offers, I must leave you to your own devices hereafter."

When I heard him speak so plainly, I was very afraid for my future, for what can a young woman do on her own? Especially a young woman like me, who had lived, if not in the lap of luxury, in very comfortable circumstances. In the house of my guardian, a noble mansion in the best part of town, I lacked nothing. His servants were at my beck and call, I enjoyed rooms that were exquisitely furnished and food that was expertly prepared, and I incurred no expense beyond my personal needs.

"What is your advice, then?" I asked, trembling inwardly that he would show me the door immediately and exile me to the countryside or, Heaven forbid, ask me to attend some old lady of his acquaintance. And that is exactly what he suggested.

"An aunt of mine, who is in poor health, stands in need of a companion — if you wish, I will recommend you to her. Her establishment is modest, but you would incur no cost as far as food and accommodation is concerned. I might even be able to negotiate a small remuneration for your services. And you could comfortably pay for your personal expenses out of the interest on the capital you father left you. My aunt is old, however, and given her poor health, liable to die sooner rather than later, at which time you would have to shift for yourself and find another suitable arrangement."

He pushed back his chair and stood, his hands against the small of his back, looking down at me quietly to make sure I grasped the full meaning of his words.

I understood him very well. My future did not look rosy. I did not have the temperament or patience to look after a sick old lady, and there was no security in that arrangement. We might quarrel and she could send me away without ado or, as my guardian said, she might die and leave me without resort.

I looked around his study, a pleasant room with tall windows draped with green damask curtains sweeping down to the floor; the bookcases full of valuable tomes, gilded and leather-bound; the venerable dark oil paintings on the walls — all the beauty and luxury I was in imminent danger of losing.

"Is that the only choice I have?" I asked.

"The alternative is to invest your money with the Clares and enter their convent. Life as a nun may not be as easy and pleasant as you are used to, or as you might find in the house of my aunt, but such an arrangement would offer you security and permanence. You will not have to worry about the future. Once you take your vows there, you will be taken care of for the rest of your life."

I thanked my guardian for his advice and, after thinking it over for a day and weighing the advantages and disadvantages of the two choices he had presented, I opted for the security of the cloister.

"A wise decision," he said.

"I hope so," I said, "although I am afraid it will be an austere life. But if I attended your aunt and she died and I had to set up by myself, I might fare worse."

He calmed my fears about life in the cloister. "Some people think of convents as sacred prisons, where nuns live behind bars, deprived of all enjoyment of life. And indeed bare cells and a life of toil await postulants without money, but a young woman like yourself who has money to invest can make a very tolerable life for herself in a convent."

His words reassured me, and I asked him to make the necessary arrangements with the Clares.

The first step, my guardian said, was to compose a letter of application, requesting admittance as a postulant. He told me what to say and supplied a few nice phrases, the sort of thing the abbess would expect to hear: that I "had felt the call of God," had "long wanted to be a nun," and was embarking on this path "after mature deliberation, with great desire, and to ensure the salvation of my soul." I did wish to make a good impression on the abbess, but I suspected even then that the letter was only a formality. It was my investment that mattered. Now that I am in charge of the convent myself, I know that it is so. When a young woman applies to become a postulant in our house, it is more important to me to find out what she can add to our budget than why she wants to become a nun. Never mind the letter of application! Ideally, the postulant offers us an annuity — or, to put it another way, a "dowry" to become the bride of Christ, and brings a substantial bridal trousseau: a dozen wimples, twenty yards of material for the habits she will need once she has taken the vows, a sufficient quantity of stockings and shoes, a dozen black veils, bedding and furniture, etc., etc. Of course I don't want a postulant who is a troublesome complainer or a spiteful shrew, but I would take her in if her bad temper was balanced by a sufficiently rich endowment. After all, once a postulant has taken the vows, she is in my power and can be punished or locked up if needed.

Some people frown upon the worldliness of the Church today and disapprove of my calculations as mercenary thinking, but what would noble families do with their unmarried daughters and their widows if we did not take them in? And how could we afford to take them without the necessary funds and an appropriate endowment? As it is, we offer them a life of quiet dignity with only a little bending of the rules. Yes, the rules speak of a cloistered existence, but that is an ideal laid up in Heaven. Here on Earth, no woman could stand being shut up in a house for the rest of her life. Of course it is necessary to allow outings and visits from friends and relatives with whom we might share a good meal and pleasant conversation, but those nice things have to be paid for. And who is harmed if we live the life of wealthy pensioners? No one, surely. On the contrary, we keep a great many tradesmen in business!

It was certainly the right decision for me to join the Clares. My life turned out well. I entered as a postulant and advanced to become a regular nun. The abbess recognized my talents and soon made me provisioner. As provisioner, I was in charge of keeping a running inventory of food and drink consumed, the contents of the larder and the cellar, and the furnishings of the convent: the beds, the tables and chairs, the desks, mirrors, and paintings and other valuables. Seeing my efficiency in that post, the abbess made me treasurer and put me in charge of keeping the accounts. After her death, finally, I succeeded her to the position of abbess — the ruler of the convent, you might say.

It was for the honour of the Order that I refurbished my predecessor's quarters with care. She had become negligent in her old age. A little refreshing of her room and her office was urgently needed. Of course, such renovations cannot be done without hiring workmen, and they don't come cheap. But how much more pleasant are my surroundings now! Among other improvements, I had the ancient oil painting of Saint Clare cleaned. She looks down upon me now from her place of honour above the fireplace, freshly gleaming and surrounded by an intricately carved frame of gold. The saint would be pleased with the changes, I think, even if the old painter has given her melancholy features and a simple dress. She was the daughter of a count, after all, a member of old Roman nobility, and would be able to appreciate the little luxuries I introduced — the Flemish tapestries on the walls, the finely crafted oak table, and the polished chests with their darkly glowing brass handles. She had been well travelled, making pilgrimages to the Holy Land and other shrines, and would no doubt recognize the oriental carpets I put down and prefer them to a bare floor.

She is said to have defended her monastery against invaders, and I am merely following her example in spirit, defending her legacy. An abbess must take charge and develop a certain hardness in dealing with the world. When I think of the responsibilities I bear, the personnel I must keep in line, the suppliers who forever seek to gain an advantage over us because they believe a woman can easily be cheated — when I consider all my duties, I sometimes think it would have been better to be born a man. Then my resolute efficiency would have been praised, and no one would have raised questions as to whether it was appropriate for me to spend so much time calculating our wealth and investing our money wisely. They think a nun must always be meek, with her thoughts eternally at prayer. That may be advisable for those who enter our convent without contributing any substance to the upkeep of the institution, but for the likes of me, that kind of thinking would not do.

But here is the lawyer's letter waiting to be dealt with. It seems Don Francisco, so simple-minded otherwise, got the better of me in this case. I should not have listened to him, all those years ago, when he came to our convent with that young mulatta, Luisa. She was carrying in her arms a baby in swaddling clothes, no older than three months. I made her wait in the hall while I talked to Don Francisco in the privacy of my room.

"Not another one!" I said to him. "I told you we have all we can handle."

Two years earlier, we had started an orphanage in the old part of the convent, which was so dilapidated that we feared it would collapse before long. The grout had come out between the stones, so that the ceiling joists had moved and the roof leaked. The floor tiles were cracked and mould was everywhere. Our convent had been designed on a grand scale and endowed by a devout member of the royal family. It was built around an interior court, with the convent church forming one side and our living quarters a second. The third side housed the stables, the wine press, and the sleeping quarters for the field hands. On the fourth side, a wrought-iron fence and gate provided a view of the countryside, the vineyards, and fields that belonged to the house then but have since been sold off, when the provisions of the founder proved no longer adequate and were exhausted at last.

After the land had been sold and converted into working capital, there was no more need for barns, stables, or rooms to accommodate farm workers. The unused wing fell into disrepair. Over the years, it deteriorated and finally reached the sorry state that made it necessary for me to take action or let it go to ruin completely.

We did not have the money for the needed repairs, but then I had a brilliant idea. I would turn the wing into an orphanage and start collecting donations for the necessary renovations. The plan succeeded wonderfully well, and I have to give Don Francisco his due. It was his preaching that made people open their wallets and their hearts. Within a year, we had fixed up the walls and the leaking roof and set up a row of cots on the floor in two long lines, and began taking in waifs. For the next two years, all went well, but then the goodwill of our patrons slowed to a trickle, and even though we made every possible economy in feeding the orphans and even hired out the older children to work and sold off the dark-skinned ones we suspected of being the children of wayward slaves, even after taking all those measures, we couldn't make a profit, and the orphanage turned into a charity for good.

So, when Don Francisco brought the mulatta with the baby, it was all I could do not to slam the door in his face. It was only in view of the services he had done us — or, rather, his knowledge that a couple of the "orphans" were the fruit of the wombs of errant nuns, who had been careless enough to allow themselves to be impregnated — that, to keep his goodwill and discretion, I put on a friendly face and asked him politely to step into my room. But once I had closed the door, I could no longer contain my chagrin.

"You know our coffers are empty," I said to him. "That orphanage turned out to be bad business. We have to reduce the number of children in our care to balance the books. So, why are you bringing me yet another one?"

"Because this one doesn't come empty-handed," he said. "The baby is an orphan, whom Luisa has taken in, but she is about to be married and will go with her husband to Mexico, and he doesn't want to be burdened with another man's child. In any case, it is unlikely that a babe of three months would survive the journey. So I suggested boarding the child with you."

"And you believe that story about the child being an orphan? If you ask me, he is the mulatta's son. She had the child out of wedlock and wants to get rid of him now that she has a chance to marry, or maybe her prospective marriage is another story she is trying to pass off on you."

"The story may be false, but the money offered is real," he said.

The mother, or whoever she was, apparently wanted to leave the child with us for five years.

"Then she will have to pay in advance for his upkeep," I said to Don Francisco.

"She is willing to pay twenty ducats," he said, "and I believe that is fair."

"Fair to her, perhaps, but not to us," I said. "With all due respect, Father, you do not know the cost of maintaining a child. I would have expected twenty-five ducats."

"I do know about the cost of living," he said. He had this quiet manner of speaking, as if he was holding back a reproach or a threat. It was not easy to deal with the man, and so I yielded. It was true that there was a satisfactory margin between what it would cost me to raise the child and what the woman offered to pay, but it wasn't wise to let on to Don Francisco, who put too high a value on Christian charity.

"So be it," I said, "but I am being more than charitable to the woman. Call her in and let me inspect the child first, because sometimes they try to palm off a cripple on us or, God forbid, a leper."

"The child is in sound health and well cared for," he said.

"But perhaps dark-skinned?"

"Black or white, he is a child of God," he answered. He was in the habit of spouting such drivel, but I ignored him. Unlike him, I know the ways of the world.

We called in the woman. She was tolerably light-skinned with a pretty face and a handsome figure with round breasts, a slim waist, and a well-padded behind. She knew how to move her hips to attract men's eyes. The baby had a white father, perhaps. His skin was so fair that he could pass for a white child.

I thought, *Never mind Don Francisco, I'll bargain with her directly*, but it wasn't as easy as I thought. She looked soft and pliable with the baby in her arms, but when I spoke to her about the money, she looked at me with a darting intelligence in her eyes and set her mouth in a hard line. Still, after some back and forth, I got her to agree to twenty ducats for four years and to send more after that if she needed an extension.

"I won't begrudge the extra money," she said, "as long as you promise to treat him well and love him like a mother."

The nerve of the woman! I don't think she understood that she was completely in my hands.

"And do you doubt my Christian charity?" I said, giving her a black look.

She gazed down at the child in her arms and softened. I guess she finally realized that she depended on my goodwill to stick to the terms we had negotiated. She became humble and apologized. She had not meant to cast doubt on my intentions, she said. After that, she clamped her mouth shut and paid out the money.

Don Francisco frowned a great deal and shot angry looks at me, but I ignored him. His disapproval couldn't hurt me. He kept grumbling: The prospective husband would feel cheated of his expectations, they needed the money to set up in the New World, I was asking a great deal for taking care of the child, and other such nonsense. I shut my ears to his complaints.

When it came to parting with the child, the woman broke down. There was a tug of war over that precious baby, with her shedding tears and hugging him, and me telling her to stop making such a fuss, and Don Francisco standing there calling on God and all the angels to protect them. I practically had to push the two of them out of the door.

All that trouble for doing people a kindness, I said to Don Francisco when he came to our convent the following Sunday to say mass for us as usual, but he gave me a stern look and said it seemed to him more a matter of business than kindness.

"She paid you good money to look after the boy, and I was disappointed when you pressed her and reduced the period of service to four years."

"You have no head for business," I said, "and with all due respect, Father, you don't know a thing about money."

He pursed his lips and said, "You are right, and it is well for a servant of God to think only of holy things."

I did not think I would see the woman again and fully expected the boy to end up a charity case, but for the time being, I did not worry about that. The first four years were paid up, and after that time I could perhaps milk Don Francisco for more money, as he was so merciful and talked so much about Christian charity. But really, who can afford to be merciful these days, when everything is so expensive?

To my surprise, the boy turned out well despite being a mulatta's child. I had anticipated problems, but he was no trouble to me at all. Sister Maria, one of our nuns, saw the baby and took an instant liking to him. She doted on him and put up a little crib in her room so she could have him with her day and night. She is a silly woman with no brains but with a large annuity and a loose understanding of money. She was a bother to me from the day she entered the convent. As she was rich, however, and did not care how she spent her money, I put up with her foolishness, her endless giggling, her strange love of pain and horror, and her odd habit of dressing up. She loved wearing gaudy clothes in the privacy of her room, clothes that would look ridiculous even on a prostitute, in wild colours, cut low to show her breasts, and tucked up to show her legs because, she said, it felt more comfortable that way, and our black habit was depressing. She had little lacy jackets and sky-blue pants made for the boy and played dress-up with him as well, making a dainty doll of him or a little prince with a crown, or a jester with a painted face. We could hear her prattling nonsense and crooning songs to him. She also insisted on feeding him by hand and letting him suck her fingers, which I found disgusting, but I said nothing because I billed her for the child's meals, of course.

Don Francisco, who looked in on the boy from time to time, disapproved of the arrangement.

"He shouldn't be left alone with Sister Maria," he said. "You know very well that she is weak in the head."

"She is a lot calmer now that she has the boy to play with," I said. "It's a great relief to us all. You know what a nuisance she can be and that I sometimes had to lock her up in her room, or she would have danced out into the street and made a spectacle of herself."

"But you are wronging the boy," he said.

I did not pay much attention to his complaints, however, because the arrangement suited me and everyone else in the convent.

When the four years were almost up, I did begin to wonder what to do about the boy, but before I could make up my mind, Don Francisco came to me in the company of a seafaring man, a certain Captain Diaz, who paid me another twenty ducats to continue taking care of the boy. Whether the man had the money from the child's mother or paid it out of his own pocket, I do not know and did not care. He said he was a friend of the mother. She had asked him to check on the boy and report back. As Sister Maria had been making a pet of him, he was in good shape and there was no problem showing him off. In fact she had dressed him up as a king, put a tin crown on his head and a tin sceptre in his hand, which he pointed merrily at anyone in his path. The captain stared a bit at that, but said nothing. There was a spot of trouble at first because Sister Maria made a fuss, afraid the captain would take the boy away with him, but Don Francisco managed to calm her down, and so all went well. The captain had also brought a present for the boy, a silver drinking cup with the initials L.A. engraved on it. I kept it, thinking I might have it melted down, because a boy like him would have no use for such a trinket and no understanding of its value.

When the child was five years old, Don Francisco reminded me that he was old enough now to learn his prayers and receive instruction in the fundamentals of religion.

"You are welcome to teach him, Don Francisco," I said.

"Very well," he said. "I will teach him every Sunday after mass, but I insist that you keep Sister Maria away from him. At the very least, do not allow him to sleep in her room. He is old enough now to notice her odd behaviour, and God forbid that he models himself after her."

I gave him only a vague reply because I had no intention of making any changes and getting into an argument with Sister Maria. If I had the boy's cot moved from her cell, she would have a fit and go into one of her mad spells. I could just picture her ripping her clothes and banging her head against the wall, clawing at her chest and shrieking loud enough to break a person's eardrums.

Nothing more was said about the matter. Don Francisco took the boy in hand and taught him not only prayers but also reading and writing, a skill quite unnecessary for an orphan and the son of a half-caste at that, but since it didn't cost me anything, I kept my mouth shut.

As for Sister Maria, it turned out that there was no need for me to interfere. When the boy turned seven, he himself began to balk at her and refused to play her games, so that she got angry with him. To teach him a lesson, she dragged his cot out into the hallway and got a puppy in his stead.

I took the opportunity to move the boy in with the porter and told him to make himself useful, to run errands for us or help out in the stable. It didn't take long for Sister Maria to repent throwing him out. The puppy she had bought to replace the boy bit her when she tried to put a shirt on him. She no longer wanted the dog in her room and begged and pleaded with the boy to move back and play games with her again, but he refused. After that scene, he cleverly avoided her, hiding as soon as he saw her coming. In the end she got desperate and started carrying on in the most annoying manner, wailing and shrieking at all hours, so that we had to put her into an asylum for lunatics.

The captain visited us once more, a year ago or so. The second four years were drawing to a close. I thought he would extend the term again, but instead he told me that he might take the boy to Mexico.

"Luisa and her husband are thinking of having the boy join them. I'll be looking into the matter to see if I can make the necessary arrangements," he said.

"Very well," I said, "but tell her not to expect a refund if she fetches the child before the term is up."

"I am sure she will not ask you for a refund," he said. "She does not weigh a child's welfare or her own love in terms of money."

"I'm glad to hear it," I said and shrugged. Another holy fool like Don Francisco, I thought.

He asked to see the child on that occasion as well, but I didn't think it was a good idea because that day I had put him to work in the stable. The captain would find him thinner than the last time and not as handsomely dressed, and more than likely filthy and stinking of manure.

"That won't be possible," I said to him, therefore. "You should have given me warning of your visit. The boy has gone to accompany one of the nuns on an outing. If you will come back in a day or two —"

"I'm afraid I can't do that. My ship sails tomorrow," he said. "But give the boy my greetings and assure him of his mother's love. She is very much looking forward to being united with him."

I said I would convey his greetings and wished him well on his journey.

When the second term was up and I had heard nothing further from the captain or the mother, I went to consult with Don

Francisco in case he had any news, but he was in poor health by then and had been moved to the hospice. They told me that he was barely conscious and not expected to live much longer. For some time he had not been able to do the parish work or even say mass. The bishop had replaced him with a young curate, a sharp fellow who knows what's what and has no interest in a charity boy. I had little hope therefore of getting any money for his continued upkeep. Still, I did not neglect my duty and looked up Don Francisco in the hospice in case he could think of a benefactor to pay for the boy, but he was in a fog and barely able to talk. In a word, he was a charity case himself.

I heard no more from the captain and got no further payment, and had no means of getting in touch with the boy's parent now that Don Francisco was too ill to answer any questions. And if he had been in his right mind, he would only have chided and harangued me to keep looking after the child whether I was paid or not, and would have counselled me to put up with being cheated out of the money I was owed. That was his definition of being a true Christian: Enjoy being poor!

I do think I did my part, looking after the child for eight years, according to the agreement I had with his mother. She struck me as shrewd enough to look after her interests. If she didn't care to renew the contract or send me instructions, why should I care? It was only right to sell the boy to a rancher when no more money was forthcoming. I didn't get a lot for him, unfortunately, because he was on the small side.

"How much work can an eight-year-old do?" the rancher said, probing the boy's arms.

"An eight-year-old grows up and turns into a lad who will give you full value for your investment. You are getting a bargain," I said.

"But in the meantime, I have to feed him," he said. "Those boys eat their weight in gold! Besides, do you have a document to show that you are entitled to sell him, that he is a slave?"

"Who will ask you for a document?" I said. "If the fact that you don't have proof of his status bothers you, call him an indentured labourer. It comes out to the same thing. He can't leave without reimbursing you for your expenses, and he can't reimburse you because he has no money. You are safe all round and getting a good deal."

I suppose he understood that I had no papers to prove that I owned the boy, but he also understood that he was getting a bargain. So, he paid me the money and took the boy away. Perhaps it wasn't a good deal for the man after all, because he tried to return the boy two months later.

He was leading him by a halter like a mule.

"He is a stubborn bastard," he said, "and tried to run away from the estate."

The boy was rail-thin and his face was marred by a red welt in the shape of an *S*.

"So you branded him?" I said.

"As a punishment and a warning to others, but he is too much bother to keep."

"The branding didn't help, then," I said.

"No," he said, "he is vicious by nature and unmanageable, and you cheated me in taking good money for him. Well, here he is. I am bringing him back to you and I expect you to return the money I laid out for him. Be glad I'm not charging you for the expense of feeding him in the meantime."

"You want me to take back damaged goods?" I said. "He looks monstrous with that scar on his cheek. He was in fine fettle when I sold him to you. Now he looks starved. You've worked him almost to death — and you have the gall to talk to me about expenses?"

I gave the man a good fight, until he ran out of arguments and took the boy away. That was a week ago. At the time I was pleased to get rid of him, but as it turns out, it was the wrong move. I'll have to get the boy back now, whatever the cost. I suppose if I go to the rancher and say I've changed my mind after praying to God and God telling me to be merciful — no, better, after Saint Clare appeared to me in a dream and told me to take pity on the child. If I tell him some such story, he'll probably hand over the boy without asking for a refund. After all, he was in a dismal condition when he tried to return him and likely is no longer of any use to the rancher. If he balks, I may have to sweeten the deal and offer to return half of the purchase price. In the end, he'll be glad to get rid of the boy — if he hasn't flogged him to death in the meantime, that is!

Of course, getting him back will not entirely solve the problem. I'll have to fatten him up. And God knows what I'm going to do about that scar on his cheek.

10

Seville, 1575:

The boy without name

WHEN TIA LUISA BROUGHT ME to her house, the scent of the candles in her shop raised a memory in my mind from way back, so far back that I think it was the very first impression I had in life: the scent of the candles in Sister Maria's room.

The memory was just a kind of mist swirling around in my brain, but later, as I was falling asleep in my new bed at Tia Luisa's house, it turned into a ghostly vision. Or perhaps I was just slipping into a dream. In any case, I was back in Sister Maria's room, with the heavy damask curtains drawn close and a dozen candles lit, casting flickering shadows on the wall. She had two silver candlesticks arranged on her chest of drawers. They gleamed mysteriously in the dark and spread out their curved arms as if to embrace and entangle me. Sister Maria liked to shut out the world from her room, to live in her dark fantasies and make up her own world. At first I was afraid of the shadows the candles cast on the armoire in her room, a hulking piece with carved heads of boars and wild men looking down on me from the top corners. I was afraid also when Sister Maria took me into the darkness of her four-poster bed, almost burying me under a mountain of pillows. The bed had its own set of heavy burgundy curtains to draw close, so that it was night at all times in its tentlike enclosure, but cozy, too, like an embrace, once you got used to it.

I did get used to living in darkness in a room illuminated only by the light of candles, but I could never shake off the fear that filled me when I looked at the paintings on the wall above her chest of drawers. I was afraid even after Sister Maria explained them to me. They depicted three martyrs.

"They are dwelling in Heaven now, at the right hand of the Father," she said. "God rewards his martyrs for their suffering and allows them to live in eternal bliss in his great mansion in the sky. They are happy in his company there and are praying to him every day, for you and me."

I was glad that God rewarded his martyrs, but I could not help thinking that he should have spared them all that horrible suffering in the first place. One of the martyrs in the paintings had his body pierced with arrows and blood trickling down his naked chest. His arms and his ankles were tied to a post with thick ropes. The shafts of the arrows stuck out of his body at all angles. The archers who had shot the arrows at him stood there laughing and pointing at him as if it were a great joke. The second martyr was a young woman with long, blond hair hanging down her back. She too was naked except for a loincloth, but with her breasts cut off and served on a platter by a laughing servant. Where her breasts had been, there were great, gaping wounds, revealing raw sinews. The third martyr was being flayed. Her skin had been cut open and peeled back like a coat, with blood dripping from every pore in her body and puddling on the ground beneath her feet.

The martyrs weren't the only horrible sight in Sister Maria's room. In one corner, right by the door so that you couldn't avoid looking at it as you went in or out of the room, was a life-sized statue of Christ carved in wood. He wore a crown of thorns and looked wretched. His body was so thin he looked starved, and there was a deep, bloody cut in his chest where a lance had pierced him and holes bored into his hands and feet where nails had been hammered in to fasten him to the cross.

"That's the way he looked after he was taken down from the cross," Sister Maria said. She liked to put her fingers into Christ's wounds and weep for him, or grasp his crown of thorns and allow the wooden spikes to dig into her palms until they bled. But the statue of Christ was not as bad to look at as the martyrs because Sister Maria liked to dress him up in a silken mantle so that his wounds were covered most of the time and only his face looked out at me, pale and suffering.

Whenever those memories come back to me, I try to blot them out and think instead of Sister Maria herself, her pudgy, round face smiling at me and her soft, milky-white hands stroking me. I was a little shy of looking into her eyes, which were round and bulging as if someone had inserted marbles into the sockets, and I became afraid also of her voice, which could change from low and gentle to piercing high in a moment of anger. But most of the time she was friendly and tried hard to amuse me — or herself — with playing dress-up games. She had a chest jumbled with clothes, wigs, and masks, and another chest full of wonderful props: crowns, swords, chains, armour, and miniature pieces of furniture that could be arranged on the floor and peopled with little dolls. I fought many devils and dragons with my toy weapons on Sister Maria's behalf, and she suffered many injuries, imagined and real, for she liked to bleed for Jesus. At other times I was the Christ child, newly born to Mary and Joseph, and she swaddled me, adorned me with a golden band that looked like a halo, and kissed my naked feet. Then again, she wanted me to be her pet kitten while she was the mother cat, and we meowed and purred together, and licked each other and ourselves clean.

As I grew older, I naturally tired of her games. I came to realize that she was a crazy old woman and started to resist her invitations to play, but she was unwilling to give up our charades and got very cross at me, calling me an ungrateful cur. I in turn talked back and stoutly refused to make silly noises, to be embraced and kissed, or sit on her lap like a baby. At last, she had a fit, threw herself on the floor and screamed until she foamed at the mouth. Then she jumped up, kicked me in the shins, scratched at my face, and pushed me out the door into the hall.

"I never want to see you again, you ungrateful boy!" she screamed and, with a strength that surprised me, dragged my little bed into the corridor and pitched my clothes across the hall, so that they flew through the air like so many birds and landed on the floor in an untidy pile.

She stood in the door and hissed at me, "You are like the proverbial dog biting the hand that feeds him. I will get myself another pet, more faithful than you."

I shouted back at her, "Yes, that's what you need, a dog you can order around, or a slave!"

She flew at me like a fury, then, and slapped at my face and my arms, screaming, "And that's what you are — nothing but a dirty, tawny slave."

I stared her down, however, and said, "I am neither dirty nor tawny nor your slave!"

I was no longer scared of her screams. She retreated into her room and slammed the door shut. I heard her turn the key in the lock to keep me out, but I had no intention of returning. I knew in my heart that I had done the right thing, defying her. I was afraid only of Mother Superior, who made all the decisions in the convent. I feared everything about her: her narrow face, her long nose, her hard black eyes, her determined step and firm voice. What would she say when she saw my bed and my clothes in a heap, blocking the hallway? She was a fierce woman. No one dared to balk at or contradict her. What if she told me to leave the convent? Where would I go?

After Sister Maria had locked me out and all was quiet, I sat for a while on my bed in the hallway. Then I took heart and thought: *If Mother Superior throws me out, I will go to Don Francisco and ask for his help.* But when I finally got up my nerve and went to tell her what had happened, she took it calmly.

"What did you do to make Sister Maria so angry?" she asked.

"She wants me to play at being her baby," I said. "It's silly. I don't want to be stroked or dandled all the time."

"You should do as she says, my boy. She has been good to you, after all. She paid for the clothes you are wearing and the food you are eating."

"But I'm not a baby," I said. "And Don Francisco said the same thing when I told him about the things she wants me to do. That she was wrong to treat me like that and should stop it."

"I see I will have to talk to Don Francisco," she said. "In the meantime, you will share the porter's room off the entrance hall. You can make yourself useful by running errands for him. I will tell him to help you move your bed and your things."

"Thank you, Reverend Mother," I said. "I think I'll like running errands."

"You will do as you are told," she said. "Whether you like it or not is beside the point."

I could tell I had said the wrong thing and was afraid she would get angry with me after all, but she only wrinkled her brow and pressed her lips together into a thin line and added, "You will take your meals in the kitchen henceforth. I will ask the porter to keep an eye on you and make sure you earn your keep."

While I was with Sister Maria, the two of us always ate like royalty. She loved a good meal. After I had been expelled from her room, there were no more delicacies for me, but the company in the kitchen was pleasant. I ate with the cook and her helper and the porter, who liked to put his arm around the cook and snuggle with her, although he was not her husband. There was always a lot of joshing around the table. I didn't like it when they made fun of me, and a few times they slapped me when I was slow to do as they told me or I talked back, but most of the time I was happy. I liked my new companions and my new freedom.

My world became filled with sunlight and expanded in all directions. During all the years I was with Sister Maria, I lived like a prisoner in her room. I was let out rarely — only if Sister Maria wanted to take a walk in the cloister garden, or on Sundays for lessons with Don Francisco. My world was

narrow. I knew only the way to the parish house, where Don
Francisco taught me reading and writing. Now, the whole city
was mine to explore. The porter taught me the names of the
streets and the location of the houses and shops where I was
to pick up parcels or drop off messages. There were a thousand
sights to look at on the way, a multitude of people, young
and old, light- and dark-skinned, able-bodied and crippled, as
well as carts pulled by mules, riders mounted on noble horses, sedan chairs carried by liveried servants, and all the wares
displayed in the shops and in the marketplace and the people
haggling over them. I would have liked to feast my eyes on
those sights, but there was never enough time. I was not allowed to linger. Mother Superior was very strict with the time
she allotted for each task, and if I was ever late returning, she
slapped me hard or beat me with a cane. So I made sure to run
straight to where I was supposed to go and hardly dared to
look to my left and right.

Sometimes I finished all my deliveries before supper, with
time to spare, and talked to the porter. He was an older man
with his hair cropped so close that he looked like a sheep
sheared of its wool. He had the aspect of a strong man because
of his thick neck and broad shoulders, but when he got up from
his bench, you realized that he was lame. His legs were crooked
so that he could not walk properly. He had to waddle, shifting
his body from side to side. He was glad that I was in charge of
running errands because, he said, he couldn't do it anymore
on account of the pain in his legs and his feet. His only job
now was to sit by the door and guard it against strangers. He
was still capable of doing that and very good at it, too, because
he knew everyone coming and going and reported to Mother
Superior on them. He locked the door at night and unlocked it

again in the morning, so that no one could pass without him or Mother Superior knowing about it.

"So, I know pretty well everything that's going on around here," he said.

When we were both at leisure, he liked to talk about the nuns, most of whom were no angels, he said.

"Of course they aren't angels," I said. "They have no wings."

He laughed at my simplicity. "How old are you, boy?" he asked.

"I don't know," I said.

"Let me see now," he said. "I remember when they brought you here. You were just a baby then. That was eight years ago, or so."

"Who brought me here?"

"Don Francisco and his girlfriend." He winked at me, but I didn't understand.

"What do you mean?" I said. "Priests don't have girlfriends."

"They are not supposed to, but some of them take lovers anyway and have babies by them."

"Are you saying that Don Francisco is my father?" I asked in wonder.

He laughed. "No, I was joking," he said. "Don Francisco is one of the good priests. He doesn't have girlfriends."

"Then who was the woman who came with him? Was she my mother?"

"Let it go, boy," he said. "You have no mother and you are nobody's son. You are a foundling. And now stop asking me questions and do your work, or we'll both be in trouble with Mother Superior."

Another time, he said to me, "It's a wonder you stuck it out with Sister Maria so long, because she is bonkers, if you ask me."

I said she had been good to me most of the time and I was even thinking of paying her a visit to see how she was doing now and whether she had forgiven me.

"You can't visit her," he said. "They have locked her up. She went nuts after the puppy she bought to replace you bit her. She was trying to put a dress on him, they say, so of course the dog turned on her and nipped her hand. When Mother Superior took the dog away, she ran after her and pummelled her back and tore her habit, so Mother Superior had her locked up and tied to the bed."

One night, not long after that conversation, we woke to blood-curdling screams and pounding on the floor above us.

"That's her, I bet you, gone berserk," the porter said. "You might as well get up because they'll want you."

But Mother Superior wanted the porter himself to go and take a message to the doctor, even though he protested that he wasn't up to it. His legs would give out.

"Then take a mule," she said, "and ride to the doctor's house, and be quick about it because that madwoman got loose and is about to smash up the furniture."

The doctor came with two helpers. They went upstairs. Then the screaming and pounding stopped and a little while later, the two men came, carrying Sister Maria between them. I peeked out of the porter's room and saw that they had bound her hands and feet with bedsheets so she couldn't kick them, but there was no need for that. She had gone limp and quiet, like one asleep. When they passed the door, however, she opened her eyes and saw me. Then she started screaming again, "That's the dog who bit me. You should take him away, too."

That's all she could say before they carried her through the gate and the porter locked up behind them.

"We won't have any problems with that one anymore," he said. "It was high time they took her away."

"Where are they taking her?" I asked him.

"To the loony bin," he said. "And that's where she belongs."

When I first started working as an errand boy, Don Francisco was displeased with the arrangement. "The porter is not the right company for you," he said, "and if you are working six days a week, you must be allowed to rest on the seventh day, as the Bible commands. I want you to spend Sundays with me from here on." He was going to talk to Mother Superior about that.

That was the beginning of a marvellous time for me because Don Francisco always had his cook give me a small tart or a flan when I came to his house. I spent the mornings in church, which was rather boring, but the afternoons made up for that. After lunch and a short siesta, we would go into Don Francisco's garden and spend the rest of the afternoon reading, writing, or just talking. Sometimes he asked me to weed the flowerbeds because his back bothered him and he couldn't do it himself.

We talked about the time I had stayed with Sister Maria. I told him that she knew many wonderful tales, of a king who had seven wives and beheaded them all; of a man who went the wrong way on the ocean and found a land full of gold and silver. She also told me of the grand mansion in which she used to live and a nobleman who had asked for her hand in marriage, but he had to fight in a battle and returned with a bloody gash in his chest, of which he died. After that, she never wanted to leave her room again, she said, and they put her into the convent.

"That is the wrong reason for a woman to enter a convent," Don Francisco said.

"What is the right reason, then?"

"To devote herself to God and help her brothers and sisters in Christ," he said. "And those tales Sister Maria told you are all very well, but there is a difference between a story and history. One is fancy and made up, the other is true and accurate."

"Then she made up the story of the king with the seven wives?"

"Not entirely," he said, "but it isn't accurate."

"I don't care whether she made it up or not," I said. "It was a good story, and I still miss Sister Maria sometimes because she loved me, until she began to hate me — I don't know why."

"Because you outgrew her," Don Francisco said. "But enough of that. We have our lessons to go through."

He had started to teach me reading and writing. We read the gospels, mostly, and he made me memorize them to exercise my "God-given brain, so I could use it the way He had intended it."

"What did He intend it for?"

"To find ways of helping other people and to love them like your brothers and sisters."

"Even if they hate you?"

"Even if they hate you," he said. "It is your duty to look after others as best you can."

"Is that why you are teaching me, Don Francisco, because it is your duty to help others?"

"Because it is my duty," he said, "and also because you are a likeable boy."

I had been trying to work up the courage to ask him about the story the porter had told me of the woman who brought me to the convent when I was a baby. I wanted to know whether that was a story or history. If it was true, I also wanted to know whether the woman was my mother and why she had given me up to the nuns. When Don Francisco said I was a "likeable boy," I took heart and was on the point of asking him those questions, but I'd left it too late. He was already putting away the Bible and said it was time for me to go back to the convent. So I let it go and thought I'd ask him another time, but I never got around to it because Don Francisco fell ill and our Sunday lessons came to an end.

He had been weak for some time, but then he fell seriously ill and could no longer teach me. He had to keep to his bed and rest. For a few weeks, I visited him and spent Sunday afternoons at his bedside, watching his still face and his hands on the bed pane, as white as the linen of the bedding but so transparent that you could see the blue veins throbbing under the skin. Sometimes he opened his eyes and said a few words to me; sometimes he only smiled. He no longer came to the convent to say mass for the nuns. The bishop had appointed another man in his stead, a young priest by the name of Orlando, who wore rings on his fingers and walked as softly as a woman and spoke very elegantly.

One Sunday, when I came for a visit, Don Orlando was waiting for me. He told me that he had been obliged to move Don Francisco into the hospice across the way because he needed more care than could be given him at the parish house.

I went across the road, knocked on the door of the hospice, and asked to see Don Francisco, but they told me that he was too sick to have visitors.

"Will he die?" I asked the woman who had opened the gate to me.

"Everyone dies sooner or later." She pursed her lips.

"But is he close to death?"

"How am I supposed to know?" she said. "He may live another year or die tomorrow."

Two weeks later, when I came home from an errand, I found my bed in the porter's room stripped and my clothes bundled up and sitting on top of the mattress.

"What's going on?" I asked the porter.

"*She* wants to talk to you," he said, pointing in the direction of Mother Superior's office. "Good luck!"

I racked my brain what I had done wrong, but when I stood in front of Mother Superior's desk, afraid of a caning, she surprised me by looking at me quite pleased. She told me that I was eight years old now, old enough to earn my bread, and so she had hired me out to work on an estate.

"It will do you good to be outdoors all day and grow up in the company of men, as a boy should," she said and sent me off.

The estate manager was waiting for me outside in his cart, but he did not invite me to sit up front with him. He told me to get into the back of the cart, where two ebony-black men were lying with their feet shackled.

After we got under way, one of the men asked me if I had any food in my bundle. I said no, it was only my clothes.

"Why are you shackled?" I asked him in turn.

"Because the manager is afraid we'll run off. Are you an idiot, or what?"

"An idiot? Why?"

"Because you ask idiotic questions," he said, and tried to kick at me with his shackled feet, but I was too fast for him and moved out of the way.

"I wonder how much he paid for that child," the second man said. "He is as scrawny as an old hen."

"Not much," the first one said, "seeing that he can't even be bothered to shackle him."

I didn't understand what they meant, but I was afraid to ask and make them angry or be told that I was an idiot.

After a while, the first one addressed me again. "Why don't you jump off and run?" he asked. "Or are you too stupid even for that?"

I was puzzled by his words but found out very soon, and without asking any more questions, that Mother Superior had sold me to the estate manager and that I, like the Black men, was now a slave. I never saw the two of them again, for the estate was very large and employed some hundred people, both slaves and free men.

At first, the manager wanted to assign me to a crew digging irrigation ditches, but the foreman wouldn't have me. He protested that I wasn't strong enough and couldn't do a day's work like the others, although I would no doubt eat my portion of food like them. He wasn't going to be punished for not delivering on his contract because he didn't have able-bodied men.

So the manager sent me down to the shore to help with the salt production. The food rations for that job were very small because the crew were all youngsters like me. Even so, I had to fight for my portion and often lost out because I was the youngest and smallest of them. My job was to scrape sand off the beach, bag it, and carry it to a storage shed. When we had gathered enough sand, we poured water on it to make a brine, which we drained off into a reservoir. Once the brine developed a crust, we shovelled it into iron pans and heated it over a wood fire until all the liquid evaporated and left only the coarse salt. Sometimes I was sent into the fields to feed lumps of salt to the cattle, because that way they would drink more and could be sold for more money because the water in their bellies added to their weight. The cattle resisted eating the salt because it was bitter, so that I had to prop their mouths open with a stick and shove it in and watch out that they didn't kick me while I was at it.

At night, as I lay in my corner of the barn, I often thought of the good life I'd had in the convent. It was hard to fall asleep because we were allowed to spread only a thin layer of straw on the trampled earth floor. I lay there, my stomach growling with hunger and my back hurting from the blows the foreman dealt out if I was too slow by his measure. One day I remembered the Black slave on the cart who said I was too stupid even to run away, and decided to smarten up. I would take off the next time they told me to go and feed salt to the cattle. It was my best chance, I thought, because there was a wheat field next to the pasture. The stalks were tall enough now to offer me cover.

Everything went as planned: I ducked down among the cattle, bellied up to the fence, swung over it, and rolled into the wheat field, all in the blink of an eye. From there I made my way to the road, slipped into the ditch, and waited until the sun went down before I started walking. But my freedom lasted no more than three days. By then my feet were blistered and bleeding. I staggered on, not knowing even what direction to go, until I could barely stand for hunger and tiredness. I had stolen turnips from a field and drunk water from a brook, but it gave me such stomach troubles that I was obliged to squat down every half-hour and relieve myself. Then I was too exhausted to do even that and lay down by the side of the road, letting it all run out of me and expecting to die. That's where the men from the estate found me.

They took me back to the farm, beat the last of the shit and piss out of me, and left me lying in the barn, expecting me to die, perhaps, but some of the salt boys shared their soup with me in the evening and gave me little bits of bread and, once, a tin cup of goat's milk — God knows where they got that from. When it looked like I was going to live, I got up and went down to the beach again to resume my work, but the foreman said, "You think you can run away, boy, and come back as if nothing had happened?"

"I suppose I'll be whipped," I said.

"Whipped and branded," he said, "to teach you and the others a lesson."

He looked around to see that everyone had heard what he had said, and although the other boys were already kneeling on the ground, scraping sand, they ducked down even further and made themselves very small so as not to be noticed and singled out for exemplary punishment. But he did nothing further.

Later, when I shovelled the crust onto the pan, I noticed that someone had stuck an iron rod into the fire underneath.

"That's for you," the foreman said.

Then he told me to stand against a tree and tied me to the trunk, hand and foot, with a rope. Next, he laid a length of cloth across my forehead and another around my neck, winding the strands around the tree two or three times so that I couldn't move my head. Then he took the iron rod out of the fire. I saw that it had a piece at the end shaped like an *S*. It was red hot and sizzled when he pressed it against my cheek. The pain was such that I blacked out for a moment, until I heard the foreman say, "Took your breath away, boy, did it? Made you forget to scream, hey?"

That's when I finally screamed and couldn't stop screaming and fell to the ground as soon as he loosened the ropes that held me upright.

"You see that, boys?" he said to the others. "Take care it doesn't happen to you."

I thought I was done in now for sure, and everyone would shun me. That's what they did in front of the foreman, backing away from me and avoiding looking at my face. But their shunning was only for show, because I was somebody now. The *S* branded on my cheek was a badge of honour among slaves. Now I commanded respect. The *S* showed that I was a mean fighter. I was honoured with donations of bread and looked after as I was lying in the barn in a fever and with yellow pus draining from the wound in my cheek. They took turns putting a wet rag on my forehead. Someone even stole a hunk of lard from the stable, the kind put on horses when their legs are chafed by the gear, and smeared the fat onto my wound. With all this care, my fever abated after a few days and the wound stopped oozing and began to form a scab. So I went back to scraping sand to get my ration of food.

I could do only a few hours of work, though, and then dropped down where I was, too tired to care whether the foreman gave me a beating. But he ignored me. I guess he knew he couldn't get any more work out of me, whether he beat me or not.

One day, however, the manager himself came riding up. He saw me lying there on the bench and told me to get up. He was carrying a piece of rope looped at the end, a sort of leash, which he put around my neck. Then he led me to the horse, tied me to his saddle, and made me trot along beside him, as he rode into town. People stared at me and pointed and some of them spat at me, but I was too tired to care and just kept my head down and watched the cobblestones so as not to stub my toes more than necessary.

When we came to a stop and I looked up, we were in the yard of the convent and the ostler took the manager's horse and eyed me curiously.

The manager dragged me into the house by the rope and to the office of Mother Superior. He didn't bother to knock. He barged in and started shouting at her that I was the very devil, that she had tricked him and he wanted his money back. But she would have none of that and shouted right back and argued doggedly, so that he was obliged to retreat at last and take me back with him. He cursed me roundly. I expected him to take his whip to my back, but I think he was afraid I'd collapse on the spot and he wouldn't be able to walk me back to the farm. He only shook his fist at me and said, "Get moving, you bastard, before I kill you."

From there on, I worked only a few hours a day and slept the rest of the time without anyone interfering because they thought I would not live much longer, anyway.

But all that changed when Mother Superior came in person a week later to take me away in a cart. It was the kind of cart that had a black cover to shield the nuns from the eyes of the common people, when they travelled outside the convent. The porter was in the driver's seat, staring at me curiously. Mother Superior told me to get into the back with her and closed the flap of the cover. As we got moving, she made me strip off the rags I was wearing. She told me to use the rags to wipe the dust and dirt off my skin and then to put on the new shirt and pants and sandals she had brought along.

"Where are you taking me?" I asked.

"Back to the convent," she said, as we rattled along. She told me a tale that was almost as good as the ones Sister Maria used to tell. She said Saint Clare had appeared to her in a dream. She had come down from Heaven in full angelic glory with a golden halo, playing a harp, and told her to rescue me from the clutches of the man who was cruelly maltreating me.

"But you could see that he was maltreating me when he brought me to the convent a week ago," I said.

"I suppose I was too angry at the impertinence of that man to pay much attention to you. It was only when Saint Clare told me to help you that I understood my duty."

"Then Don Francisco was right when he said that it was our duty to find ways of helping others."

She started up violently. "Don Francisco is an old —" But then she stopped and softened her voice: "… An old priest who expects everyone to be perfect. But we can't all be saints."

"Will I be allowed to sleep in the porter's room again?" I asked.

"You will sleep in my room," she said, "and I will look after you."

I wasn't sure I liked being around Mother Superior that much, but I changed my mind when we arrived and I saw the bed prepared for me in her room. It had the thickest mattress I had ever seen in my life, and pillows and coverlets filled with eiderdown. The room was twice as large as Sister Maria's and furnished with such luxury that I thought I was in a castle — or, rather, in a dream. There were carpets covering the floors, delicate wall hangings depicting dancing maidens, a glittering crystal chandelier with three tiers of candles, and a mirror as tall as a grown man, with a carved and gilded frame. Mother Superior's bed was a four-poster like Sister Maria's but with a purple baldachin on top and the curtains looped back to show coverlets of the finest silk. I had time only to pass my eyes over these wonders once before I fell asleep in my new bed.

I did not wake up until late the next morning, when the maid brought in a copper tub and washed me down and dried me with a piece of cloth as soft as lamb's wool. Then she returned and brought me a bowl of beef soup with an egg mixed into it and bread so white it looked like it had never seen the inside of a baker's oven.

After a few days of being fed the most heavenly meals, delicate fish fillets, roast meats, sweet figs, and honey tartlets, I felt strong enough to get up and started walking around and inspecting the room once Mother Superior had gone to her office. It was at this time that I looked into the mirror and saw how wretched I was, as thin and pale as the Christ figure in Sister Maria's room, and with my face marred by a red welt in the shape of the letter *S*. I also discovered that I was locked in. I was not sure why Mother Superior took such precautions. Surely she did not think I was going to run away when I was treated so well. I merely wanted to go out into the hall to talk to the porter, or into the kitchen to have a chat with the cook, because I was getting tired of being on my own.

The next time Mother Superior looked in on me, I told her that I felt quite well again and could run errands for her as I had done before, but she didn't want me to work. She had other plans.

"Indeed, I have good news for you," she said.

I wondered whether this news had anything to do with the velvet bag she was holding in her hand.

"What news?" I asked. I was curious about the contents of the bag but also a little suspicious of the "good news." After all, what could be better than the life I was leading now? I was even prepared to suffer loneliness and boredom if that was the price to pay for it.

"I have found a foster mother for you," she said.

"I don't need a foster mother," I said in alarm. "I'm quite content to stay here with you." I was afraid she was going to sell me a second time and turn me over to a mistress as harsh as the estate manager.

"You are a silly boy," she said. "I don't know if you deserve the good luck that has come your way. The woman who wants to adopt you is a well-to-do widow, a half-caste like you." I had never realized I was a half-caste until I was treated like one at the estate, but even now I wondered how that could be, for my skin had been milky white until I began working outdoors, and even now I looked more like a tanned white man than a mulatto.

"She has no children of her own," the abbess continued. "Her name is Luisa Abrego, and she promises to treat you like a son. She will look after your education and leave you all her possessions on her death, so that you may even become a wealthy man one day. And as a token of her goodwill, she has sent you this present."

She opened the velvet bag and took out a silver drinking cup etched with the initials L.A. It looked valuable and must have cost a great deal of money. But why would anyone make me an expensive present? *It's a trick of some kind*, I thought. I had no other explanation.

"Why would anyone send me a present like that without even knowing me?" I said to Mother Superior.

She looked at me sideways. "Well, that is the problem," she said. "That she doesn't know you and has never set eyes on you. I told Doña Luisa that you are a good-natured and well-behaved boy and that Don Francisco taught you to read and write, but I did not tell her about the scar on your face. I am sure you will be on your best behaviour when you meet Doña Luisa, but I'm afraid she'll be put off by your looks. So we have to do something about that."

"What?" I said. "I can't change my face."

"I talked to the doctor," she said. "He has thought of a way to improve your looks."

She put the silver cup back into the velvet bag and handed it to me.

"Take good care of it," she said. "It's a valuable present. Put it in the drawer with your clothes, for the time being."

After she had left, I took another look at the cup. It was a smooth and shiny thing and no doubt precious, but I could not shake off the notion that I would have to pay for it one way or another. I did not trust Mother Superior. She was treating me well for a reason, whatever it was — I couldn't figure it out.

A few days later, she came to me in the company of the doctor and a surgeon. They told me to lie down on the bed and proceeded to put my head into a kind of vise clamp. Then they tied my arms and legs to the bedposts and began their preparations. When I saw the surgeon heating a knife over the flame of a candle, I cried out in fear. They were going to brand me again! They were going to mutilate me! I was going to be like one of the martyrs in Sister Maria's paintings and have parts of my body cut away. I knew it all along! The silver cup was a decoy. Mother Superior was playing a horrible trick on me.

"Better gag him," the doctor said, "or he will alarm the whole house with his crying."

The surgeon stuffed a piece of cloth into my mouth to stifle my cries.

"Now this will hurt a bit," he said, "but you must be brave, and when it's all over, you'll look a lot better."

Then he put the hot knife to my cheek, and it hurt every bit as much as the branding iron, so that I blacked out once again. When I came to, they were taking the clamp off so I could again move my head freely. They also untied my feet, but left my arms bound because, the doctor said, "We don't want you to touch your face."

I had no desire to touch my face because it hurt badly, just as badly as after the branding, but the doctor came every day and changed the dressing on the wound and put ointment on it so it wouldn't get infected.

"You've been a very brave young man," he said. "What's your name?"

"I don't know," I said. "Everybody just calls me 'boy.'"

"His name is Diego," Mother Superior said, and that's the first time I heard my name. She seemed anxious and hovered after the doctor left and asked how I felt and was there anything I wanted — any special food or drink? I only needed to tell her, and she would get it for me.

"Why did you let the doctor do that to me?" I said.

"For your own good," she said. "To improve your looks. We talked about that, didn't we? We don't want to shock your prospective foster mother."

She spent a lot of time with me and was very obliging. I had never seen her like that. She brought me dinner herself and felt my head every so often, saying, "Thank God, no fever," and in every way behaved as if she were my servant. If I had to relieve myself, she brought me the chamber pot and emptied it herself. When I said I was hungry or thirsty, she herself put the cup to my lips and brought me choice foods on a tray. After a few days, she allowed me to get up and look at myself in the mirror.

My cheek was red and swollen, but the *S*-shaped welt was gone — or rather, replaced with a cross-hatch of cuts.

"I don't see how that makes me look any better," I said.

"It will, once the swelling goes down, but what's more important, it doesn't look like an *S*, which is the mark of a vicious runaway," she said. "And when your foster mother comes and asks you what happened to your cheek, you must say that a mule kicked you. Just make sure you get the story straight, or she may not adopt you. The doctor will talk to her as well and assure her that the scar will flatten out and be barely visible by the time you are a grown man."

"Is that true?" I asked.

"Let's hope so. Are you worried that the girls will not like you?" she said and laughed.

"No, I'm worried I will run into the manager one day and he will recognize me and force me to work for him again when he sees that I have regained my strength."

"Don't worry about that," she said. "I've straightened it all out with him."

After I recovered from the operation and my cheek was no longer very sore, I got bored again and asked Mother Superior to find some occupation for me.

"You may walk in the courtyard with me," she said, "or look at books in the library."

I would have preferred to walk in the courtyard alone, but she was like a shadow, never leaving my side and shooing away the other nuns, who eyed me curiously. I didn't mind spending time in the library. It was a large, vaulted room, with shelves full of books on three sides and two recessed windows on the fourth with cushioned benches where you could sit and read or look out into the courtyard. The bookshelves went all the way up to the ceiling, so that you had to climb a ladder to reach the top row. There was a large, polished oaken table in the centre and a dozen chairs arranged around it, so that you might have had a feast there, but no one ever used the library except Mother Superior and me and, once or twice, a young man who did her accounts. The first time we went to the library, she took down a few books for me to look at. They were heavy tomes bound in stamped and patterned leather with metal clasps. Inside, the words were arranged in two columns and written in ink, rather than printed like the books in Sister Maria's room or the Bible I had read with Don Francisco. The letters were as regular as if they had been printed but I could see that they were handwritten because the ink was flaking off in places and left a black smudge on my finger if I rubbed the spot. The letters at the beginning of each chapter were written in red ink and skillfully worked into a gilded picture, illustrating the story. That was my guess, at any rate, because I couldn't make out the meaning of the words. Perhaps they were misspelled, because they looked familiar but didn't quite make sense. I guessed that *deus* was *deo* and *fuerunt* was *fuere* and so on, but it made for cumbersome reading.

I didn't like to ask Mother Superior for help because she looked cross most of the time, or impatient, at least, like someone who had better things to do than keep me company. I could see she wanted to be somewhere else, and I wished she would leave me alone, but she stuck to me.

One day, when I was sitting in one corner, leafing through books, and she in the other going through some lists with her accountant, she said to him, "You strike me as a cultured man, Don Baltasar — almost too good for the counting house."

I was surprised to hear her talk so civilly to someone in her pay. Perhaps he was a man of standing. He was certainly well dressed, in a smart embroidered jerkin, a lacy collar, and tidy black hose. His dark hair was brushed to a sheen and he moved elegantly, but he couldn't have been very important, because he was only a youth.

"I wish my uncle saw it your way, Reverend Mother," he said. "I am tired of the counting house already and wish I was back at university. Life in Paris wasn't entirely to my liking because the courses you need for the degree are boring, to say the least, but no one kept me from reading the poets in my spare time, whereas now I have no spare time. I have to account to my uncle for every minute of the day."

"Then how would you like to spend two hours here in the afternoon and look after the boy for me?" She nodded in my direction. "Read poetry with him, if that's what you like — I don't care."

He laughed. "A most gratifying offer," he said, "but I doubt my uncle will give me time off to spend in your library and read poetry."

"You may bill me for the hours, of course," she said.

"Ah," he said, "that makes all the difference. In that case, my uncle will have no objections. But who is the boy?"

Then they put their heads together and whispered. He looked in my direction a few times and said, "I see, I see." The upshot was that he came every afternoon for two hours and practised reading and writing with me.

It was a great relief to be rid of my "shadow" for a bit. The two hours went fast because Don Baltasar was very friendly, and we had some fun together.

Mother Superior kept on at me for the rest of the day. I was never allowed to be by myself, not even at mealtimes. She sat with me, "making sure the maid doesn't talk nonsense to you," she said. I guessed then that she did not want me to talk to anyone in the household and spread the story of my suffering because she might be blamed for it. In fact, the more I thought about the matter, the more convinced I became that she had wronged me, that she had no right to sell me into captivity. But I had no idea why she had brought me back and only half believed the story of Saint Clare appearing to her in a dream. I wished I could speak with Don Francisco and ask him whether he thought it was a story or history.

"How is Don Francisco?" I asked Mother Superior. "Could we pay him a visit, perhaps?"

"The hospice doesn't allow visitors," she said, "and for all I know, he might be dead. I haven't heard from him in a long time."

I was sad when I heard that he might no longer be among the living, but Mother Superior was unwilling to entertain any more questions on the subject of Don Francisco's health.

I carried on my lessons with Don Baltasar until she called me into her office one day. She had a visitor, and that was when I first met Tia Luisa.

Mother Superior introduced us.

"Doña Luisa has come to take you home with her," she said.

The moment had come. I was afraid to look at the woman who would have me in her power from now on. Was she worse than Mother Superior or better? Cruel like the estate manager, crazy like Sister Maria, or good-hearted like Don Francisco? I raised my eyes and saw that she had a kind face and a smile like an angel. Her eyes had the same expression as Saint Clare, whose painted picture hangs in the convent chapel: as if she was listening very carefully to every single word I said, so she could tell God afterward and make sure my prayers were answered. Tia Luisa had the same wish-granting eyes. I knew immediately that it would be heaven to live with her, and that made me very anxious. I was afraid of spoiling my chances. I could hardly push out a word in answer to her questions for fear that I would make the wrong impression and be rejected.

"Don't you want to thank Doña Luisa for her present?" Mother Superior said.

I was glad she reminded me because I had been too nervous to think of the silver cup, and I certainly did not want to appear ungrateful.

"It is a very beautiful cup," I said, embarrassed by my forgetfulness. "And the most precious thing I own."

"I am glad you like it," she said, and every word entered my heart directly, like food going into my stomach. It was as if she was feeding me with her words.

"But tell me, what happened to your cheek?" she asked.

I told her the story of the mule kicking me. She only nodded. Then, to my enormous relief, she told me to get my things together and come along. Her cart was waiting in the courtyard.

Mother Superior said goodbye to her with a mincing smile. "I am glad to see you so content, Doña Luisa," she said. "You look much happier than when I saw you the last time."

"It is the happiness of bringing home a child and also the happiness of good conscience," Doña Luisa said, "for I was a sinner once and afraid of God's wrath."

"We are all sinners," Mother Superior said piously.

"But I atoned for my sins and have been acquitted," Doña Luisa said. "You should do the same."

Then a strange thing happened. Mother Superior blushed. At least, I think she did. Her cheeks flushed, but within a heartbeat, the pink changed to a purple rage, and I expected her to give us a terrible dressing-down.

Doña Luisa, however, had already turned to the door and beckoned me to come along and, strange to say, Mother Superior kept the peace. So I last saw her standing very upright, fury in her eyes, lips compressed as if she had to hold in her breath, hands tightly clasped as if she had to keep herself from committing an act of violence.

I slipped out behind Tia Luisa, keeping a respectful distance as I followed her with my bundle of clothes. I still thought of her as my mistress, then, although she looked at me with the loving eyes of a mother, and Mother Superior had said she would adopt me.

We went quite a distance in her cart, to a part of town I had never been in before and where almost everyone I saw was dark-skinned. That part of town was called San Bernardo, she told me. When we got to her house, which was made of adobe and had a red-tiled roof, she took me by the hand and showed me around. There was a shop in front with a counter running the full length, where she sold all kinds of candles. Behind that was a storeroom with shelves and baskets that held more candles. Then came the kitchen with a big hearth and kettles hanging from hooks inside. There was a set of baskets lined up along the wall with fruit and vegetables, and shelves with earthenware and a sturdy table with four chairs. Behind the kitchen was a bedroom that we would share, Tia Luisa said. It had two bedsteads, a large wardrobe, and a washstand with a mirror above it. I looked into the mirror and saw my face staring back at me in all its ugliness, and behind my shoulder, Tia Luisa, smiling and beautiful. In the back of the house, overlooking a courtyard planted with flowers and trees, was another large, whitewashed room where you could sit comfortably. There were two cushioned chairs facing each other and a small table beside one of them, holding a work basket full of sewing. Two paintings hung on the wall behind the table, but unlike the paintings in the convent, which were mostly of saints doing holy things, these depicted ships, one with the sails billowing and racing along under a blue sky, the other with bare masts and being tossed by huge waves under a stormy sky. I looked at everything but was afraid of liking it too much until I had an answer to the question that filled my mind.

I finally asked: "Are you adopting me, then, Doña Luisa?"

She didn't say anything in reply. She reached out and stroked my hair very gently. Her touch was like velvet. She chucked me under the chin and made me look into her eyes. Then she kissed me on the forehead and pulled me close. She held me for a long time until I squirmed away, and then I saw that there were tears in her eyes.

"Do I make you sad, Doña Luisa?" I asked.

"No, no," she said.

"Then why are you crying?"

"I will explain it to you when you are older," she said. "In the meantime, you can call me *Tia* Luisa."

Then I understood that she expected me to be with her for a long time, and that her house was my home now.

11

Seville, 1575:

Baltasar Ruiz, accountant

PEOPLE THINK FORTUNE MUST BE smiling on me because I
am a member of the Ruiz family and a grandson of the legend-
ary Simon Ruiz, banker to the king, but fortune isn't smiling
so broadly if you are, like me, a younger son of a minor branch
of the family and have no head for figures. Then the allowance
you get isn't as generous as people think and not nearly enough
to keep you in style. No one asks what you would like to do
with your life. They give you two choices: Enter the family
business and spend your days hunched over a desk, counting
sums, or enter the church and say goodbye to getting laid, at
least officially.

Because you need some education, however, whether you
become a bean-counter or a priest, they send you to university
for a few years, and that's the only time you are allowed to

have fun. Or, rather, you get away with having fun because they can't keep track of you every hour of the day and night. By "they," I mean my father, first of all, but also the old tutor he hired to keep me in line until I was allowed to depart for Paris. "They" includes the parish priest nattering at me in the confessional, my mother and her sisters, and the whole family council reminding me of the duty I owe to God and to each one of them, whereas nobody owes *me* anything, apparently. The tutor was the worst of the lot because he was always around and in my way. After my older brother turned sixteen and escaped his grip, I was the only victim left in the schoolroom. I had the full and unceasing attention of Old Bones. His tyranny became intolerable. Every morning he made me read aloud the motto of the day, some pious pitch he had got out of a worm-eaten book: exhortations to be good and honest and serve others and say your prayers and honour your elders, and other stuff so sweet it made your teeth hurt. Then we got on to the poets — his kind of poets, the holy Prudentius and the boring Lucretius. Not a single girl's name in either one. As for the historians, I wouldn't have minded reading about Nero in Tacitus, but no, that was too steamy for Old Bones. We read Livy's battle speeches instead, the most high-flown tripe you've ever heard. No soldier I know talks like that. For one thing, none of them says five words in a row without swearing, and they always get around eventually to telling you how they got drunk and laid some girl and enjoyed themselves immensely because "life is short." Now that is a motto I can subscribe to. Ovid wrote a splendid poem about it, "Carpe Diem," but of course that was too pagan for my tutor's taste.

Finally, everyone agreed that I knew enough to go to university, and I escaped the clutches of Old Bones.

Of course, my father thought he had me under lock and key in Paris as well. He arranged for me to live in a boarding house for students supervised by a dour theologian-in-training, but we managed to escape over the garden wall at night and drink to the health of the wenches in the local tavern and get into some healthy brawling to work off our frustrations. During the day, we looked studious, but whenever we had a chance, we left off the dreary textbooks and read our poetic effusions to each other. We had high hopes of finding a printer willing to stake his money on us because, except for a few keeners, we were all poets at heart. But no luck with the printers. They are a mercenary lot and take on only what is a sure bet and has the imprimatur of the Church because they are afraid of their stuff ending up on the Index of Forbidden Books. In any case, we all agreed: To hell with Aristotle and the rest of the philosophers and damn Aelius's grammar and Isidore of Seville's etymology! They are useless for any kind of real living unless you want to become a professor, wearing a shabby beret and a black gown hanging down to your ankles, and spend the rest of your days in the lecture hall, droning on, while the students on the benches before you sleep off last night's hangover. Even my father conceded that getting a degree and calling yourself a bachelor doesn't help anyone running a business.

"But getting a degree from Paris is the done thing in our family. It's expected," he said. "You'll learn the business fast enough once you are apprenticed to your uncle and start working in his counting house. You'll be doing the books for his clients in no time at all and be able to make an honest living."

I said "yes, sir," of course, and did what I had to do, but I feel I am wasting my time. It is boring as hell to sit over the accounts all day, so I make sure I have a sheet of paper handy to write down any verses that come into my head. Whenever the muse strikes and I am inspired and no one is breathing down my neck, I pull a sheet of paper out from under the accounting books and compose a poem or two.

A few times a week I enjoy a little relief and amusement, teaching a boy who was brought up in the convent of the Clares. When I first met him, I thought he was the love child of a nun. Was he the offspring of Mother Superior, I wondered. Nah, I thought, I can't imagine any man being brave enough to fuck that dragon lady or get it up in the first place, given her age. I bet you her breasts are as wrinkled as her cheeks, and her quim is drier than a creek in August. I've been looking after the accounts of the convent for the past year — well, helped Mother Superior with her accounts. She is savvy enough to keep them herself and wants me to look only at a page here and there. I bet you there is a great deal in those books she doesn't want me to see and a great deal also that never makes it into the books in the first place. But that is none of my business. I am paid to go to the convent once a month and that's just fine with me. I escape the counting house for an afternoon.

She usually receives me in the library — a place that offers complete privacy because no one ever sets foot in there, whereas her office is always busy with a lot of coming and going.

A few weeks ago, I arrived and found her waiting in the library with a boy at her elbow. I remembered seeing the kid before, hanging around in the entrance hall. As far as I know, he was the porter's errand boy. He looked a little thinner than the last time I saw him, and his right cheek was covered by a large scab.

"This is Diego," the abbess said to me.

The boy stepped up and bowed to me politely.

"Hey," I said, "what happened to your cheek?"

Before he could answer, the abbess put in, "A mule kicked him. For a while, he was quite ill on account of the wound suppurating."

"But you are okay again, little man?" I asked.

He only nodded and looked at the abbess as if he needed a cue to say more. I was wondering if he was weak in the head.

"He is well again," she said, "but a little tired. I thought he might use the time of convalescence to practise his reading and writing."

"You know how to read and write?" I asked him. I guess he wasn't weak in the head, after all, but I was surprised nevertheless that he had learned those skills. When I had seen him with the porter, I had thought of him as no more than an errand boy, an urchin who might end up on the street one day. Now it looked as if he had special standing with Mother Superior.

"Don Francisco, the parish priest, taught me," he said in answer to my question.

"And I thought I could engage your services for the next few weeks to tutor him," the abbess put in. "For a fee, of course, and if your uncle is willing to let you off work for ... let's say ... two hours, twice a week."

That would make for a nice change in my routine, I thought.

"I'm sure my uncle will be amenable," I said. "He wouldn't refuse you a favour, Reverend Mother, if you asked him yourself."

"Very well," she said, and added after a pause, "You once mentioned that I should have a catalogue drawn up for the library. Perhaps you could make a beginning and engage Diego's help. His handwriting is excellent, or so Don Francisco said."

Ah, I thought, she is up to her old tricks, trying to get something for nothing. I had indeed suggested drawing up a catalogue some time ago, but of course I expected to be paid for the job if she wanted me to do it. Now she was trying to get a little extra out of me, combining that job with tutoring the boy. The convent library was substantial. Some of her predecessors must have been book lovers, or else the convent had received a large legacy of books at some time. A cursory look around had shown me that the holdings were valuable, even if most of the stuff was of no interest to anyone other than a bibliophile. I could see that nothing had been bought or added over the past thirty years, and there were none of the humanistic books that are all the rage now, and none of the editions of the classics that have been published to great acclaim by the Italians and the French. Maybe that's not to be expected in a convent library, but I saw some very old manuscripts that are valuable now that printed books are everywhere and manuscripts have become rare. And once you start looking, who knows what treasures are stored somewhere in a corner of the library with the worms quietly gnawing away at them.

"I am not sure that drawing up a catalogue is a suitable exercise for a boy of Diego's age," I said. "I believe we should do something more conventional, like reading Cato's *Seven Sages*, or a book of adages." Or something unconventional, like my poems, I thought.

"I leave that up to you," she said, a little reluctantly.

"And may I suggest six afternoons a week? Practice has to be constant to be effective," I said, thinking the more often I could get away from my desk, the better. And so I ended up looking after the boy two hours every weekday, during which

I made him read and copy out an old primer I had. At first, it looked like I had to forget about reading poetry as planned, because the abbess wouldn't leave us alone. She lingered in the background and listened in on what we said. I guess she wanted to make sure the boy didn't tell me anything embarrassing about the nuns. She had warned me that he was an inveterate liar, but I think she was just afraid he would tell me more about life in the convent than she wanted me to know. To guard her reputation, she made him out a liar. That way, she could always deny his words and say he was fibbing.

After a few days, I had an idea of how to get rid of her.

"You heard that Mother Superior wants us to make a catalogue for her library," I said to Diego, "but for that, you will have to learn the elements of Latin, for most of the titles are in that language."

I fetched some of the old Bibles and Church Fathers from the shelves, blew the dust off the leather covers, and went through the titles with the boy, translating them word for word. He was pretty quick on the uptake and soon recognized some of the words like *opera omnia, anno Domini, epistolae,* and so forth, noting the case endings on the nouns and the tenses of the verbs.

"Now we'll make up simple sentences," I said to him and made him write down *puer bonus est* and *puer malus est* and repeat the declensions and conjugations, until the abbess looked annoyed because she couldn't understand a word, and finally decided to leave us alone.

Then, at last, we got on to poetry, and I recited a few of my things to him, which he liked a lot because, as it turned out, he was a smart kid. I also showed him a love poem by Catullus.

"That's to teach you the numbers," I said.

Da mi basia mille, deinde centum
Dein mille altera, dein secunda centum
Deinde usque altera mille, deinde centum.

Give me a thousand kisses, then another hundred,
then another thousand, then a second hundred,
then yet another thousand more, then another
hundred ...

I read it to him in Latin and translated it for him and made him swear to keep it a secret from Mother Superior, because it was "hot to trot."

He was delighted.

"Hot to trot!" he exclaimed and couldn't stop giggling. "And how do you say that in Latin?"

"*Calidum ad eundum,*" I said, making it up on the spot, because it wasn't a phrase found in the ancient orators.

He volunteered to write that phrase out twenty times, but I said it was too risky to put such naughty words on his slate. What if Mother Superior came in and wanted to check what he was doing?

"Just keep it stored in your mind, where nobody can get at it," I told him.

He was pleased to no end to have such a dangerous secret.

In a word, the kid and I had a good time. It was a hell of a lot better than sitting in the counting house.

At the end of the fifth week, Diego told me that he might not see me again because a woman by the name of Luisa Abrego was going to adopt him.

"But Mother Superior says she is well-to-do and will treat me like her own son, so perhaps she won't object to paying for your time. Then we could continue our lessons."

For a moment, I thought he was fibbing and the abbess had been right to warn me, but the name Luisa Abrego sounded familiar. *Where have I heard that name before?* I thought.

"Does she live in Seville?" I asked him.

"I don't know," he said, "but if you tell me where you live, I could visit you from time to time because I feel you are a friend, and I don't have any other friends."

He was a very trusting boy and, if I didn't know better, I'd call him simple-minded. But when it came to studying his lessons, he was razor-sharp.

He was certainly no liar, because I finally remembered where I had heard of Luisa Abrego: at the counting house, from the company lawyer, Miguel Aguirre. He told us a story I would not have believed if I didn't know that the man is too prosaic to make up things. He doesn't have a creative bone in his body. He is all facts and figures. This Luisa, he told us, was a slave in the household of a rich man, who got her pregnant. He freed her and set aside a tidy sum for her and the child before he bit the grass. But she left the baby with the nuns and ran off to Mexico and — here comes the unbelievable part — never collected a peso of the sum owed. Now she was on her way back and wanted to cash in on her loot and retrieve her child from the nuns. Everybody at the counting house was amazed at the story. What was she like, this Luisa Abrego? we wanted to know. A dazzling beauty? A siren?

"I met her only once," the lawyer said, "and that is almost a decade ago, before she took off for Mexico. She was a good-looking woman, that's for sure, but she never opened her mouth, and you can't tell what those half-castes are thinking. I suspect she didn't understand a word I said to her, and of course she can't read. I don't know who wised her up to the fact that she's owed money."

"It's not just the half-castes who can't understand your legal mumbo-jumbo," I said.

"Or, for that matter, your poetic mumbo-jumbo," he said smartly.

When Diego told me that Luisa Abrego was going to adopt him, I put two and two together. He must be the child she left behind, and yes, the boy's complexion is a little on the tawny side, but I had never thought much of that before. Doña Luisa, as everyone calls her now that she is in funds, collected her money from Aguirre and bought a house with a candle shop. Then she picked up the boy and moved him in with her. Lucky for me, she agreed to pay for his lessons, and so I still get out of the drudgery of accounting. I went to her house to talk about the terms.

I was rather curious to lay eyes on the formidable "Tia" Luisa, as Diego calls her. He absolutely worships her. Hearing him talk, you'd think she was the most beautiful as well as the kindest and wisest woman ever born. She is nothing like that, of course, but I must say she did make a good impression on me, like a woman who knows what she is about — a businesswoman, in other words. Perhaps she was beautiful at some time, ten or fifteen years ago, but no woman her age is beautiful to me. They remind me too much of my mother and my aunts. Lovable, of course, but in a dull way. In any case, Doña Luisa and I had a pleasant enough conversation and settled on the terms, and after talking to her for a bit, I'd say she has the right voice to sell candles — smooth as beeswax.

Twice a week, then, Diego and I retreat to my room above the counting house. It's not the nicest place. My uncle doesn't believe in pampering his apprentices. It's an attic room, blazing hot in summer and cold and drafty in winter. It wouldn't impress even a kitchen maid (if I could smuggle one in). I suspect it was used for storage at one time. The furniture is ancestral, let's say — a rickety bed that would collapse under the weight of passion, a couple of hard chairs, and a table with one short leg that needs to be shimmed to keep it from wobbling. Above the bed is a shelf for the books I cannot live without, among them Ovid's *The Art of Love*, a kind of guide to picking up girls. It's of no practical help with girls nowadays, except maybe the bit where he recommends brushing imaginary crumbs from her bosom, although I suspect I would get slapped if I tried that. But even if Ovid's strategies are outdated, the book is doubly valuable to me now that it is on the Index of Forbidden Books. Life is boring if you don't take a little risk here and there. At least, that's what I think, although my uncle would have a heart attack if he ever found out that I am keeping an illegal book on his premises.

Whatever the shortcomings of the room, Diego and I can do our studying there in privacy and with no one telling us what we can or can't read or talk about. The boy is getting to be quite a good Latinist. I bet he'll be composing his own verses in no time at all, or writing down the story of his life, which would make for an excellent picaresque novel.

The whole adventurous story of his life came out one day when I quoted him the proverb *Tempora mutantur, et nos mutamur in illis*, "The times are changing, and we change with them."

"Yes," he said in all seriousness. "I have experienced that myself."

"Oh sure," I said, "over the course of your enormously long lifespan of nine years."

"No, seriously, Don Baltasar," he said. "There have been enormously big changes in my life."

"From convent to candle store, I know."

"From absolute misery to total bliss," he said and spilled the beans: Mother Superior had sold him into slavery.

"What?" I said. "You are making it up! You are trying out a theme for a poem, right?"

"No, it's true," he said, but Mother Superior had cautioned him not to tell anyone about it, or Doña Luisa would not adopt him. So, for a long time, he kept his mouth shut, but now that he was sure Doña Luisa loved him and would never give him up, he could tell me the secret story of his life.

"Go ahead," I said. "Maybe we can make a heroic poem of it."

I never guessed what was coming. First, he said, he had shared a room with a crazy nun, who was into stories of blood and gore and liked to prick her fingers until they bled.

"But those years weren't so bad, when I think of them now," he said. "I believe Sister Maria was genuinely fond of me. It's just that she was mad and couldn't help herself."

Next, he shared a room with the porter and ran errands. That was all right as well, he said.

"It was when Mother Superior sold me to a rancher that my life turned into a horror story."

Then he told me the real reason for that ugly scar on his cheek. It made my skin crawl. That bitch of a nun who had sold him, that "Reverend Mother," ought to have her ugly face reworked as well.

"Then my life changed again," Diego said. "Tia Luisa adopted me. And now I am so happy I wish there were no more changes, and everything stayed exactly the same forever!"

I could see that he still believed he was adopted. I guess the woman is a little shy about telling him that he is her son and was born out of wedlock, but no doubt he will find out eventually. It wasn't for me to enlighten him on that point.

The proverb turned out to be right, however, as proverbs often are. *Tempora mutantur*, times change, and there is another big one coming up in Diego's life.

One day last week, he came running up the stairs and burst into my room, all excited, waving two sheets of paper at me.

"Guess what," he said. "Tia Luisa got a letter!"

We had started reading a letter-writing manual with examples of every type of letter. We went over the table of contents first. There were reference letters that praised a candidate's suitability for a certain position, letters of consolation on losing one's child or one's spouse, warnings against taking religious vows rashly, letters for and against marriage, exhortations to young men to lead a virtuous life and abandon their vices, and many more.

"Whew!" Diego said after we'd gone through the table of contents. "That's a lot of different kinds of letters."

"True," I said, "but there are only two kinds that are of real importance and that an ordinary person is likely to receive or write: love letters and letters announcing the death of a loved one."

"In that case," he said, "let's read only those samples and skip the rest."

"Unless, of course, you end up being a teacher," I said, "in which case you need to know every single kind of letter. Or if you become a lawyer, in which case you will be called upon to compose many different letters. Or if you are a lover of language, in which case you *want* to know every phrase that can possibly be of use in a letter."

"Then let's read the whole book," he said, "because I do love words and hope to be a poet one day, like you. But Tia Luisa says I'd better learn how to figure out the accounts, because she thinks I have what it takes to be a merchant, and not just someone dealing in candles and the like, but a big merchant who imports spices or silks or wine or wheat, or all of it. And such a merchant needs to have a head for figures and calculate the cost of everything, she says."

"That's how elders talk," I said. "They always want to push you into some boring profession, just because it makes money. But Doña Luisa is dreaming if she thinks you can set up as a merchant. It takes a great deal of capital to start an enterprise like that. Besides, dealing with import and export is the most boring job imaginable. If you want my advice, stick to poetry and hire an assistant once you are in charge of the candle shop. Let someone else do the drudgery. You are cut out for better things."

"That's just what I said to Tia Luisa — that I didn't want to be a merchant. I want to be a poet. But she said there was no need to settle that question now. First you learn your letters and your figures, she said, and whatever else your tutor tells you to study, and then we'll see. But here is the letter I was telling you about, Don Baltasar, the letter that was delivered to her yesterday."

"All right, let's read it, then," I said, seeing the boy's excitement and his impatience.

He put the two sheets of paper in front of me.

"They were folded over and sealed," he said, "so that Tia Luisa would be able to tell if anyone opened it and took a peek at the lines. I remembered what you said to me, that the ordinary person receives only two kinds of letters, and I wondered whether it was about love or about death, but with all respect, Don Baltasar, you were wrong. It was neither. The letter contained news of her husband."

"Her husband! I thought she was a widow."

"She thought so too, but now she is no longer a widow. When the messenger handed her the letter, she turned it front to back and over again and took a hard look at her name, which was written on the outside, but that's all she could read, and only because I taught her to write her name. Then she broke the seal and we saw that there were two letters, one inside the other, one stiff and written in black ink and in perfectly shaped letters, the other in an elegant humanistic hand as from a scholar. She unfolded them and looked at the lines and finally had to admit that she was helpless. So then she asked me to read the letters to her. And here they are. I have her permission to show them to you, because I said to her: I have to tell someone about this or I'll burst."

"All right," I said, "show me the letters."

The first one was from Doña Luisa's lawyer, the one who works for my uncle as well. It said:

> *Esteemed Doña Luisa, I enclose a letter from*
> *Mexico City addressed to you and delivered to*
> *me by a messenger of the Holy Office. It bears, I*
> *understand, happy tidings. I await your instruc-*
> *tions, should you wish me to make any prepara-*
> *tions on your behalf.*
>
> *Sincerely yours,*
> *Miguel Aguirre*

The second letter was signed by "Alonso de Herrera, fiscal of the Holy Office" and said:

To Doña Luisa, with my felicitations.

My dear friend, I write to tell you of a miracle and hope that the happy news will reach you speedily through the hands of your lawyer. Two days ago, I received a letter from a physician in Zacatecas, informing me that your husband, Jorge, has not died in the mine accident, as I had been told when I departed for Mexico City. He was found the next day in the rubble of the collapsed tunnel, still alive and breathing.

I rode at once to Zacatecas to see for myself how Jorge is faring, not wanting to trust in any further correspondence, since you and I had already been deceived once by false information, with the most unfortunate result — that is, your precipitate return to Spain.

I still blame myself for neglecting to investigate the matter myself then and there instead of trusting to hearsay. Thus it is with certainty now that I can inform you: Your husband is indeed alive. It was his servant, Chulo, who was killed in the accident.

Jorge was in grave condition when the rescuers found him, but there is hope that he will recover. He is tended by the grandmother of Chulo, who is very knowledgeable about herbs. The dressing she put on Jorge's wounds seems

*to have had the desired effect. He is now free
of fever, although still very weak. I should caution you, moreover: Even if he recovers from his
wounds, he does not expect to have the use of his
left arm ever again.*

*We talked at some length about your ordeal
and his plans and prospects. He told me that
the two of you had, after the death of your child,
talked about returning to Spain and setting up
shop there. He will take steps now to sell the
house in Zacatecas and his mining rights, collect
his savings and follow you to Seville as soon as
his condition allows.*

*He begs you to be of good cheer and sends
you his love.*

"You see," I said to Diego, "I was right after all. The letter
is about love."

"Maybe you are right," he said, "but you wouldn't have
known it if you looked at Tia Luisa because she started sobbing
and wept a flood of tears. I wanted to embrace and console her,
even though I didn't understand why she was crying, but she
told me, 'never mind, go on with the letter.'"

The fiscal's letter continued:

*I am sending you this message through Miguel
Aguirre, the lawyer handling your affairs. I
hope, as does your husband, to receive a speedy
reply telling us how you are faring. I did tell Jorge
about the funds your former master left to your
son and the income to which you are entitled.*

Jorge was, of course, happy in the knowledge that you have sufficient means of support for the time being and until he can join you.

I am longing to return to Spain myself. I have given notice to my superior and informed him that I wish to resign my position on the tribunal. I believe that I have done my duty to God here and have earned my release. I will therefore gladly accompany Jorge on his way back to Spain, if it can be arranged, and give him what assistance he may need. Indeed, I feel it is my duty to do so, to make up for my negligence, which has caused you so much grief.

With all best wishes and Godspeed!
Alonso de Herrera

"Then she wiped away her tears," Diego said, "and embraced and kissed me and said many times over: Dear boy, dear boy, I'm so happy, so happy, I can't tell you! She said it would be a great day for me too when her husband arrived, because he would be like a father to me."

"My God," I said. "What a story, Diego! I swear you and I will make a heroic poem of it to rival Homer and Virgil! It will be better than the Odyssey."

"But wait for the rest," Diego said. "My name is no longer Diego. Tia Luisa said she was very sad that Chulo died in the mine accident. She had a great liking for her husband's helper. He was an excellent young man, open and honest and hardworking, the kind of man she hoped I'd grow up to be. Because she was so sad, I put my arms around her and said I would try very hard to be like Chulo and I was sorry that he was dead. Then she said there was a simple way of reviving him. How? I asked. By changing your name to Chulo, she said. And if you grow up to be like him, it will be like bringing him back to life. So now you must call me Chulo, Don Baltasar."

"If you say so, but it's a strange idea," I said. "Do you even like your new name?"

"I've thought about it," he said. "It's only a short time ago that I learned my name was Diego. Until then everyone just called me 'boy' or 'hey, you.' I haven't had enough time to become attached to the name Diego. 'Chulo' is certainly a strange name, but if it pleases Tia Luisa to call me Chulo, so be it, for I would never think of denying her anything."

"You are a very obliging son," I said to him.

"And she is a very good mother to someone like me, who never had one before. She said she'd call me 'Chulo' in private and 'Diego' in public. And since I've been nameless for so long, I don't mind having two names now."

"Oh, well," I said. "*Tempora mutantur.*"

"*Et nos mutamur in illis,*" he chimed in.

POSTSCRIPT

The harbour of Seville, 1576:

Captain Juan Diaz

IT WAS A QUIET VOYAGE back to Spain. On the way out-
bound, I had delivered another hopeful group of settlers, eager
to make a new life in Mexico. On the return journey, the hold
of the *Marisa* was filled with silver bars, and I had only two
passengers: Jorge Abrego and Alonso de Herrera. Almost a decade had gone by since that voyage in 1567 when Don Alonso
took up his post as prosecutor in Mexico City and Jorge, Luisa,
and I made our way to Zacatecas. Don Alonso had not changed
much. He looked vigorous. His eyes were clear, and he still had
a full head of hair, even if the first strains of grey had made
their appearance. Jorge, of course, was much altered since I
had seen him last — in body as well as in mind. He was a cripple. His illness had aged him prematurely and given his face a
weathered look. I don't mean like a seaman's face coarsened by
sun, salt, and wind, but a face marked by misfortune. Yet his

mind was newly illuminated, or so he told me. I had offered to share my cabin with him on the voyage, for we were keen on each other's company after so many years had passed.

On the first night, as soon as we were alone, he told me about his "enlightenment": He loved Luisa!

"What?" I said, "You didn't love her before?"

"I loved her all along," he said, "but I didn't know it, and now I do."

"And how did this new insight come about?"

"I had a kind of rallying of the mind," he said. "I was as good as dead when the mine shaft collapsed, and I am still half-dead as far as my body is concerned. But my mind had a resurrection. You might say I was a child before the mine collapsed — or had the understanding of a child. I am a man now and know myself a lot better. The most important thing I have learned is that I love Luisa with every fibre in my body and with my whole mind and soul, and I will be the happiest man alive if I find that she is still in love with me."

With Don Alonso, it was the other way round. He had fallen out of love and was as eager as Jorge to tell me of his enlightenment on this point. First, he told me his part in the story of Luisa's suffering — that she had insisted on being judged by the Inquisition and that he had complied with her wishes unwillingly, for he had taken an earnest interest in her well-being. He then confessed that on the voyage to Mexico he had become enamoured of Luisa. Foolishly enamoured, he said.

His confession did not surprise me. Luisa had captivated many hearts on that crossing. Her honeyed voice and gracious movements charmed everyone. I had seen the covetous gleam in the eyes of the men watching her. Indeed I was afraid that the feelings she aroused in them might lead to trouble, but

Luisa had a way of filling men with a longing for her touch and at the same time with an awe that made them keep their distance.

When Don Alonso said he had been "foolishly" in love, I objected, however: "You were too late, you mean. Jorge was her husband by then. I wouldn't call it foolish to fall in love with Luisa. She is a remarkable woman."

"I won't deny that she is remarkable," he said, "but as to my folly, I must beg to differ." He spoke in that voice of authority that made you think he had swallowed wisdom whole, and it was flowing in his veins now instead of blood.

"Luisa is no doubt remarkable for one of her class," he said, "but to love a woman — and I mean not just be charmed by her — she must have first and foremost an admirable mind. You will agree with me in that point, captain: There is nothing to admire in Luisa's mind. That is why I said I was 'foolishly' in love with her."

"Oh, you know her mind?" I said. "Then you are wiser than I, for I at any rate could never understand Luisa. Indeed you may be unique, my friend. At least I don't know any other man who has perfected the skill of reading people's minds."

"You willfully misconstrue my words, captain," he said. "I am not talking about knowing the chance thoughts that might cross a person's mind, which I can guess as little as you. I am talking about the habits of thought, logic, and ratiocination based on learning, which continually manifests itself in a person's conversation."

"Oh, well," I said, "then you are right. Luisa is not an educated woman, and I wish you luck finding a female philosopher who has mastered logic and will always follow the call of reason."

"I am not looking for a woman rivalling Plato or Aristotle," he said. "I am perfectly willing to settle for a well-bred woman, who will speak to me of things of the mind in an intelligent manner, although of course I hope that we may love each other body and soul."

In other words, he was looking for a woman of his own class, who would defer to his wisdom and produce an heir. He meant to say: Luisa was not of that class, and so it was foolish of him to fall in love. But I let it go. However much Don Alonso and I differed in our opinion of Luisa, I had to like a man who put his own interests aside to aid Jorge. Don Alonso had been anxious to leave for Spain and could have done so sooner had he not waited until Jorge was well enough to travel. Nor did he balk at being a passenger on my ship, which offered few comforts, when he could have taken a royal mail boat, which would have been faster and better able to accommodate a gentleman of his standing. He had no obligation to defer to Jorge's wishes and no motive to help him other than Christian charity, for Jorge's life was complicated at every step by his poor health and his lame arm.

When we sailed into the harbour of Seville after an uneventful journey, Don Alonso's father was waiting for him at the pier and welcomed his son joyfully. He had made arrangements with the harbourmaster to let him know as soon as the *Marisa* came in sight. His servants were waiting to take care of Don Alonso's luggage and had brought along two splendid horses to carry father and son back to the family estate.

Jorge and I repaired to the nearest inn and arranged for a mule driver and a cart to take us and our gear to Luisa's candle shop in San Bernardo. As we rattled along, I could see that Jorge was turning sentimental, a side of him that was new to me and no doubt another consequence of his long illness.

He looked around in wonder. "How greatly changed every-thing is," he said. "Or rather, how different it appears to me now!" And there was a sheen in his eyes as of tears.

I suppose it had to do with his newly gained insight. He looked at everything with the eyes of a loving man: the bust-ling harbour, the bridge to the city proper, which had indeed become grander over the last decade and displayed the wealth of its citizens. Then we passed into the suburbs, through the narrower streets of San Bernardo, with its modest houses, and at length arrived at Luisa's store.

As we entered, a boy — Diego, I guessed — called out, "I think that's them!"

Of Luisa we had only a glimpse as she fled to the back of the store, her cheeks flushed and her skirts rustling. I under-stood. She did not want her reunion with Jorge to become a public spectacle. Two customers at the counter, a kerchiefed old woman and a priest in a black robe, eyed us curiously.

The boy came out from behind the counter and made us a bow. "You must be Don Jorge," he said, his eyes on my friend's arm, which hung useless by his side.

Jorge only nodded. He had no words for anyone but Luisa. He looked longingly toward the door through which she had disappeared.

The boy then turned to me. "And you are Captain Diaz," he said. "I met you once, years ago. I remember that I was afraid of you because you were so tall and your beard was grizzled."

"Yes," I said, "we met when you were a little boy. But go on now and announce us to Doña Luisa."

He led us to the storeroom, where Luisa stood trembling among her stock of candles until Jorge stepped up to her and put his good arm around her tenderly. I myself had halted at the door and beckoned the boy to leave the pair alone.

"Your customers need attending," I said to him.

He served them, grinning happily all the time. When the old woman and the priest had picked up their wares and left, he locked up, for it was the end of the workday. He pulled out a stool for me to sit down and talked to me politely, but it was hard going. We didn't have much to say to each other. In truth, we were both impatient, waiting to be called into the presence of the couple and eager to accept our share of their happiness.

"It's been a long journey to bring the two of them together," I said, to make conversation.

"It's almost like having a father and mother now," he said. "Not that I lacked anything after Tia Luisa brought me home with her, but now that Don Jorge has come, we are a real family. I have never had one, you know."

When we were finally invited to join the couple and Luisa served us a celebratory glass of sherry and little cakes, I saw how changed she was — not wholly changed, for her gentle manner and soft voice were still the same. There were the usual signs of aging — she had grown sturdier around the middle; her face seemed a little more lined — but the greatest change was in her eyes. Gone was that opaqueness I had noticed when I first met her, which hinted at a lingering sadness, or even a guilty conscience. She had always been quick to cast her eyes down, as if to bar you from seeing what she felt. I never was a good judge of women, but her reserve made it even more difficult to understand her. It was as if she had wanted to keep me and everyone else at bay.

That furtiveness was gone now. She held my gaze steadily. There was a new clarity in her eyes and a new certainty. Then, for the first time, I understood Luisa, for who can fail to understand the signs of love and happiness?

ACKNOWLEDGEMENTS

I WOULD LIKE TO THANK my friends who read the manuscript at various stages and helped me shape the story: Cynthia Reyes, Heide Franke, Patti Katzman, Roberta Johnson, Karin MacHardy, Beverly Graf, and Gregor Medinger, who drew my attention to Luisa de Abrego's life. I also want to thank everyone at Dundurn Press, especially Russell Smith, Erin Pinksen, and Vicky Bell, for guiding this book through the editing and publishing process. I am very much in your debt and grateful to all of you for taking me under your wing.

ABOUT THE AUTHOR

ERIKA RUMMEL HAS TAUGHT HIS-
tory at the University of Toronto and
Wilfrid Laurier University, Waterloo.
She has accumulated a great deal of
useless knowledge about ancient times,
dead languages, old memes before they
were called memes, and old souls. She
grew up in Vienna, immigrated to
Canada, and explored life in villages
in Argentina, Romania, and Bulgaria. She found urban life
preferable and now divides her time between Toronto and Los
Angeles. Rummel is the author of more than a dozen books on
social history and nine novels, some of them autofiction, others
historical. She has been the recipient of international awards
and fellowships and in 2018 was honoured with a lifetime
achievement award by the Renaissance Society of America.

DISCUSSION
QUESTIONS

1. What qualities in Luisa fascinate Alonso de Herrera?
2. What helped Luisa's son cope with the hardships he encountered?
3. What do you think of the relationship between Luisa and Don Diego while she was still enslaved by him? What struck you about the reaction of Doña Ana to this relationship and to the content of Don Diego's will?
4. When Luisa is caught in the nets of the Inquisition, what motivates Alonso de Herrera to protect her and to stand by her after the trial?
5. Captain Juan Diaz thinks that people from different ethnic backgrounds cannot truly understand each other. Why do you think he believes this, and do you agree?
6. What role did the Catholic Church play in the lives of people in the sixteenth century? In what ways is Father Francisco not a typical representative of the Catholic Church from that time?

7. Compared to the sixteenth century, how have attitudes toward "The Other" changed in our time, and in what ways have they remained similar? How has the role of the Church changed?

8. Discuss the relationship between Luisa and Jorge. In what ways does it change over the years?

9. What is the significance of the novel's title? What does it tell you about the author's approach to the subject and her method of telling Luisa's story?

10. Do you think your own gender and ethnicity influenced your approach to and enjoyment of the novel? In what ways?

11. Do any of the characters in the novel who observe and comment on Luisa change their opinion of her? If so, what causes them to change their mind?

12. To what extent should historical novels stick to known historical facts? How much leeway would you give the author to fictionalize the story?